MISTAKEN

Tania Park

National Library of Australia Cataloguing-in-Publication entry
Creator: Park, Tania, author.
Title: Mistaken : why do they want her dead? / Tania Park.
ISBN: 9780994284709 (Paperback)
ISBN: 9780994284716 (Ebook)
Subjects: Suspense fiction.
Dewey Number: A823.4

Printed & Channel Distribution
Lightning Source | Ingram (USA/UK/EUROPE/AUS)

Dedicated to my friends at my writer's group, 'Just Write', who have, over the past ten years, encouraged me, read my first attempts then picked my work to pieces. They've then made suggestions for improvement, not all of which I have taken on board. They are an invaluable group of like-minded people who have a love for the written word. Each one seems to have developed their own individual styles and many have had success in various competitions. Special thanks to Rosie, Sue, Penny, Lyndal and Ted, who have been with me on the entire ten year journey.

Thank you also to my husband, James, who puts up with me spending hours locked away in my office, tapping on a keyboard. At least he always knows where to find me. His support is much appreciated and too often unacknowledged.

Chapter One

The instant he noticed Jared's fingers spinning around in the air, King turned and raced from the room. He was halfway to the helicopter before Jared finished scrawling details of the garbled message on the pad kept by the phone for that purpose. Wishing Buck were back from his annual physical check-up, Jared ripped the page from the pad then shot out the door, tearing after King. They were short-staffed – again and his prayer that they weren't called out today had gone unanswered.

Within minutes they were lifting off the ground. 'Some guy, a Mr Bart Hudson, called in to tell us a woman, his secretary I think he said, has fallen over the edge of Reyne's Lookout. What do you reckon the drop there would be? A hundred metres?'

Concentrating on the controls, King didn't turn his head. 'Eighty. Straight down. Nobody could survive that kind of fall. I think we might be looking for a body.' Flying straight ahead, he turned to glance at Jared. 'That place is fenced off isn't it? How could anyone fall from the top?'

'I've never been there. What is the terrain like? Can we fly up the valley?' Jared reached for the pile of maps stored in a locker above his head, rifling through them until he found the correct one. He studied the printed plans. 'I can't see a spot to land. The valley is covered with virgin forest, which means tall eucalypts and thick undergrowth. Damn, there's also a high voltage power line across the top of the lookout. Jeeze, I hope it isn't in the way. At a pinch I suppose we could land in the car park.'

'Fat lot of good that will do us if the body is down in the valley,' King mumbled as he gave a quick glance towards Jared then refocussed on where he was going. 'Are we going to need Buck?'

'If it's a body I can manage on my own. How about we skim across the trees in the valley to check it out, we might be lucky. I can retrieve the body using the sling.'

Refolding the maps he stuffed them back into the locker then settled back in his seat.

Approaching the valley from the west, King flew low while Jared scanned the ground with his eyes and a pair of binoculars, searching amongst the dense treetops for any signs of damage or for the sight of a female body on the ground. After several sweeps up and down the valley floor he could spot no evidence of broken branches or bushes intimating something or someone had crashed through.

'Are you sure this was the place, Jared?'

Jared frowned as he unfolded the notes he'd scribbled down and studied them. 'This is where he said. Reyne's

Lookout is directly above us and to the left.'

'I hope this isn't another lousy crank call,' muttered King under his breath as he swooped the aircraft around to head back to the actual lookout.

'It sounded genuine. Why don't we go up top, land then search the ground for any disturbance, that way we can ascertain exactly where the body should have landed, if in fact this call is genuine. If we fly in from land-side then we shouldn't whip up the dirt. Inspecting the ground should give us an indication one way or the other.'

'Good idea,' said King as he shifted practised hands and feet on the controls. The chopper rose with the curved front window facing the rocky cliff face while the two men flicked their eyes from side to side. Nearing the top, King said, 'Keep a lookout for the powerlines.'

Leaning sideways Jared glanced upwards, seeking the heavy curve of thick wires and, spotting one of the enormous pylons, began giving details of the position as King manoeuvred, allowing plenty of room to avoid the lines.

When the machine jerked suddenly Jared grabbed hold of the handle on the overhead locker to steady himself. 'What are you doing, mate, trying to turf me out?'

'Sorry but have a look over there, to your right a bit. Let me just swing this baby around further. Look straight ahead now.'

'Strewth!' Unable to believe his eyes, Jared stared at a hollowed out section in the side of the cliff. Carved out by the wind was a small cave backing into the rock face from a narrow rocky ledge about eight metres down from the top of the lookout. Lying at the bottom of the spooned out cave was the body of a woman.

'Do you think she's still alive?' asked Jared as he leant forwards for a closer inspection and using the binoculars to spot any small sign of movement.

'If she is, she shouldn't ever buy a lottery ticket 'cause she's used up all the luck she's entitled to. What are the chances of going over the edge and hitting the only ledge for miles? Let's see how close we can get, you look for any movement.'

***

Thwack, thwack, thwack. Annabella Perez groaned. Somewhere in the depths of her semi-consciousness, she could hear a noise. A steady rhythm of sounds sent messages along her nerves that didn't quite register in a brain that felt as though it were stuffed with pillow filling. She felt desperate to wake up to see what the noise was, but her subconscious told her that waking meant something really unpleasant. She forced one eyelid to open, then the other. Then she tried to focus through her pain. Come on girl, ignore it, and concentrate on the noise. Forcing her brain to function and take stock, Annabella stared ahead. All she saw was dirt; plain red dirt. Dirt doesn't make that kind of noise, she thought. Too afraid to move her head, she rolled her eyeballs, seeking out anything else, but the only other things she spied were rocks - just dirt and rocks.

Look behind you girl, the noise is behind you. Every part of Annabella's body hurt. Even breathing hurt, telling her she was in a great deal of trouble but she had to find out exactly what was making the noise. Was it the noise that caused her to hurt so much? She wracked her brain to see if she could recall what happened, why she ended up looking at rocks and dirt, lying on her side in sheer agony. Was she run over? Did she have a car accident?

What the hell was that noise? Swallowing down cries of pain, Annabella shifted. A wave of moisture spread across her eyes as memory came crashing back. Bart Hudson. 'Oh, God, why?' she whispered, the words coming out harsh and crackly. She coughed to clear her throat as she recalled hitting the ground with an agonising jolt of pain then nothing, until now. Tears welled as her eyelids slid closed and she sank back into the black abyss of darkness.

Chapter Two

Keeping an eye on the woman from the glass dome of the helicopter, Jared saw a fluttering hand rise up, an arm fling backwards, followed by a shoulder twitching then slowly flicking over. Even above the noise of the chopper engine he heard the loud scream when the top part of the woman rolled onto her back. One leg flopped over but the other stayed on the ground at such an awkward angle Jared knew it was fractured. Sweeping his eyes over the woman seeking other injuries, his cursory examination stopped when he found himself looking into rich, dark brown eyes staring right back at him. Pain was etched on her face with her mouth drawn in a tight grimace.

'She's alive!' Sliding the door open, Jared hooked on his safety line then picked up the loud hailer, placing the microphone hard up against his mouth. 'Try not to move.

You are near the edge of a very steep cliff. Wait there and we'll come down from the top to get you. Wave if you understand.'

Leaning out the side of the helicopter, Jared spied a couple of tears slide down the beautiful dust covered face, leaving red streaks as gravity led the droplets on a path downwards, over the cheeks then plopping into the dirt. He noticed the effort it took for the woman to lift her hand in acknowledgement then he continued staring as the eyes slid closed. He prayed it was into unconsciousness – at least then she wouldn't move.

'Okay, King, take her straight up a couple of metres as slow as you can so I can figure out how the hell I'm supposed to get down there. That cave can't be more than two metres long and doesn't look very wide.'

'What about the cables?'

Jared scanned the area above his head then cursed. 'Damn! Stop! They're almost directly above us. You can't go any higher. Go left.' Calling directions as the chopper swung left, Jared kept an eye on the lines until the aircraft was clear. Then he concentrated on studying the wall of the cliff.

As they rose, he became more and more alarmed as more and more methods of rescue were eliminated one by one. Dense overhanging foliage from ancient native trees along the top of the lookout meant he couldn't be lowered from the hovering chopper. Even if he was able to negotiate a way through the trees on the way down, the winch wire would become entangled in the branches and they wouldn't be able to winch back up again. The high voltage powerlines were a bigger problem. A single gust of wind could very easily have the winch wire brushing against them causing an instant fry up. Shuddering at the thought, he knew that option was out of the question.

'Okay, let's arch around to land so the rotors don't blow away any marks,' Jared said when he was satisfied they were clear. As King turned away Jared began pulling objects from neatly packed stowage areas. Everything they would ever need to affect a rescue from the air was stowed in readiness in various compartments inside the specially outfitted aircraft. They had everything except manpower, an ongoing problem since two men resigned a few weeks ago, leaving them mortally short-staffed.

Thank God the parking area was devoid of cars or human beings, which enabled King to settle the chopper with ease. The two men had their seat belts unbuckled and were out of the aircraft before the rotors had ceased spinning. Jared Mann stretched out his six foot two, powerfully built body to iron out the tension and kinks.

King stretched even taller, his rangy body belying the power and strength of very fit muscles. Sandy haired and hazel eyed, King gave the appearance of being a fiery tempered red-head but in actual fact Jared found him to be one of the most genial men he had ever met. The only time he had seen the man scowl and show a terse side to his nature was when Jared had first met him nine months earlier and asked what the A.J. stood for. King had refused to impart the information and Jared still didn't know, although he had his suspicions after a bout of name guessing and King had shifted uneasily at the name Aloysius.

Side by side, they strode across the bitumen towards a man-made wooden structure. From the lookout, the scenery in almost every direction was breathtaking. The deep valley spread for several kilometres to the right then arched around in meandering curves in the other direction. It was a good half a kilometre across with the point they were standing being the highest.

King reached the decking first then peered with his face snug against the safety wire netting 'Can't see the ledge from here.' As though not keen to have to be the one to climb over the security fencing, he added, 'If you go over the fence you can use a safety harness and rope to prevent accidentally slipping on the loose gravel.'

'Gee, thanks!' Jared said as he turned away.

With haste a priority, Jared returned to the chopper to gather all they needed for their initial inspection while King radioed for backup assistance. There was little doubt they were going to need more manpower to execute a safe retrieval. Armed with harness and ropes they sidled along the fenced pathway searching for any signs of ground disturbance. After finding a scuffed area, each man in turn tested the fence for strength by tugging it to and fro rapidly.

King rattled it again. 'I'm not sure this will hold your weight if you lose you footing. Let's fix the end of the ropes to that tree.' He pointed to a large Redgum about three metres away. 'Then we can wind the rope around the upright steel strut of the fence.'

'Sounds fine but why am I the one climbing fences?' Jared sent his friend a supercilious smile while he secured a harness over bright orange overalls, taking care to double check every mechanism.

King grinned back as he tied and wound then tied again. 'Because you're the rescue expert while I'm the pilot.'

As he struggled to reach the top of the two metre high fence, it baffled Jared how anyone could climb over the darn thing, swing a leg over the three strands of barbed wire then drop down the other side. He swore under his breath when a barb penetrated the two layers of fabric he was wearing then wriggled his torn pant leg free and dropped back to the ground. 'I need to cut these wires. Can you find the wire-cutters?'

It took another ten minutes before Jared managed to manoeuvre to the other side of the fence. Squatting, he studied the earth before gingerly making his way to where he could peer over the edge.

King remained on the other side of the wire, easing out just enough rope for Jared to take the next step, echoing Jared's curses every time his foot slipped in the loose gravely scree.

Adrenaline pumped at every footfall on the slippery, dangerous ground. Even though he knew what he was doing and the rope ensured he wouldn't fall to his death, Jared's pulse was pounding by the time he reached the edge.

Peering over, he saw the unconscious woman directly below. He brushed away the cold sweat from his brow as he stared. A shiver coiled down his body at the thought of how close to death the poor woman had come and by the looks of things there was no way he could guarantee she was going to get out of this mess alive.

Studying the ground, he noticed long streaks in the red dirt where the loose stones had been scraped away. There were remnants of a few shrubs that had been torn from the soil, giving him the impression the poor woman must have slipped at the top and slid down with the front of her body against the face of the earth, feet first, trying to grapple for something to grab a hold of. He tried to imagine the fear she would have felt then screwed his face in consternation wondering how, or why she was in such a position to start with. He glanced at the woman and then back at the fence several times. How on earth did she clamber over?

Glancing skywards, he studied the tree canopy and powerlines then swung his eyes downwards again, calling his observations over his shoulder. 'The only way to reach her is to abseil down. But, jeez, King, I don't like the look of this dirt. We're going to need help. Man, this is going to be difficult. The dirt here is too friable. How long before they reach us?'

'By road, about an hour but they're already on the way,' King yelled back as Jared slid one foot closer to the edge.

He swore as he jerked his foot away when the dirt under his foot crumbled. He felt the jerk of the rope attached to his harness as King reacted instantly to his foolish action. 'We can't wait that long. By the angle of her leg, I'd say she has a compound fracture. I'm guessing she's in shock. I can see a lot of grazes and there's a nasty gash on the side of her head. After a fall like that there could be internal bleeding. Okay, I'm done here. Help me up.'

Tensing at every step, Jared made his way back towards the fence knowing that if the cliff gave way it would mean certain death for the woman. Before clambering back over the fence he studied the wire and surrounds, searching for some clue as to how the woman had reached her precarious destination. The moment he was on the other side he felt a sense of relief he shouldn't have – after all this was his job. But there was no doubt this was going to be a difficult rescue and the thought niggled at his innards.

As King readied the equipment, Jared collected a backpack filled with medical items, some high energy food and water. As an afterthought, he shoved in a lightweight warm jacket before slipping one arm through the straps of the pack and flinging it onto his back he tightened the straps so he could abseil unhindered.

Hours of training and experience had the two men working with methodical efficiency to set up three abseiling ropes, each a hundred metres long. Securely anchored, each was tossed over the edge, the loops unfurling as they snaked their way through the air to the valley floor below and taking loose dirt and rocks with them. In surprisingly quick time Jared's harness was secured to the central rope and he began inching down the side of the cliff at such a slow pace it felt ridiculous but gut instinct told him to ensure he didn't loosen too much soil. Every time a handful of stones rained down, he tensed, worried sick the entire cliff would follow.

Close up, the woman had an ethereal beauty. She looked so pale and angelic as dust encrusted brown curls fanned out around her head. Kneeling beside her, Jared reached for the spot on her neck to check for a pulse. It worried him when he felt her soft, pale skin was somewhat clammy. *Damn, she's close to being in shock.* He felt the slight bumps of a thready pulse before calling to her.

'Hey, pretty lady, wake up.'

There was no response. Congealed blood on her temple meant the blood flow had stopped so he centred his attention onto the unusual angle of the right leg and decided he had no choice but to stabilise the fracture before he attended to any of her other injuries. Guilt suffused him as he lifted clothes to check for signs of internal bleeding that would require special attention. *Christ, Mann, you've done this dozens of times before, so why the guilt trip?*

Sending up a prayer of thanks that his patient was unaware of what was about to happen, Jared gently lifted her body, moving it to one end and closer to the wall of their tiny cave to give himself room to work. Even though she was a dead weight, she seemed so tiny and so light to lift. Slipping off his backpack, he dropped it to the ground then removed the plastic self-inflating leg brace. With incredible tenderness, he felt all the way down and around the injured leg, seeking out the nature of the break and which way he was going to have to twist it to set it back into place. He hated what he was going to have to do next.

He placed one large booted foot against the woman's groin, the scrunched jacket padding her from injury. He braced his other foot against the back wall of the cave, wedging it against an imbedded rock. While he wrapped the fingers of one hand around the ankle of her injured leg, the other circled her leg just above the fracture. Three big breaths, a fervent prayer then he yanked backwards as he twisted slightly to the right before easing her leg back into place: his eyes ensuring her leg looked to be in correct alignment. As long as the tibia was in alignment: the fibula wasn't so important at this stage. It would be set in place during the essential operation this lady was going to have.

He felt the sickening grinding of the bones at the same time as he heard the shrill scream of agony. Long, black eyelashes flew apart and dark brown eyes stared at him in abject terror.

'I'm here to help you, though I guess you find it hard to believe when I've just hurt you so badly but your leg needed to be put back into alignment. The pain should ease off a bit now. I'm Jared Mann from Air and Sea Rescue. Let me tell you, I'm very glad to be talking to you. We thought it would be impossible for you to have survived such a fall. Do you have any idea how lucky you are?'

'Lucky?' The word was a squeak. 'Like hell,' came out much stronger. Her eyes scrunched as her mouth screwed in a tense, white line. She gulped then sucked in a long hissing breath through her nose. 'Call me, Bella.' There was a long pause before she swallowed. 'I feel so nauseous,' she whispered.

The woman needed comforting but speed was essential and took priority. Even though Bella gave the impression of being strong willed by her terse response he needed to keep her calm.

'Bella, a pretty name, it suits you. Now, I need to get this brace on your leg to stabilise your fracture. I'm afraid it is going to hurt.' He glanced at her ashen face then added, 'a lot.'

He didn't miss her wince. 'The nausea is probably from the pain but let me know if you need to vomit so I can help you turn over.'

She nodded, a couple of barely there movements. 'Then we need to figure out how to get you out of here. We either climb up, or go down.' He waved a hand upwards. 'Up, is about eight or nine metres but a very difficult climb, especially since you only have the use of one leg. Under normal circumstances we would use a metal cage stretcher, but I don't think we will be able to get it up, the ground at the edge of the cliff near the top appears to be unstable.'

At the sound of her indrawn breath, Jared cursed to himself. Damn but he shouldn't have said that. Spreading his open hand on her clenched fist, he gave it a gentle squeeze. 'We're going to get you down safely. Down, is about seventy metres. It's still difficult but probably the best option. I will go down with you. Are you thirsty? I'd prefer you not eat because you will need surgery on your leg.'

Without waiting for an answer, Jared unscrewed the top from a plastic flask containing water and additives to help with shock and held it to Bella's lips, slipping his large hand under her head and raising it so she could sip. Once her thirst was sated, Bella lay back with her eyes closed while Jared began easing the plastic brace up her leg. He knew by the grimace on her face and the tight clenched fists, she was hurting badly. He paused to wipe the glisten of sweat from her brow with the back of his hand.

'Tell me if it's too much.'

The nod of her head was the only indication she had heard his words. Her eyes remained shut as he eased the plastic up over her ankle.

'Your fingers are warm,' she whispered hoarsely indicating a dry throat, which caused him to wonder exactly how long she had been here. Had the man called it in straight away or had there been a delay?

Glancing at her face, Jared saw the lines of tension had eased a tad, but she was very pale. He smiled as he tightened his hold on the fractured section of her leg with one hand and tugged on the top edge of the plastic until he was satisfied it was in the correct position. When the painstaking process was over, they both let out a loud sigh of relief at the same time. Smiling to re-assure his patient, Jared released the self-inflating valve, checking there was enough pressure exerted against her leg to prevent the bones from moving but not so much as to block blood flow.

'How does it feel now?' he asked.

'A bit better, more like a constant throb instead of the jarring grind.'

'Good, now let me check you over for other injuries.' Working quickly but with care, Jared traversed Bella's body from her head downwards inspecting every single cut and graze: cleaning, anointing and covering where needed. His main concern was spinal injury but after a lot of probing and satisfactory answers to questions he felt certain her spine was fine. And she had turned over earlier. While he worked he chatted quietly to keep her calm and kept watching her face for any sign of her losing consciousness. Once happy with her condition, he slipped the jacket around her body, helping her slide her arms in the sleeves before zipping it up.

Despite the sudden increased warmth from the jacket, Bella began shivering. 'Damn, you're in shock. I need to get you warm.' She made no comment when he budged his body alongside her, eased her into his lap then wrapped his arms around her slight frame to warm her with his body heat. He felt her tension ease as he rubbed her undamaged limbs vigorously to increase blood flow to her extremities.

'Jared, what is your status, over?'

When the disembodied voice came through his helmet, Bella jolted in his arms. Jared ceased his constant rubbing and reached over to switch on the transmitter of the radio built inside his hard helmet.

'Bella…' He glanced at her with a quizzical frown.

As though understanding his unasked question Bella answered. 'Perez.'

'Bella Perez is conscious. Closed compound fracture of the tibia and fibula – stabilised. Nasty contusion on left side of head – bleeding ceased. Numerous cuts and abrasions but none serious. I suspect concussion and she is showing signs that her body is in shock. I've not noticed any signs of major internal bleeding. She is unable to climb and I suspect the ground is not stable enough to use a papoose so we are going down. I'd prefer another man here to help.'

There was a pause while he studied the dirt around them. 'I'm not sure how stable this ledge is. I'm secured but Bella isn't so can you lower me down a harness for her then we're out of here. I'll need three men on the ground with a papoose as soon as you can get them there. Check the map for the nearest clear spot where you can either land or use the winch. Mark out the course for me. We'll carry Bella out. Over.'

'Bella, have you ever been abseiling?'

Bella started as she realised Jared was addressing her then she visibly trembled. 'Yes, twice - on a leadership course. I hated it the first time and didn't feel a whole lot better the second, but I know the basics.' There was a pause before she added, 'Don't you think I'm scared enough without you telling me this ledge isn't safe?'

'I'm sorry you had to hear that. Normally I'd move away to give King a status report.' He pointed to the edge of the cave. 'Unfortunately there's no-where for me to go. To be honest, I'm not sure about the stability of the ledge. It's probably safe enough with your weight but I weigh twice as much and I don't like taking unnecessary chances. I could swing out there, the rope will hold me, but there's no way I would leave you alone. When we get the harness on you, I'll attach you to your own rope then guide you down. We'll take it very slow.'

Clods of dirt flying past them had Bella's body tauten. The sudden tension eased at the sight of a thin nylon rope coming into view from above. Attached to it was a second abseiling harness. Easing up from his uncomfortable sitting position against the end of the cave, Jared lifted Bella in his arms then settled her on her one good leg, propped up against the rear wall as far away from the edge as possible. As he watched waves of pain sweep across her face, unusual indecision filled his mind. To reach the harness he would have to release her for a moment. If he slipped or the ground gave way, he needed to have a firm hold of her. 'Stand against the back wall and don't move. I need to release you for only a second while I grab your harness.'

He felt her body stiffen again as her eyes closed. She didn't even look as though she was breathing. He watched her for a moment then eyed the dangling rope before positioning his body so that he would have the minimum of movement to grab the harness. Taking one step towards the edge, he reached out then gripped tight around the rope. He stilled when he felt the slight shifting of the dirt beneath his foot. Swinging his weight back onto the other leg, he lifted his foot in the air while slinging his free arm back around Bella's waist and grasping her in a tight hold with his fingers. His blood surged as he remained still, eyeing the ground near the edge of the ledge.

His held breath hissed through his clenched teeth when the ground remained intact. Fear thrummed along his nerves as he edged Bella as close to the wall of the cave as possible. Keeping the harness secured to the rope in case either of them dropped it, Jared opened it out and slipped one part over the end of Bella's broken leg. Grasping her around her waist with one arm, he then lifted her off the ground and slipped the other side up over her good leg.

Bella sucked in a very audible breath at the pain from the sudden movement. Jared continued working while he spoke. 'Are you all right? It's okay to scream – you don't have to be brave. I know any movement causes you a lot of pain, so yell if you need to.'

'No, I'm not all right.' She paused as she moaned then sucked in another breath. No way was she all right.

'I learnt years ago that complaining about how you feel doesn't make you feel any better. Making the most of a bad situation and smiling is a far better option so keep going. I'm smiling.'

Jared grinned at the exaggerated smile she planted on her face before she added, 'I have a compelling desire to get out of here. You really don't think it's safe do you? I felt you stiffen.'

Glancing at her face, Jared smiled again at Bella's feisty words. 'I want to lie to you and tell you I'm not worried. But lying will achieve nothing and I'm guessing you wouldn't appreciate it. Yes, I'm concerned enough to want to hurry. Right now, getting this harness on you is a priority. Move as little as you can.' He deftly drew the harness up with one hand, slipped her arms through the correct spaces in the webbing then buckled her up; yanking on the catches to ensure the harness was secure then tightened each strap so it clung to Bella in a snug fit. She looked ridiculous with her skirt bunched up around her hips but he figured Bella was in no mind to be worrying about how she looked.

He paused before the hard bit, reaching out for one of the other ropes hanging down the cliff wall then attaching it to her harness. Untying the knot in the short rope that had been secured to the harness, Jared then wrapped his arm tight around Bella's waist. He eyed the two ropes on either side of his then studied the ground to ascertain which rope was the best option. Deep down, he didn't like either. He was about to step out to the left when he paused. Something told him Bella wasn't secure enough. Releasing his hold he slipped one arm between the harness and her back then eased her against his body.

'Hold tight,' he murmured in her ear as he stretched out with his free arm to grasp the second abseiling rope. He inched one foot towards the edge. The moment he put all his weight on that foot, the earth moved.

Chapter Three

It was difficult to work out which was louder, the roar of the earth ripping apart, Bella's scream of terror or his shouted curse when the entire ledge gave way. Jared swung wildly around in the air with Bella's body clung to him, his arms instinctively clamping tight around her torso, not daring to let her slip one single centimetre.

Dust billowed up around them, not only from the capsized ledge but also from soil loosened from further above as his rope jerked and tightened under their combined weight, pulling the loose scree from above on top of them. With the ledge gone, part of the cliff face above the cave tore free, tumbling down the rocky face in a mini landslide.

While wildly tilting one way then the other, Jared stretched his legs out at ninety degrees from his body to protect Bella from hitting the wall. Again and again, they bounced off the face of the cliff, the rope between them jerking, causing the polyester fibres to rub and chafe against his body. It jerked so hard he wondered if he had torn his skin for the searing burn felt as though he was being skinned alive.

Clods of hard soil, small boulders and dirt rained down over them, causing whimpers of pain from Bella. Harsher agonising cries were torn from her throat every time they jolted against the ragged but sheer cliff wall. Not caring about the severe bruising his own body received Jared instinctively tucked his head over Bella to protect her as much as he could.

It seemed like an eternity before they finally came to a standstill. After the echoing sounds of Bella's screams and the thundering of the earth falling, the silence was sudden and eerily absolute. In total disbelief they clung to each other with heaving chests. Jared felt adrenaline galloping through the maze of blood vessels in his body and he imagined Bella felt the same. Time seemed to stand still while he clung to her in a tight embrace, instinctively not daring to ease the tension in his muscles.

Jared stirred first, forcing calmness to his voice but waves of fear gripped his innards. He knew he was in one hell of a pickle but somehow he couldn't let the already battered woman know how serious things were. 'Bella, look at my eyes.' He waited until he was staring into the brown depths, the terror in them unable to be masked. 'Now reach up with both hands and wrap them around my neck.'

Bella reached. Her eyes remained staring while her lips squeezed together in a thin white line of tension as she slid her arms around his neck then grasped her wrists tight.

'Good girl, now grip your fingers around the harness at the back of my shoulders.'

He felt her force her fingers between his iridescent orange jacket and the nylon webbing then she wrapped her fingers tight around the strands of webbing. Jared figured by her determined actions, nothing on this earth was going to make her let go.

'Now the hard bit, sweetheart.'

'Hard? This isn't already hard?' she squeaked.

He forced a grin. 'This is about as hard as it gets but see if you can lever yourself up far enough so I can get your harness clip to latch onto mine. We need to be head to head. Then you will be safe, attached to me. I won't let you go, I promise, but I have to release one hand so please don't panic. Ready, on three.' Before beginning the countdown Jared paused a moment to ensure Bella understood his instructions. At the small nod of her head he used the arm still wrapped around her waist and under her harness, to help lever her up.

The count was slow and deliberate but on three, Bella heaved. Taking his eyes away from her face for the first time, Jared glanced down, found her clip, reached down and slid the clip over his own in one fast, almighty effort, his muscles aching with the strain, his nerves screaming and his body burning underneath the straps of his harness from the deep bruising he could already feel. Clip on he whipped his arm back around Bella's waist. Her face was scrunched in tension. Who could blame her? The ordeal she was going through would test even the strongest of people. It was certainly testing him and he was used to scaling mountains and had even taken a fall leaving him hanging in mid-air as he was now. But then, his climbing partner had been safely secured above and not clung to him like a limpet.

'Bella, look at me.' It took a few seconds for her to open her eyes. 'You did very well so now listen carefully while I explain what's going to happen next. The rope we have to slide down is between us. If we slide the way we are friction will cause it to burn through our clothes and skin. Do you understand?'

All she could do was nod. He could tell by the terror in her eyes that speech was beyond her.

'Good. Now bring your hands, one at a time, around to grip the front of my harness. Force your arms through the straps as far as you can so you can clasp your fingers together. Then I'm going to bring my legs up, one between your legs, which you can use to put some of your weight on. I need my hands free to release the brake behind me.'

He paused, still staring into her eyes until he was certain she understood. Even though he could feel her shocked muscles trembling he saw her visibly try to relax her body. She blew out a couple of breaths as though seeking courage.

'Jared, are you there? Over.' King's voice broke the tension but with no free hand, Jared wasn't able to respond to the call. He swore under his breath at the Government department that had refused to fund the new helmets they'd requested. This was exactly the type of incident he'd detailed in his submission.

'Aren't you going to answer?' asked Bella.

'Can't without letting you go.' Pausing to look at her he saw her throat work but no words came out for a few seconds..

'Then yell!'

Jared laughed then yelled. 'I'm here!' He then added to Bella, 'King knows not to panic if I don't answer straight away. He'll know by the tension on the rope that I am still attached. He also understands that I need a free hand to flick the switch. Now, after you have a firm hold, I want you to lean away from my body so the rope isn't touching you. You won't fall. You are clipped to my harness. I'll be using my feet to bounce us off the cliff face as we go down and I imagine you are going to be in intense pain from the jarring but there is not a lot I can do about it right now. Believe me, I wish there was some other way but there isn't.'

'Just do it!' she yelled then softened her tone. 'The pain I can handle. Hanging up here like the bullseye on a target I can't. Just get us down.'

For a moment she stared then a look of resignation swept over her features. 'We're not going to make it are we? I'm smart enough to figure out the impossibility of you being able to abseil down the cliff with me clinging to you like an abalone on the reef.'

Jared jolted her as his arms tightened. She couldn't give up. 'Don't even think like that. We'll make it.'

'Maybe I should just let go,' she whispered.

'You do that then I will spend the rest of my life filled with guilt.' Somehow he had to convince this gutsy woman to keep fighting. 'Besides you are now attached to me harness to harness so if you fall then so do I. Look at me.'

Lifting her eyes, she stared then smiled. 'I trust you, Jared.'

The simple statement was said with such compassion and solemnity that Jared ceased to breathe, her words reaching deep into his soul. Of all the things he had done in his life and all the rescues he had made, never before had any person put so much faith in him. He held her life in his hands and he wasn't at all sure he would be able to get them down to the ground alive. The manoeuvre he was contemplating was one he thought up on the spur of the moment, it certainly wasn't one he had ever done before or even heard of being undertaken, but he didn't have a lot of choice. There was no way he could transfer a badly injured woman across to another abseiling rope in mid air, seventy odd metres off the ground, especially without assistance.

Bella obeyed every one of Jared's instructions implicitly. She forced her hands under the webbing before tucking her fingers around the front of his harness, gripping so tight her knuckles glowed white while her trusting eyes stared at his face. Jared swung his legs up, allowed Bella to rest her weight on his thigh then he released her waist by slowly easing his arm through the straps.

All the time he wriggled his arm out he was ready to regain a tight hold in case the sudden strain on the one piece of metal holding them together was too much. He held his breath as he slid his arm the final few centimetres. Breathing ceased as he waited for that small piece of curved metal to give way. A well-engineered, strongly constructed clip, built to take the strain – but when your life depended on it working – it took an enormous amount of faith and courage to rely on it. And how strong was the harness webbing after being jerked so tight?

The moment his arm was free, Bella's death grip on his harness tightened even more. Hearing her gulp he looked at her just in time to see her eyes squeeze shut. He heard her whispered words.

'Please, God, keep us safe.'

Jared's heart flipped in his chest at her whispered prayer then not wanting to prolong this agony and waste any more time, he reached for the rope behind with one hand while his other hand grasped the same rope in front just above his head. An audible sigh of relief expelled from his lungs when he jerked the rope hard and the brake mechanism released. He hadn't been sure it would after the tremendous jolt during the fall. He willed his heart rate to slow then paused before whispering, 'On the count of three, ease your body away from me, keep your head back but not so far that you can't watch the rope. Yell if you feel it burning and don't, whatever you do, let go of my harness. Ready?' He waited until she acknowledged with a determined nod of her head.

'One, two, three.'

Bella pulled back as far as the clipped harnesses would allow, leaning backwards and outwards with her fingers still clamped together.

Jared released the braking mechanism on the rope behind his backside to allow his body to freefall at a slow but steady pace, down the rope, his legs stretched at right angles to his body, knees slightly bent, his eyes on the wall of the cliff watching it whiz past as they zipped down through the air. Each hit against the wall brought down more dirt from above. With his eyes swinging from the rock wall to Bella's face he felt the air whipping against his skin, heard the zinging of the rope passing through the metal loops of his harness and smelt the friction of the rope as it heated. Bella was unable to hold back her yelps of pain every time he hit the cliff face with his feet.

A second eternity passed before they jolted when he slowed them down near the bottom, braking to bring them to a complete standstill just before they hit the ground.

Releasing the brake as his legs straightened, his feet settled on the ground taking the weight of both bodies. Taking as much care as he could to be gentle, Jared gathered Bella into his arms to ease her to the ground, careful to minimize movement of the fractured bones he knew must be almost unendurable. Just minor movement on a newly fractured limb was agonising so what Bella had endured must be unbearable.

His body ached, his muscles strained beyond their limits and he could feel the sting where his harness had cut into him. After settling Bella onto the ground, he unhitched his harness from the rope and then sank down beside her with his eyes closed while he sent up a silent prayer of gratitude and tried to steady his thumping heart. He had been in scary situations before, but never anything as frightening as what he had just been through. That they were still alive, he knew, was a miracle.

Bella was as silent as he and he wondered if the sheer terror of the past few minutes was racing through her brain as rapidly as it was his.

A crackling of Jared's radio broke the intense atmosphere. 'Jared, give me a status report. What the hell happened? Are you all right? Over.' King's disembodied voice sounded frantic.

Knowing the slackening of the rope would have alerted King, Jared lifted one arm that felt like jellified lead, heavy and liquid, but it took tremendous effort to reach over to his radio to flick the switch of the transmitter. 'King, that was one hell of a ride. The ledge collapsed but we're safe. By some miracle we are both on the ground. How long before you can get the men down here? I've got to tell you, man, that was the scariest thing I've ever done in my life and right now my old job is looking pretty damn good. Over.'

'A close call, eh? You had me really worried when I saw a huge chunk of the cliff fall away, almost back to the fence. I have to tell you mate, you scared the sh…, err sorry ma'am, scared me to death. Help should be there in about fifteen minutes. You'll have about an hour's walk due east to the first clear spot where I can lift you out. What's the status on Bella? Over.'

Jared's hands dropped to the ground as he stared at the lady in question. Her face was deathly white underneath a thick coating of red dust. Her wound was seeping blood through the plaster he had administered, but he could see the smallest of wry smiles turning up at the corner of her mouth.

'I've flown over the side of a cliff twice in one day, busted my leg, am covered in blood, dirt, dust and God knows what else, making me look like a freak show. Every bone and muscle in my body feels like it's been torn apart. I've been terrified out of my wits and he wants to know how I am.' Bella couldn't suppress the ironic grin from spreading across her face.

Jared let out a shout of laughter then switched on his transmitter. 'She's the gutsiest woman I've ever met. Same injuries as before, no adrenaline left in her body and feisty as hell. She wants to know how you would feel after flying over the same cliff twice in one day – the second time with a broken leg? Over.'

'Can't figure out why she went so close to the edge to start with. Over'

Jared was alarmed when he saw a rush of unbidden tears wash across Bella's eyes and her already ashen face pale even further. It was like watching a dam burst, the way the blood drained from her face with such rapidity. With a great effort he pulled his tortured body up to crawl nearer.

'I was pushed,' she whispered in a voice that cracked on a sob of fear or pain. He couldn't tell which.

Chapter Four

'Pardon? What do you mean pushed?' Forgetting about his own pain, Jared squatted right in front of Bella's face, reached out with the fingers of one hand and cupped her chin, forcing her face up to look at him.

'Pushed means pushed!' Bella yelled. 'You don't think I would be stupid enough to climb over that fence for fun do you? I'm terrified of heights. I couldn't even walk out on that darned viewing platform. I was bloody well dragged over the fence and pushed.' Reaching up with one hand she ran her shaking fingers along the deep contusion on the side of her head. 'How do you think I got this? He hit me with a branch.' Unable to control her wildly seesawing emotions any longer, Bella burst into tears.

Crawling on his knees and too stunned to say a word, Jared gathered the distraught woman into his lap, settled on the ground and wrapped his arms around her in a tight embrace then held her securely. It was several minutes before he dared release one hand. He reached up to turn on his transmitter. 'Come in, King, over.'

'Yeah, man, what can I do for you, over?'

'Do you have any police officers with you, over?'

'Not yet, why? I didn't think we would need any, over.'

'We're going to need them. Bella was pushed over the cliff. We have an attempted murder on our hands. While you are waiting, look around for a branch big enough to be used to whack someone over the head. It should have blood on one end. If you find it, see if you can't stow it in the chopper without telling anyone why, but be careful not to compromise the evidence, over. Oh, sorry, keep this to yourself. Have the police meet me at the hospital. Over.'

'Damn it man. Pushed? I'm on it now, over.'

Silence reigned while Jared mulled over what Bella had told him. He needed answers before he took this unbelievable story to the police. Knowing he needed to keep her calm he maintained a quiet conversational tone as he began probing questions. 'Bella, who did this to you?'

'My boss, Bart Hudson.'

'Why? It was he who rang us that you had gone over the edge. It doesn't seem logical for him to call it in.'

'I'm not sure why, he never got around to telling me why he wanted me dead!' Sarcasm dripped from her tongue. She paused for a moment before continuing in a quieter voice, her frustration and continuing pain obvious. 'He thinks I'm dead so why not call it in. Dead people can't talk. In fact, thinking about it, with me gone everyone will believe whatever he says. He has no idea I landed on that stupid ledge. I'll bet he wasn't waiting for you.' The laugh accompanying her words was derisive. 'He needed to call it in so there would be a body to explain my absence. If I disappeared off the face of the earth people would ask questions. We were seen together leaving the office. I spoke to some of my friends as we walked outside to the car park. They knew I was with him.'

'You have no idea why? There wasn't something you overheard, or saw that you shouldn't have? What kind of business is he in?' For some reason, Jared believed every word of her inconceivable story. It was too fantastic to make up and her manner told him she was being honest. With years of experience behind him, he knew when people were lying and this woman certainly wasn't.

'You're not a copper are you, why all the questions?'

Jared hesitated while he contemplated her question. He considered telling her about his real profession, but what if she was making it up? Discretion won his inner battle. 'Sorry, Bella, but I need to know a few facts to tell the police when we meet up with them. I need to understand this crazy situation.'

She sighed then hesitated as though she didn't really want to talk, which sent a wave of doubt through his mind. 'Bart Hudson runs a combination of businesses: real estate, insurance and finances, under the name of Hudson Enterprises. I work as an accountant in Head Office. I'm not the head accountant, James Carthew is.' Her face screwed while she thought. 'The only thing I can think of where something was a bit strange was two days ago when I walked into Bart's office.'

'You just walked in without knocking?'

'It was after hours. He wanted a report on the monthly balance of payments completed so I stayed back a few minutes. I thought only the two of us were still in the building so I knocked at the same time as I pushed the door open and walked in.'

'What happened when you entered the office?'

'There were three other men with him. I think they were having some kind of a meeting. They all looked edgy when they saw me. You know, startled eyes, one man blushed, that instant tense silence. I don't know but they just looked guilty. What really made me feel something was up was that Bart yelled at me, asked me what the hell I was doing there. He's never done that before. I explained how he had insisted on the report ASAP, handed it to him, apologised for the intrusion then left.'

Jared shifted his body to a more comfortable position. 'Did he say anything to you about the meeting, you know… afterwards?'

'Not once.'

'I'm mystified. Why were you up there this morning?' Releasing one arm he pointed skywards.

Bella couldn't suppress a shudder. 'He asked me to attend a meeting with him to take notes and give financial advice. I queried why we were driving up to the hills. He said his client lived in the hills. When we neared the lookout, he asked if I had ever seen it. When I said no he stopped the car and walked me to the lookout showing me the view. I couldn't go out on the wooden platform hanging out over the valley because I suffer from vertigo, so turned back. Next thing I knew I was being whacked over the head with a branch. It stunned me. I fell to the ground but when I looked up Bart was standing there. He just leered then whacked me again. I must have lost consciousness for a while. I can vaguely remember being dragged along the ground. He had his hands under my armpits and I could feel my heels dragging in the dirt.'

There was a long pause while Bella appeared to search her mind for details. 'I recall the sensation of being pushed. It must have been over the fence because I remember being jolted and the pain when I landed on the hard ground.'

'That would explain some of your injuries,' Jared interrupted. 'You have a few long gouges on your abdominal region. At a guess, I'd say they were caused by the barbed wire.'

For a moment Bella just stared at him, her jaw slack. 'Barbed wire! He dragged me over barbed wire?'

'Sorry, but there was barbed wire all the way along the top of the security fence. I attempted to climb over it to reach you but ended up having to cut it away. I couldn't figure out how you managed to reach the top. Go on.'

'Things are a bit hazy. I must have come around because I remember lying on my stomach stretched out.' Her eyes closed and her troubled fingers brushed against her brow. Then her eyes flew open and her hand clenched into a fist and hit her thigh. 'He was gripping my fingers with one hand through the wire. I recall struggling but I couldn't get my feet on solid ground. I realised my feet were hanging over the edge of the cliff. When I looked at him, he… oh, he… he simply released my hands then shoved my head with… I think it was his foot, but it might have been a stick or something else.'

Bella's voice faded away so much Jared had to strain to catch her words. She sat staring into space, her eyes unblinking. Bile surged and anger boiled. He'd seen and heard a lot of grizzly details in his life but this one was close to the top of the list of horror stories.

Her next words sounded robotic. 'I felt myself falling, screamed, tried to find something to grab a hold of then felt the pain when I guess I landed on the ledge. The pain …

was excruciating. The next thing I knew was hearing your helicopter.'

The pain in her voice caused Jared to tighten his hold. Unbidden, he dropped his face towards her head and planted a kiss on her dusty curls and instinctively rocked her. 'These other three men, did you recognise them?' he asked as a surge of warmth and intense feeling of protectiveness engulfed him. His voice was muffled against her hair.

'I've never seen them before and have no idea who they are.'

Feeling her tremble, Jared realised what he had done and lifted his head, chastising himself for his unbidden action. She was a patient, and beyond caring for her injuries and safety he had no right to any other feelings towards her. As he put some distance between as much of their bodies as he could, he said, 'It sounds to me like something untoward was going on. Why else would he try to get rid of you? I have a couple of friends in the police force.' Hell, he had oodles of friends in the police force. 'I'll ask them to make some enquiries and I think it might be best if we make out, to your boss, that we retrieved your body.'

A weird sound, something between a snort and a groan, rumbled from her throat. 'Well you wouldn't be lying would you? You needn't mention that the body was still kicking and screaming, although the way it feels right now, you wouldn't be far wrong. Is there any chance you have some painkillers?'

'Sorry, my backpack went over the edge. I could try to find it but it is probably buried under a tonne of dirt. I think it might be quicker to wait for help. I'm sorry. Tell me how I can make it easier for you.'

'My leg throbs so much, but I have another more pressing problem.'

'What's that?'

He felt her squirm. 'I feel so embarrassed but I need to pee and I'm not quite up to walking away from here and squatting behind a bush.'

Jared was unable to suppress a grin. Bella Perez was quite something. How many women would be so open about such a rather delicate problem? When he first saw her lying unconscious up on the ledge she looked so angelic and fragile, like an injured butterfly. After the ordeal she had been through, he figured her to be very tenacious. He liked her spirit. Most women he knew wouldn't have been able to withstand the torturous suffering Bella had been through without becoming hysterical. Taking care not to hurt her any more than he had to, he moved her from his lap, stood tall then assisted her to her feet, holding her steady when she swayed.

'I can close my eyes while I help you with your… err… nickers and promise faithfully not to tell a soul.'

Her glance was quick, catching the grin he didn't have time to mask. 'Very funny,' she muttered sarcastically. 'It's an act of nature – even the queen has to pee, but I normally prefer some privacy. You men have it so easy at times. How about getting this ridiculous contraption off me first and then I can handle my own nickers thank you very much?'

Jared's grin widened. He just couldn't suppress it. He was finding it very difficult not to laugh out aloud. 'That ridiculous contraption, as you call it, just saved your life.' He unbuckled the harness then slipped it from her body then eased it downwards before grasping her under her arms and lifting her feet off the ground as he removed it entirely and tossed it aside. As he eased his hands into her armpits, her rumpled skirt unfolded but still hovered high on her thighs. 'Slip your nickers down and I'll lower you. I promise to close my eyes.'

A rising redness in her cheeks told Jared that the only thing keeping Bella's mouth shut while she shimmied her lacy bikini nickers down to her knees, was utter embarrassment at her predicament. The glimpse of the barely there underclothes, sent a different kind of heat surging through him, a heat he hadn't experienced in quite a while. Why now? Why this woman when no other woman had particularly interested him for eighteen months?

'Okay, lower away and don't you dare peek or laugh.'

"Keep your leg out straight,' said Jared as he used all the strength in his arms to lower her downwards and backwards on her one bent knee. The manoeuvre was more difficult than he'd thought, taking a considerable time to undertake. Job completed, Bella asked him to lift her up again. He knew his body was shaking from suppressed laughter, so he wasn't surprised when she shot him a comment under her breath while she pulled her underwear back into place.

'You're laughing. I sincerely hope I didn't miss your foot.'

Unable to control himself any longer, Jared let loose with loud laughter. 'And you are an incredibly sassy lady. I'm only sorry we had to meet under such dastardly circumstances. I think I like you a lot, Miss Bella Perez.'

'That would be Mrs Perez. Mrs Annabella Perez. I'm a widow.'

Chapter Five

Feeling a strange desperation, Bella tried to drag her mind from the depths of a dark, swirling fog. This time it was an unfamiliar smell invading her nostrils that her subconscious was attempting to put a name to. When she forced her eyes open all she could see was a dim light and she had no idea where she was, her surroundings unfamiliar. Turning her head sideways she could make out the features of a large man sitting slumped in a chair next to her. Full consciousness hit. She was in hospital and the man next her had brought her here.

Memories of her ride out of the valley surged to the fore. He'd said it would be an easy ride for her. Yeah, right, Mr Mann, very easy ride. An hour of jolting, strapped into a ridiculous, narrow aluminium frame – a papoose, Jared called it. More like a torture chamber. The bush had been very thick, the path rough. In fact there had been no clear path. The four men had clambered over boulders and waded through prickly scrub, forging their own pathway, every bump and jerk jarring the broken bones of her leg together and sending wave after agonising wave of pain through every nerve ending in her body. All the while the over-hot sun had sent down scorching rays even though the direct light had been shielded from her body by a cotton sheet. This had caused her breath to be stifling, further exacerbating the amount of perspiration oozing from her pores. The only upside had been the filtering shade from the huge trees of virgin forest, the reason the helicopter hadn't been able to winch them out safely.

She knew it hadn't been easy for the men either. They did their best to ease her discomfort and she knew their muscles must have been aching by the time they reached the small clearing where the helicopter had been waiting. Not only did they carry her all the way, much of the time they had lifted the papoose head high over obstacles to keep her from being scratched or whipped by branches from the dense underbrush.

It was only after being strapped into the helicopter that the ride had become anywhere near easy but the flight through the air kept giving her visions and sensations of her two flights down the cliff face and she had kept her eyes shut tight until they had landed on the roof of the hospital. Being transferred from the papoose to the trolley was not without its trials and tribulations, everyone taking it slow to keep her pain to the minimum. All she wanted was one quick movement. The pain would have been just as bad but much shorter. It wasn't until after a thorough examination that anyone thought to give her a shot of painkiller to end the continuous throbbing.

Attempting to move to a more comfortable position, Bella found her actions restricted. With her hands, she felt around. A drip in her arm had her attached to machinery and her leg elevated on cushions and obviously now in plaster, was anchoring her down. She felt her head, which was beginning to ache and found a bandage holding down a large swab.

'Bella?' Jared sat up and leant over, reaching out in the dim light for her hand.

'Just don't ask me how I'm feeling. Although my leg doesn't ache quite as much, I still feel like I've been flattened by a giant steam-roller.'

'You're probably due for more pethidine.' Jared's hand moved over to press the call button for the medical staff to attend. 'Your leg has been set. They've checked you over for internal injuries and found none. You are a mass of bruises and scrapes but the doctor is happy you will make a full recovery. You are one very lucky lady. I've talked with the police; they want to speak to you when you feel up to it. As far as I know, your boss hasn't been told about you being alive. King found the branch, which is being tested at forensics for your blood, and if we are lucky, DNA from Hudson.'

Jared said no more, leaving the room while the incoming doctor checked Bella's readings while asking pertinent questions about her condition. He assisted her to sip water through a straw to moisten her arid mouth then gave her a shot of some painkiller to ease her growing pain. The moment the doctor walked out the door, Jared moved back in, settling back into her bedside chair: a chair that seemed incapable of holding the mass of his large muscular frame.

'Go home, Jared. You must be exhausted. Go and get some sleep.'

'I've had enough sleep. I'm staying to make sure you are safe. There is one thing I'm curious about, you said you had been married?'

'Yes, briefly, Raoul died.'

'How briefly?'

'Six months.' Her eyes slid closed. Memories of her life with Raoul were too painful to talk about. He had been such a wonderful, kind, funny, adorable man. Her feigned pretence didn't last long as she fell into a deep, drug induced sleep.

***

Completely mystified, Jared sat watching the ever-changing expressions flit across her face. He'd read her medical report. The second last line stated that Mrs Annabella Perez was still a virgin. What kind of marriage did she have? The last thing he could ever imagine happening would be to be married to such a beautiful strong woman for six months and not take her to his bed. He wouldn't have lasted one night. The very thought of this beautiful woman in his bed sent his hormones surging, causing an uncomfortable hardness. Willing his body to behave, he shifted in his seat to ease the discomfort then settled back to study her.

Now that she wasn't covered in a layer of red dirt and blood, Jared inspected Bella's features. Reaching over, he turned on the bedside light to gain a better look. He knew her closed eyes were a deep, rich brown. Long black eyelashes fanned them. A cute nose, slightly tilting up at the end gave her face a perky look, a perkiness that suited her strong, determined personality. High cheekbones now had a bit more colour from the warmth of the blanket and air controlled temperature rather than the coolness of the brisk breeze that had kept their bodies chilled while perched precariously on the side of the cliff. Jared shuddered at the memory of the ledge collapsing. He closed his eyes; remembering the sensation of flying through the air, Bella clasped against his body, praying the brake on his harness would work. It was a moment he would never forget; a moment when he had felt sure they were going to die.

After forcing the unpleasant thoughts from his mind, he opened his eyes to continue his close study. Bella's lips were the next item for his scrutiny. Not too thin, not too pouty, very kissable, very inviting. How many men had had the privilege? He dared to run the pad of his index finger along the bottom lip then up over the top, finding them soft and warm. His finger continued on a journey of exploration down Bella's cheek, along her jaw-line to her ear where it touched the tiny diamond stud in the centre of the soft lobe. He wondered if her lobes were sexually sensitive and what parts of her neck would arouse a deep passion in her when they were kissed. He couldn't imagine her being anything else but very passionate.

Quit it, he remonstrated with his mind, then thought that his newly aroused desire might be because he'd been too long without a woman but after his last humiliating experience at a relationship, women hadn't been on his agenda.

Shaking bad memories from his mind he went back to his study of the woman causing his libido to return with a vengeance. The white hospital gown spoiled the effect, preventing him from searching further. He'd seen further during his examination of her injuries but at the time his perusal had been purely clinical. There was nothing clinical about the feelings the sight of her were creating inside him now. He recognised them for exactly what they were.

Reclining against the cold vinyl of the uncomfortable hospital chair he remembered the feel of Bella's slim waist as he had held her in a tight embrace, not daring to ease his hold in case he dropped her. He knew without a doubt that he would never have forgiven himself if that had happened. Shaking his head to rid his brain of the horrible thought, Jared recalled the cute little backside when he had held her shivering body in his lap to warm her up.

Did he desire her? Too right! And it surprised him but Annabella Perez was one very sexy, very beautiful and very desirable woman. Would he pursue her? He sure wanted to but knew he wouldn't - at least not yet. Bella didn't know it but logic told him her life was still in grave danger. Once Bart Hudson discovered she was alive, Jared felt certain that whatever had driven the man to attempt murder, hadn't gone away and the fact Bella had been bashed and flung over the edge of a mountain by Hudson would only make her life a lot more vulnerable. She had recognised the perpetrator.

Lifting his long legs, Jared rested his feet on the edge of the bed as he sank further backwards into the chair, his hands resting in his lap, his elbows leaning on the hard curved arms of the chair. He felt desperate for more sleep but thoughts of what he could do to help Bella kept sleep at bay. He felt certain she was going to need some sort of assistance. With no idea about her family situation and until he was sure she was in safe hands, he wasn't letting her out of his sight. Until she was fit to talk more, her safety was his only concern.

When Bella awoke not long before dawn Jared was still slumped in the chair attempting sleep, but he was aware of her stirring. A nurse, who took Bella's pulse and blood pressure every hour, had doused the light by the bed during the night. He watched under hooded eyes while Bella wriggled then hoisted her body up onto the pillows behind her head before inspecting her surroundings. She was still attached to the drip, making it impossible to move from the bed. A sudden flush of pinkness rose up her cheeks as her eyes settled on him.

'Jared,' she whispered.

He straightened, groaning as sore cramped muscles protested. 'Bella, you're looking much better.' But if she felt anything like him, she probably wasn't feeling a whole lot better.

'How come you are the only one around every time I need to pee?' she groaned.

He had no control over his grin. It just slipped out before he could mask his features as he reached over to press the call button. 'It's nice to know I'm useful for some things. You want me to help again or would you rather wait for a nurse?'

'I think I'll wait for the nurse and you can damn well disappear when she does come.'

He laughed. 'Good morning to you as well. I'm glad to see you are suffering no ill effects from your little adventure yesterday. I'll leave you in peace but don't think for one minute I won't be back. I'd be lost without your charming sweet words.' In one swift movement, he stood, bent and planted a kiss on the top of Bella's head then strode out of the room.

***

A sudden burst of male laughter as he strode down the corridor was explained when Bella's nurse entered the room – a male nurse. She sighed in resignation as the man began tending her. Being roughly the same age as she was, didn't ease her chagrin one iota as she was stripped, bed-bathed then a bedpan was slid under her backside.

The young man had only just returned from emptying the pan in the en-suite bathroom when Jared stuck his head around the edge of the door. 'Can I come in?'

Still feeling mortified, Bella was about to say no when the door opened wide. Jared stood back and an orderly walked in carrying Bella's breakfast. Jared followed the woman across the floor. He had showered, shaved and had on a fresh set of clothes.

He stood back until the orderly had settled Bella's tray on the table overhanging her bed then he tugged at the sleeve of her clean hospital gown. 'Sweet, Annabella, I have as much medical training as your nurse so I can't figure out why I couldn't have been the one to denude you of your gorgeous sexy nightwear, sponge you down and dress your wounds. My feelings are mortally wounded.' The chuckle accompanying Jared's words earned him a withering glare.

Bella kept her eyes down, assiduous in her study of the food she was pushing around her plate while ruminating on his words. He was probably right and she knew for sure he would have allowed her to use the bathroom despite the difficulty of being hooked up to a drip. One thing she'd already learnt about the man was that he was very caring and considerate and he would have found a way for her to get to the bathroom. But she wasn't about to let him know that she would have preferred his ministrations.

When she pushed the tray containing her uneaten breakfast to the end of her trolley, Jared's sarcastic demeanour altered in an instant. 'You must eat something: you've had nothing for almost twenty-four hours.'

'You eat it, I'm not hungry.'

'You must eat. Here, let me help you.' Jared settled on the side of the bed to butter the toast, cutting it into narrow fingers before gently pressing the long slivers against her mouth.

Smiling at his determination, Bella relented and slowly nibbled her way through each offering until all the toast had disappeared but she refused any more food for she still felt nauseous and wasn't all that hungry.

Jared had no qualms about polishing off her cereal and poached eggs but they shared the orange juice and lukewarm, bitter coffee, Bella screwing up her face at the acrid taste.

Once settled back amongst the plumped up pillows, Bella wavered her fingers up and down and asked, 'Where did the clothes come from?'

'I always carry a change of clothes and toilet bag in my car. In this job, even though we wear protective overalls, we get dunked in water, our clothes get torn, bloodied or filthy and more often than not we need to shower and change. I've left a message for the police to let them know they can come to interview you after eleven this morning. But right now, I'm going to leave you for a couple of hours. Do you have any personal belongings at work?'

'Yes, why? My handbag was in Bart's car and there are a few things on my desk.'

'I want to use that as an excuse to ask your boss a couple of questions. I'll make out your family asked me to pick up your belongings.'

'My parents live overseas so you'd better say you spoke to them on the phone.'

'Even better, it makes my visit more genuine. I'll be back before ten. Do you have a mobile phone?'

'Yes, but it's still in my handbag.'

He hesitated a moment then withdrew his own phone from his shirt pocket. After punching in a series of numbers he handed the instrument to Bella. 'I'm leaving you my mobile phone. If you need me press this button.' He held the phone to show her. 'It will automatically page me on this pager.' Pointing to the small black instrument attached to his belt, Jared placed the phone on her bedside table before departing.

Chapter Six

From his position sprawled in a blue upholstered chair in the reception area, Jared spied a man with a smug grin on his face, swaggering down the corridor and somehow he knew it was Bart Hudson. There was a pause then the grin altered the moment Bart and Jared caught each other's eye. Jared didn't miss the shiver of apprehension as Hudson took one more step then paused mid-stride before renewing his forward journey, but the swagger had been replaced by hesitancy. As Bart neared, Jared unfolded his body, found his feet then pulled himself up to his full height to give the impression of intimidation while he assessed the man. It was a tactic he often used when confronting people he felt he needed to read their body language. Why not use your God given build to your advantage?

The first impression was that Bart Hudson was an overweight, podgy man of no more than five feet eight. Jared imagined the man was considered good looking by most females, but he gave the appearance of being in the habit of overindulging in both food and alcohol. There was an unhealthy redness to his nose and cheeks and a definite beer belly. Premature thinning of blond hair aged him. He looked fifty but Jared guessed he was probably younger.

'Good morning, Bart Hudson?' Jared outstretched his hand as a sign of greeting. It would be fascinating to see how the man reacted. If he was any judge of character, and after the life he'd experienced Jared considered he was a better judge than average, then this man should be very nervous. Hell, if the man could drop a female worker over the edge of a cliff, then he would have to have some sort of a guilty conscience and be wary of strangers.

'It depends on who is asking.'

The surly response didn't auger well for an amicable meeting nor did the refusal to shake hands. It did give Jared the instant knowledge this man was indeed afraid and had something to hide. So to put Hudson off kilter even further, Jared planted his feet shoulder width apart, stood firm and lifted his hands to his hips in a threatening stance. As Jared hoped, the manoeuvre brought Hudson to a halt. The man had no choice since Jared had deliberately positioned himself between the main entry and the closed door with Hudson's name printed on a large gaudy brass plate. The sight of the ostentatious nameplate had indicated exactly the type of man he was dealing with.

'My name is Jared Mann.' He paused to see if Hudson recalled speaking to him over the phone only the day before. The man didn't even blink in recognition. 'I work for Air and Sea Rescue.'

Hudson's eyes flared before the man attempted to compose his features. Determined not to make it easy for the man, Jared took his time before disclosing the reason for the visit. Let the man stew.

'I believe it was you who phoned us yesterday in regards to the woman we retrieved from below Reyne's Lookout.' He chose his words with care; deliberately not mentioning a body so there would be no recourse later, and he was now more than certain there was going to be a later: a very long winded and complicated later if his gut instinct was correct - especially since Hudson overreacted with vigorous head nodding and tsking.

'Your secretary, I seem to recall you saying. Her family has asked me to pick up any personal effects.' Could Bella be regarded as her own family? He hoped so as he wasn't in the habit of lying. Deliberate lies always caught up with you in the end.

There was an instant change of demeanour. Hudson wasn't able to completely mask a smug grin of satisfaction before he thought better of it and schooled his features to sobriety then muttered platitudes of sorrow. 'Nasty business. I'm sorry to have lost such a wonderful member of my staff but she was one of our accountants, not my secretary. If you wait just one minute I'll get my real secretary to gather Bella's things together.'

When Jared took a step to follow, Hudson held up a hand to stop. 'Wait here.'

It was obvious by the way Hudson spun on his heel, but not quick enough to hide the grin of satisfaction from his face, that he was eager to escape this confrontation. But he had taken the bait by presuming Bella was no longer in the land of the living and Jared wasn't in the mood to let the creep have any relief from a situation created by his own evil doing.

'One minute, if you don't mind, Mr Hudson?' Jared called after him. He waited until the man stopped, which he did, but he didn't turn so Jared continued, 'I need to fill out my report: a necessary evil, all this paperwork. Are you able to tell me exactly what happened, why you were both up there to start with? It seems rather an unusual place to be in the middle of a working day.'

Jared studied Hudson's demeanour as the man paused with his back to him. There was a definite tremor across the shoulders followed by a straightening of the back. The shoulders hitched back a fraction and the head lifted. Hudson was taking an inordinate amount of time to gather his wits together and Jared imagined the man's mind was spinning to search for a plausible explanation. When he finally turned around there was a look of confusion in Hudson's eyes. What amazed Jared was the fact that Hudson hadn't yet realised, or wasn't smart enough to know, that only the police should be asking for such details. When Hudson opened his mouth to answer, Jared released his held breath.

'Oh! Oh, certainly. Mrs Perez was overwrought when she arrived at work. She… um… she said she'd had a bad dream about her husband. He was killed in an accident you know. So sudden and only a week after they were married. She never got over his untimely death. I suggested a pleasant drive followed by lunch so she could regain her composure. It was her idea to go up into the hills. When we stopped at the lookout, she just flew out of my car and ran, screaming that she couldn't take it anymore. I couldn't stop her. She just went crazy – over the fence and jumped. What could I do?'

Taken aback by the glib lie, it took Jared a moment to come up with something plausible to carry on the conversation. 'I see. No, there's not a lot one can do in those circumstances. It was good of you to ring it in straight away. Now, her personal effects?'

Jared was left standing while fighting to prevent his face from revealing his anger at the man. Didn't he realise it would have been virtually impossible for a woman of Bella's build to have even climbed the fence let alone get over the top. Like perimeter fences in prisons the three strands of barbed wire were bent over the fence at such an angle that scaling it was not viable: an unfortunate necessity this day and age to prevent hooligans from tempting fate. He tracked Bart Hudson as he sped towards his office, giving his secretary instructions as he raced past her then slamming the door thus putting a solid wall between them.

It took only a couple of minutes before the secretary, a skinny woman dressed too young for her obvious middle age, was back carrying a small cardboard box. After being handed the box, Jared browsed through the contents; two photographs, he presumed of her parents on the one facing upwards, a wet vase that had obviously had its contents only just tipped out and a conglomeration of small odds and ends as one would find on the majority of office desks around the world. Nothing projected a red flag as being out of place. But the one item he had come for was missing.

In the short time it took him to scan the contents, the secretary had returned to her post. Jared strode towards her then tapped on the desk to gain her attention. When she finally glanced up, there was a rising blush on the woman's cheeks. Why? Did it indicate guilt? Was she involved?

'Sorry to disturb you but surely Mrs Perez must have had her handbag at work.' He smiled to lighten the tense atmosphere. 'I'm yet to meet a lady who doesn't carry some kind of purse with her credit cards, licence, keys and money. It wasn't at the scene. Her family would appreciate it.'

Not wanting to be seen he was making a big deal of his request, Jared smiled again while thinking of Bella's words. Her bag had been in Hudson's car. He was about to mention this when, without saying a word, the secretary turned and tapped on Hudson's door. Her flicker of unease and rising redness didn't go un-noticed giving Jared the impression she was definitely hiding something. Maybe she already knew where the handbag was. How he would love to hear the conversation going on in that room.

It was a full fifteen minutes of Jared pacing around the reception area staring at inexpensive prints on the walls and noting the worn carpet that was beginning to show threads at the seams. Hudson Enterprises was showing signs of either neglect or financial hardship. So why was Bella the victim in all this? Did she know something about the financial status of the company? Were they robbing Peter to pay Paul? Is that what this was all about? But it didn't make sense. You don't kill somebody for having knowledge of financial hardship. You might sack them but you don't drop them over the edge of a sheer rock-face. There had to be more.

His mind spinning over all sorts of scenarios, Jared ambled around. He couldn't help but think about the discrepancy between the two stories. Bella had said she had been married for six months, yet Hudson mentioned only a week. If she had jumped, the momentum would have taken her at least a metre from the edge. It wouldn't have allowed her to land on the ledge since it only stuck out for about two metres and her injuries confirmed her having slid with her front against the face of the cliff. There was no other way she would have received so many scrapes along her torso and torn fingertips. There was also the question of the fence. There was no way Bella would have been able to scale it without assistance. He hadn't managed it and he was a good deal taller and a lot stronger.

Jared ceased pacing, turned then stared at the still closed door. Mr Hudson was not as smart as he made out but then again he wasn't yet aware that Bella Perez was still alive.

When, at last, the secretary returned, she carried a small black leather shoulder bag, her words breaking Jared from his puzzled reverie. 'Mr Hudson found it in his car yesterday and had to search around to find where he had put it. He says to apologise, he had forgotten all about it. Would that be all?'

Shifty eyes and edgy movements told Jared the woman was lying through her teeth. He settled the bag on top of the box, bade the woman farewell, turned on his heel and left. His own suspicious mind told him the bag had been searched, but for what reason he didn't have a clue. What was Bella hiding? Was she keeping something from him? It was a strong possibility and to that end he decided he would have to question her carefully to see if there were any inconsistencies to her story. And why were these people so cagey? Over the next few hours, he hoped to find out.

Tempted to go through the bag, Jared resisted the urge. In his experience, most women knew exactly what they carried around in their bags and could lay their finger on any one item in an instant. Bella would know if things were as she had left them so he figured it was better to not further tamper with the contents. He headed back to the hospital, ensuring he would have a few minutes alone with Bella before the police arrived.

To his chagrin, heavy traffic and a sudden deluge of rain created chaos on the roads through the city, slowing Jared to a frustrating crawl and forcing him to concentrate on the dicey road conditions and set aside his concerns about what sort of a mess Bella may have gotten herself mixed up in.

By the time he pulled into the car park of the hospital and found a vacant parking spot, a quick glance at his watch told him he had run out of time. Breaking into a run, Jared sped across the puddled hospital grounds, through the entry and up three flights of stairs, taking them two at a time. He managed to reach the door to Bella's hospital room at the same time as two men wearing cheap rumpled suits. If his guess was right, they were plain-clothed detectives. His thoughts were confirmed when one showed a badge Jared recognised immediately as that of the local police force.

'Gentlemen, a moment?' Balancing the box on one arm, he reached into his back pocket, withdrew his wallet then juggled it between both hands until he managed to withdraw a business card, holding it in two fingers as he flashed it in front of the two men for their perusal, but not long enough for them to actually read the words. 'I wish to be in attendance when Mrs Perez is questioned but first I would appreciate ten minutes with her alone. I have something of importance to discuss with her, facts she will probably want to impart to you.'

The two men glanced at each other before the elder of the two agreed. 'Go ahead, we'll see if the coffee here is better than at headquarters, which wouldn't be hard to beat.'

'Try the machine in the waiting room downstairs. It was reasonably drinkable last night. Far better than the one down this passage.' Jared waved to the right then turned towards the door of Bella's room. He knocked but didn't wait for a response before entering. Encouraging the men to move to another floor meant they wouldn't be tempted to eavesdrop. To ensure this didn't occur, he left the door ajar a few centimetres.

Bella was perched up in her bed with a mound of plumped pillows behind her shoulders, her eyes on the overhead television screen but he heard no sound.

She turned her head and studied him as he strode across the linoleum.

'You have a bit more colour in your face. Are you feeling any better?' said Jared as he neared the bed.

'The painkillers have helped and this concoction of fluids they are feeding me seems to be having some effect, so yes, I do feel better. How did you go with Bart?'

'These are what they gave me.' Jared settled the box in her lap. 'Before you go through it, I would like you to take care when you open your bag to see if it has been tampered with. Then go through the contents to see if anything is missing. Hudson was reluctant to hand the bag over. I had to ask for it specifically and then he took quite some time to locate it, or that's what his secretary said. He seemed pleased we found a body and at the moment is unaware you are still alive.'

Shaking fingers pulled the bag from the top of the box. Bella unzipped the top then eased it open, taking care, as asked, to not disturb the contents. A look of consternation crossed over her features as she studied the innards. 'Someone has gone through everything, but why? The only things in here are my own personal belongings.' Upending her bag, she tipped the contents onto the blanket across her lap then one by one, inspected each item before replacing it in, what Jared could only assume, the correct home.

As Jared watched he kept an eye on the expressions flitting across her face. When she reached a small bundle of keys, she fingered each one as she slid it around the circular metal keeper then looked up at Jared, a worried frown creasing her brow.

'Two keys are missing, my office key and my house key. Which reminds me, my car is parked at the office.'

'I'll sort your car for you if you give me your car keys. In one sense I can understand them taking your office key since they think you are dead and you won't need it again but why would they want your house key?' He paused as he settled onto the edge of the mattress. 'Do you have any work papers at home? Maybe some computer discs? Files? Correspondence?' It was a logical explanation. Maybe she had taken something home that contained some important information. It made sense.

'Nothing. I never take any work gear home. My private life is exactly that, private.'

It wasn't what he hoped to hear. 'Can you give me your home address? I'd like to check your house.' And search it at the same time but she didn't need to know.

'I'll write my address down for you. There is a spare key hidden outside,' said Bella as she continued going through her personal effects. The readiness for him to enter her home surprised him. There was no argument, no hesitation and he was virtually a stranger. She wouldn't have agreed so quickly if she had something to hide. So what was going on?

While Jared mused over the problem, he continued to monitor Bella's actions and body language. She paused when she opened up the wallet side to her money purse.

'These cards are all in the wrong places. Why does anyone need to go through these?' Lifting her eyes she stared

Jared in the face so fiercely he began to feel uncomfortable. 'What is going on? Why do I have this strange feeling something is very wrong? All the time you were away, I didn't feel safe. Now I'm really scared.' She scrabbled together her remaining belongings and dumped them back into the bag, zipping it up before tossing it onto the bedside table as though she didn't care. Her actions indicated she wasn't as blasé as she was pretending. He bet she was more than scared but wasn't the type to reveal the true depth of her feelings.

In an endeavour to ease her terror, he leant forward and took one hand. 'Bella, how did your husband die, and when? Was it an accident?'

'Why all the questions? What has Raoul's death got to do with this?'

'Hudson mentioned that your husband was killed in an accident and you have never gotten over his death.'

There was a long hiss of an indrawn breath before Bella screwed her eyes and her nostrils flared. 'What the hell would he know? Nobody at Hudson Enterprises knows. I've never spoken about it to any one at work. My private life is none of their darn business and no, it wasn't an accident. As for getting over it, does anyone get over losing someone they love?' Her breath caught and a rush of moisture washed over her eyes. 'Raoul meant the world to me but it's been four years since he passed away. Do I dwell on it? No, I accepted his death long ago. I knew he was going to die before I even married him. He had a very aggressive form of spinal cancer.' She fell silent while staring at some far away vision in her memory.

Stunned by her words, Jared had trouble trying to swallow the lump of emotion that had lodged firmly in his throat. There was no way she was lying. He would be able to tell. She was too quick in her response – too sincere. He reached out to re-grasp the hand Bella had pulled free in her angst.

'Hey, I'm really sorry, Bella. It couldn't have been an easy time for you.'

A knock at the door had him jerk his hand away. Standing, he strode over to the door, pushing it wide to allow entry to two detectives. He hadn't gotten the information he needed but of the two, Bella and Hudson, he bet Hudson was the one hiding something. So far it certainly wasn't Bella.

It was like watching two panthers stalk their prey the way the two men prowled close to Bella's head, impinging on her personal space and way too close for a normal conversation. The hair on the back of Jared's neck bristled. Something wasn't right here. He knew the tactics for what they were - to threaten. He'd used them himself often enough. But why make Bella feel so uncomfortable? And she was uneasy for she wriggled backwards a bit to give herself more personal space as she glanced warily at each man in turn. His radar alert, Jared deliberately hustled his way at the head of the bed, shoving the younger man down the side then he took Bella's hand as though comforting her was his reason for budging into the space. Two could play these games and he was well aware of the tactics being played. He'd seen it all before.

The older man pulled out his badge and spoke. 'Mrs Perez, I'm Detective Sergeant Bill Travers and this is Constable Kim Jennings. We'd like to ask you a few questions about what happened yesterday. Do you feel up to it?' The other man briefly held out his identification tag then both pocketed their badges.

'I'm fine, nothing that isn't going to mend given time. This is Jared Mann, the wonderful brave person who saved my life yesterday.'

Jared nodded to the two men, ignoring their quick glances of surprise, for he had deliberately given the impression of being someone in authority.

Travers recovered first and turned his attention back to Bella. 'Ma'am, can you tell us the details about what happened yesterday? Explain why you think someone tried to kill you?'

Jared didn't like the way the tone of voice had altered from passive and genial to cynical and patronising, and he figured when Bella responded with a loud outburst, she had also picked up on the same unsaid nuance.

'I don't think it – I know it! Being bashed over the head with a piece of wood, dragged along the ground, shoved over a high fence then dropped over the edge of a sheer cliff – what does that tell you?'

At the detectives' silence, her face showed utter disbelief. 'You think I would do that to myself? I couldn't even face going anywhere near that wretched platform to look at the view. I'm terrified of heights.'

'Why were you up there to start with?' asked Travers.

Jared rocked back on his heels. This was something he had been intending to ask again since her story was nothing like Hudson's.

As she related her story in minute detail, Jared positioned his body so he could study the facial expressions and body language of both officers. Something just didn't gel about the entire thing. About the only person he believed was Bella. All the time she spoke the young constable looked edgy, the fingers of one hand twitching and picking at the side-seam of his trousers in between jotting down notes.

He was edging backwards as though he didn't really want to be there. He didn't say a word. Catching the man's eye, Jared noted how his eyeballs flared then a blush swept up the man's neck before he dropped his gaze.

Turning his eyes to the Travers, Jared knew the man couldn't be trusted. He gave the appearance of being supercilious and made scoffing sounds during Bella's statements. The rolling of his eyes was overacted.

'Why would a man in his position do that to you? Your story sounds a bit far fetched don't you think?' Travers asked in a derisive tone, confirming Jared's estimation of the man.

These were not the type of questions or conclusions an officer would make in an initial enquiry. If things were above board, Travers wouldn't be so dismissive. Both the attitude and the increasingly scary sensation of something really sinister happening sent a shiver of apprehension down Jared's spine but still he said nothing. Instead, he absorbed and processed every word, every nuance and every facial expression.

It was obvious by Bella's next outburst, that she had similar concerns. 'You don't believe me do you?' She paused as she eyed first one then the other as though begging for a positive answer. When neither man responded she asked, 'what about the piece of wood with my blood on it? You think I could do that to myself?'

Jared winced. He hadn't yet handed over the piece of wood but was having it privately analysed, so when neither detective said anything about the wood, nor did he. If they asked he'd give it to them, if they didn't then he would want to know why they weren't interested. They didn't even blink, let alone ask, which meant they were ignoring crucial evidence. Why? They were experienced detectives.

The derisive tone of Travers immediately snagged Jared's attention back to the rather one-sided conversation. 'I suggest you simply fell, hitting your head as you went down. Concussion does strange things. In your dazed state, you climbed over the fence and jumped.' Travers moved closer as he spoke, his face ending up only a hand-span away from Bella, imposing even more into her personal space in an unspoken threat.

Jared eased closer, ready to push the aggressive man away but Bella shot out one hand and shoved the man back with one almighty push. 'I saw him swing the damned branch mere seconds before it hit me.' Her eyes widened as she sent the man a withering glare to accompany her terse tone. Her lips thinned and after her one shove, her tight clenched fists were forcefully held down on the covers as she wriggled to the far side of the bed to gain distance from the intimidation.

Jared wanted the interview to end but wasn't about to interfere, interested to see what would happen next. In one sense he prayed Bella wouldn't let fly with the fist he knew was itching to wipe the smug smile from the detective, for assaulting an officer would see her arrested. But at the same time he wished she would punch the man fair square in his sneering mouth even if it did mean she'd probably end up in handcuffs. Getting her off would be a breeze.

Bella's voice was frosty. 'I think this interview is over. You asked for my version of events. I've told you exactly what happened but it is obvious to me you don't want to believe me. I've done absolutely nothing wrong, have been the victim of attempted murder and yet you are treating me as though I am the criminal. Would you leave now? That maniac thinks I am dead but as soon as he finds out I'm not, he'll probably be back to finish off the job. I have no idea why he wants me dead but maybe it will take my dead body for you to believe me. Now go!'

Both officers remained still, seemingly taken aback by the outburst and unsure of what to do. Jared noted the uneasy stance of the younger man as though he didn't feel the same way as Travers. Instinct confirmed his suspicions that something really strange was going on, something unscrupulous and villainous. His attention was soon brought back to Bella when she screeched out at the top of her voice.

'Get out! Now!' Lunging over towards the side cupboard, she grabbed the panel to summon the medical staff, jabbing her finger again and again on the red emergency button.

Good on you girl, Jared thought as a doctor and two nurses came bustling in, the sudden action causing the two officers to make a hasty retreat. Bella was so angry she looked to be on the verge of hyperventilating but she waved her arms about, brushing away all attempts by the medical staff to calm her.

Knowing it was now time to take over, Jared stood tall, hoping he appeared much calmer than he felt. He grasped Bella's trembling hand as he addressed the three staff members. 'Bella is fine, just a bit agitated.' More like ready to throw something at anyone in sight, he mused. 'Those two detectives gave her a hard time, pushed her too far. They wouldn't leave when she asked them to so she pressed the button to summon help. Could I suggest Bella be allowed no more visitors until she requests them. She has been through a terrible emotional and physical ordeal and it's obvious she is not up to having visitors other than me. We appreciate your prompt actions. Doctor, before you go, can I ask what Bella is being fed through her drip?'

The doctor fidgeted as though it went against the grain to not be giving medical attention to an obviously distressed patient. 'Glucose, the normal post-operative fluid and an antibiotic to avoid any infection around the fracture as well as the head contusion. The wound was quite messy with splinters of wood and bark. Mrs Perez was a little dehydrated so we need to keep up with the fluids. We like to keep it going for twenty-four hours to avoid complications. We also have to check for blood clots since she took such a battering but we are confident she will make a full recovery.'

'Thank you, Doctor,' said Jared as he yanked the chair back into position against the bed. 'You didn't by any chance keep those splinters of wood.'

'No. Should we have? It's not normal practise.'

'It would have helped but never mind. Is it possible to keep visitors away until further notice?'

'I'll see to it.' The doctor turned to follow the other staff out.

Jared settled back into the chair while the doctor made his way across the room, his shoes barely making a noise on the polished linoleum. By her position Bella looked to be still simmering. She sat hunched up, her arms folded across her chest, tension emanating from every pore in her body. Jared was in two minds about how to approach her for he still needed answers to a few questions. He reached out to take one of her hands, deliberately running his thumb around in circles against her palm in an attempt to soothe her rattled nerves. He was quite surprised she allowed him to even touch her since she was so irate.

'That was a very interesting interview,' he said.

'You think?' came back with such venom Jared couldn't help but smile.

'What I think is that I believe you were absolutely correct in your assessment of the situation. Travers didn't want to believe you and I need to know why. The other one is under his senior's thumb but I feel he was on your side.' Feeling a slight relaxation of tense muscles, Jared grasped her other hand to double the massage. 'Bella, the more I hear and see, the more I am convinced something very unsavoury is going on and you appear to be a pawn caught right in the middle. Now I am in a bit of a quandary. I have a few friends in whom I have implicit trust and who I can ask to make a few enquiries. I need to pay them a visit. I'm also curious about why Hudson wanted your house key and I have a feeling that maybe he photocopied the particulars on your cards.'

She jerked her hands away as she jack-knifed into a sitting position.

'To check on all these things I need to leave you, but I'm worried about your safety. That's why I've ordered no more visitors.' He reached out to gently push her rigid body down.

Bella complied and sank back in her pillows, taking in every word, her pallid face showing her mounting concern. Pulling her hands free, she reached over to retrieve her bag, pulled out a notebook and pencil then wrote down her home address with oral as well as written directions on where to find her spare house key. She then slipped her car key from the small bundle by winding it around and around the spiral coil.

'You go. I'd like you to check out my house while you are away. I can assure you, there is nothing concerning work inside, not even a scrap of paper with any phone numbers on. I'm as safe in here as anywhere else with this emergency button right next to me. Just remind the staff out there to come running if I press it again.' She paused then stared into Jared's eyes. 'Jared, please help me find out what is going on. I have no one else here to call on. My father was transferred back to England for work so they now live in London and it is damned obvious the police aren't interested in investigating. I'm sorry to have to ask you but I really have no idea who else I can ask.' Her eyes dropped.

She's one tough woman, Jared thought as he followed her downward glance until he saw how her agitated fingers were scrunching the blanket into a tight ball. All sheer bravado. The poor woman was giving every indication of being a nervous wreck on the inside.

Then, with her chin seeking to meld into the skin on her chest, she mumbled, 'I'm sorry. I shouldn't be asking you since this has nothing to do with you. I guess you have to go back to work. I can't believe this is happening.'

How could a woman change from being so tough to so damn vulnerable and appealing in a split second? Jared's heart went out to her. 'I'm due some leave and can take time off. I think after the battering we took yesterday, my superiors will understand.' As if we weren't short-staffed enough. But then Buck was back and they'd found someone from the weekend crew to fill his spot for today. They'll just have to change the roster around for a bit longer. Maybe this would be what it took for his superiors to pull out all stops in finding more staff.

To Bella he said, 'If you are sure you'll be all right I'll be back as soon as I can. Here,' he handed her his phone, 'keep my phone right next to you as well. If anything happens, ring me. Rest well and try not to worry. We will sort this out, I promise.' Eager to get started on his inquires, Jared left.

Chapter Seven

Earlier showers had increased to a full-blown torrential downpour. The windscreen wipers, whumping at full pace, were finding it hard to cope with the steady flood of water streaming down the glass. Jared had to peer through sheets of water to see anything other than vague shapes whilst negotiating equally frustrated drivers on the highway. A heavy shroud of clouds obliterated the sun but not all drivers had the sense to switch on headlights, making it almost impossible to see some of the oncoming traffic. Not being in familiar territory whilst trying to find the turn-off to Bella's house wasn't helping matters. Forced to slow to a crawl at each intersection, Jared peered through the slanting rain at street signs, searching for the correct one. In the end he almost missed it, his eyes and concentration having been temporarily alerted to a car that had fishtailed then spun out on the slippery road. The last thing he needed now was to waste time attending to an injured driver, but he would if needed. He sighed in relief when there was no resulting bingle and the driver was able to straighten up and drive away, although, Jared noted, at a much slower pace.

While waiting for a break in the traffic so he could turn right, Jared kept going through the list of contacts he needed. He would be calling on a couple of long-term favours owed to him. The traffic flow lessened. Easing down his foot on the accelerator, he scooted across the road, having just enough clearance to make it safely. Now he was off the main road traffic was almost non-existent, allowing him to drift down the street seeking out number twenty-seven. He pulled up in front of a neat, cream brick house, coasted past then drove further down the street before turning around and pulling up on the opposite side of the street two houses down from Bella's home. Whilst staring at the house, he wondered if Hudson had been yet. What were the chances of Jared being caught in the house? The last person he wanted to meet here was Bart Hudson. At least Jared had a right and permission to enter which was more than he could say for Mr Bart Hudson – he hoped.

Knowing he was going to get very wet, Jared stared at the unrelenting downpour while slipping his arms into the only jacket he had with him, a thin windbreaker that was not constructed of materials designed to keep out a deluge of water, but it would keep him warm, temporarily, and it was the best he had. Cursing the un-seasonal storm, he shoved the door open, stepped out then slammed it shut before racing across the street.

Seven bricks to the left of the back door there should be a feature stone that was loose from its cement foundations. Clever Bella, he thought as he reeled off the memorised directions. Don't look under the stone, but go back three stones towards the wall, lift it and he should find a small metal container. Jared vaulted over the low side fence, hunching his shoulders against the continuous onslaught of cold water then trotted around towards Bella's back door, counting off the bricks as he reached them. The key was exactly where Bella had said, hidden under a thin layer of sand. From its condition, Jared figured it was a very rare occasion Bella had been locked out of her house. Using a paving stone, he rubbed off a fine layer of rust from both sides then polished it on his already damp jeans before inserting the key in the lock.

Bella's house was as Jared expected, the only surprise being her bedroom, which was in deep contrast to the rest of her home. Where every other room was vibrant with colour her bedroom was almost clinically white. White curtains, white covers, white linen and bare of any of the quaint adornments he found in the other rooms. One lone photograph stood next to her bedside clock radio. He studied it. Straight black hair and dark brown eyes indicated the Latino look of Raoul Perez. One glance at the cheeky grin spread across the man's face and Jared knew he would have liked the man who had stolen Bella's heart then died so tragically.

A second examination of the rooms wasn't needed. Jared knew by instinct nobody had been in to search but he lingered, soaking in the atmosphere, examining her personal photographs and knickknacks, learning more about the woman who intrigued him so much; the quintessential woman who needed his help, who he believed had told him the truth. Sure, she had a few thorns constructed out of her independent and strong spirit, along with determination, but he firmly believed that when Bella loved someone, it would be an absolute love. Raoul Perez, even though he didn't live long enough to appreciate it, was one very lucky man and Jared suddenly felt very jealous of the man.

The rain had eased to a downpour when Jared ventured outside. After locking the door he returned the key to its safe hiding place, brushing over the soil with his fingers to smooth it out even though the rain would soon obliterate any sign of soil disturbance. He sauntered back across the road to his car, not caring how wet he became. Wet is wet and he was already soaked.

It was only a short drive back to the outer suburbs where Jared pulled into the driveway of an old friend and private investigator. Simon Adler was able to dig deep into many levels of government as well as seedier underworld organizations. He and his team were the men Jared could rely on to find the information he needed as quickly as anyone he knew.

After borrowing a towel from his friend to wipe off the worst of the water, Jared unbuttoned his shirt and hung it over the back of a chair in front of a heater then settled back into the plush leather cushions of a sofa, coffee in hand, relating the entire story of Bella as he knew it.

Simon Adler sat opposite, looking pleased to be catching up with his long time friend but alarmed at what he heard. 'Jeez, Jared, the story is so far fetched it is believable. Are you sure this Bella has told you the truth?'

'As certain as I can be. I keep searching for some kind of body language to indicate she's lying but all her actions and responses have been instant, open, natural. Either she's telling the truth or she's the cleverest crook I've ever encountered.'

Simon smiled. 'And you've met quite a few over the years. Okay, let's see what I can find out but I'm going to need a couple of days to set the wheels in motion. Off the cuff, it sounds like a bit of corruption to me. The meeting Bella interrupted. Why did Hudson react that way? You say this police officer seemed a bit dicey. Drugs? Maybe. If Hudson works in the financial industry then maybe some money or property scam?' Simon shrugged his shoulders as he rocked the fingers of one hand side to side in a so/ so motion. 'I'd love to know the names of those three men Bella inadvertently saw in the meeting with Hudson. Now I've heard about him and all indications are that he is one slimy bastard, which gives me the feeling that your Bella is in deep trouble if Hudson wants her dead and certain police officers are being so contemptuous. Do they know who you are?'

Jared grinned as he shook his head. 'Not yet and I want to keep it that way for a while. I did waver my card in front of their noses but it was upside down and I flashed it so quickly they wouldn't have been able to read a word.'

Simon grinned back. 'Cunning. Could I suggest you keep an eye on Bella? I wouldn't put it past Hudson to try again. I don't like it that this particular officer is so dismissive of her claims. Could he be involved with Hudson? He wouldn't be the first nor only crooked cop on our force at the moment. Did Bella recognise him as one of the men at the meeting?'

Intrigued, Jared leant forward. 'I didn't think to ask but I'm sure she would have mentioned it if she had recognised him. And she didn't react as though she knew him but I'll ask.'

'You do that just to be sure but personally I don't think your concerns are unfounded – especially since Hudson was responsible for her - accident.' He indicated quotation marks with two fingers of each hand. 'Maybe you should get Bella out of hospital as fast as you can and put her into hiding.' Simon paused then added. 'Sending her home probably isn't a good idea if Hudson has her house key.'

'I was thinking along the same lines, especially since she has a busted leg and is pretty well immobile for a while. I'll suggest she goes into hiding although right now I don't have a clue as to where.'

'There's always your place. It's pretty well remote enough that she won't be seen.'

Jerking in surprise at the suggestion Jared stood and retrieved his shirt. 'I think maybe I'll find somewhere else.' His sleeping libido had already been awakened by this intriguing woman so having her stay in his home was probably the worst thing that could happen

'Fair enough but right now I need to get onto this. I'll be in touch as soon as find something out.'

A sudden thought came to Jared as he eased his arms into the still wet sleeves that clung to his skin like greasy sunscreen. At least the shirt was warm. Simon's last words about Bella going home had given him a thought. Maybe it was why Hudson stole her key – to gain access to her home to finish her off. Another thought instantly negated his first one as being illogical since Bart Hudson was under the impression that Bella was already dead, which meant there had to be another reason. Hudson wanted something Bella had in her possession. But what?

A sudden beeping from Jared's pager had him reaching around to lift the instrument from his belt. Expecting a call from work to tell him he was needed the next day, he was alarmed to note the number of the mobile he had given Bella was showing up on the screen. 'I have to go. Bella is in trouble. I'll be in touch.'

Chapter Eight

Even before the door had closed on Jared's back, Bella practised finding his number by studying the layout of the phone face, skimming her fingers across the buttons and counting from the left and top, exactly which button to press in an emergency. To her there was no doubt that the only reason she would summon him was when there wouldn't be any time to figure out how to contact him. She then slid the phone and hospital call control by her side but hidden underneath the cotton, open weave blanket that was the only cover apart from the snowy white sheet. The weight of the blanket should hold them in place and prevent them sliding to the floor.

Earlier in the morning she had insisted the nurse keep the curtains drawn across the windows, preferring the soft glow from the small light by her bed instead of the harshness of the natural daylight that seemed to worsen the steady, dull ache in her head. The television was still running so she twiddled with the controls, found a more interesting programme and turned up the sound just a fraction so she could just make out what was being said without the noise impinging on her aching head. For one who was normally very active, she soon became bored and began wriggling around to find a more comfortable position, the heavy cast on her elevated leg hampering movement. Her boredom had her drifting off into a semi-slumber.

'Bella?'

The sudden flash of light through the crack of the opening door and the sound of a familiar voice roused Bella. Without answering, she peered through the gloom then tensed as her heart began to pound. That voice. She knew that voice but she couldn't put a name to it. Her subconscious had her searching for the reason her heart was hammering so hard all of a sudden. Sliding her eyes closed so she could feign sleep she surreptitiously peeked at the shadowy form hovering in the doorway. She didn't dare move a muscle.

With slow, stealthy movements, the dark shape approached her bed. As he neared, Bella was able to make out a white lab coat in the gloom, which was strange because most doctors didn't wear that kind of garment any longer. *Oh, God, please help me?* Male, short with a paunch, her mind computed then she suppressed the cry of alarm she felt rise up in her throat by clamping her lips together.

Bart Hudson. He'd found her. He knew where she was. How? Not knowing what to do, Bella moved her fingers at a snail's pace, seeking Jared's mobile phone while praying the subdued light and the soft sounds of the still running TV covered her movements. Fear tore through her body while she tried to think. What could she do? What was he going to do?

Bart stopped – staring at her, causing her already wildly palpitating heart to stutter then kick-start again. The look on his face frightened her even more: such hatred and hostility. But why? Hoping she could convince him that she was asleep she fought to control her breathing while forcing messages to her brain to keep calm. As if that was ever likely to happen!

Bart turned towards the stand holding up the plastic bag of fluids. The very instant he turned away, Bella ran her fingers across the control pad on the mobile phone then jammed down her index finger hard while praying she was pressing the correct button. Just to be sure, she slid her finger back to the top left hand corner and counted down then across and pressed again.

Through the narrow slits in her eyes, she kept Bart in her direct line of sight. He pulled something from the pocket of the coat but she couldn't make out what it was in the gloom. What was he doing? Why was he standing over there with his back to her? Her eyes widened in alarm when he held up a syringe at his eye level and the light from the gap in the door reflected off a tiny stream of liquid as it squirted out of the end.

Bella felt her heart miss a few beats then adrenaline surged before racing at full pelt. Her blood thrummed through the veins in her neck so much she could hear the increased pulse rate in her ears. Her nerves were stretched taut, ready to snap. Her muscles tensed. A cold sweat broke out all over her body. She dragged her eyelids back down, forced her breathing back under control. Think, woman, think. He's going to poison you. How quick would it reach her? The drip is slow so it should take a few minutes to reach her arm, or maybe it would only be a minute. How in hell's name was she supposed to know these things? She'd never had the misfortune to have even needed a drip before.

An idea blinked into her frantic brain. Moaning, she turned the top half of her body over, ensuring she tucked her right hand next to her left wrist under the blanket as though turning over in her sleep.

She felt the tension in the air as she heard the swish of Bart twisting around, probably to see if she had woken. Not daring to open her eyes even the slightest bit while she knew she was being observed, Bella waited, forcing her breathing to be soft and even. She heard a slight rustling movement and guessed Bart had turned back to the drip bag. Then, keeping her lashes down, she opened her eyes the tiniest amount while the fingers of her right hand stripped back the sticky paper holding the catheter in her vein.

Pick, pick, pick. It sounded so darn loud as she scraped at the dressing while watching Bart press the plunger on the needle he had poked into the plastic bag. Trying not to make too much movement, Bella then grasped a firm hold of the catheter and with slow and, she prayed, unobtrusive movements, pulled it out of her arm, swallowing down the twinge of pain. Dropping the catheter onto the bed sheet and holding it in place with the back of her hand so it didn't clatter to the ground and give her actions away, she pressed a firm finger where she thought the tiny hole was that she knew was leaking blood from her vein.

She felt a desperate urge to press the alarm button but figured the noise would alert Bart. Then what would he do? Would he use a pillow to suffocate her? Maybe he had time to strangle her? Wait. She had to wait. The tension was unbearable while she did just that - waited for Bart to empty the syringe.

Breathe slowly, Bella. Relax. Calm down. She kept repeating the phrases over and over in her brain, watching, waiting. Bart lowered his hands, slipped the hypodermic back into his pocket then turned to look at her. She dropped her eyelids again and listened for signs of him leaving. The silence was deafening leaving her convinced he hadn't moved. There was no rustle, no swish, no soft footfalls, nothing. Why didn't he leave? For heaven's sake, Bart, just go. You've poisoned me. Do you want to watch me die as well? Just go. Jeeze, just her luck that her silent pleas went unheeded. There wasn't a single sound to indicate he had left and knowing it was impossible, she could feel his sinister eyes staring at her. Then all of a sudden his breathing became harsh and laboured.

Realisation dawned. He was afraid. Was that good or bad? How long is this stuff supposed to take? Is she supposed to die instantly or is it a long, slow, painful death? Should she dare press the button? What if they don't come? Will he try to suffocate her? Strangle her? Did he have a gun… or a knife? Jared, please hurry?

While trying to bring some coherent thought to her addled brain, Bella attempted to reason out what her best course of action would be. Daring to lift her eyelids just a fraction, she noticed Bart send a couple of quick glances in the direction of the door, which meant he was agitated and afraid of getting caught. His actions gave her an idea. He wouldn't want to get caught in here so wouldn't wait around too long. Maybe if she hurried the process then he would go. But how did one die? What sort of effect is this stuff supposed to have? She had no idea but finally figured it wouldn't really matter. Once the alarm went, she prayed Bart Hudson would panic and flee.

Remembering snatches of talks and shows she had seen on TV about dying and sending up a fervent prayer to any God who was listening that her ruse would work, Bella started gasping in short, audible, rasping breaths as though the poison was taking effect. After a couple of sudden bodily jerks, her eyes flew open in startled alarm, staring straight at Bart. She was going to make damn sure he knew she recognised him. The bastard deserved that much. He deserved to be as panic-stricken as she was feeling. She noted the look of alarm crossing over his face before she planted her finger on the alarm button she had already found under the cloak of the blanket. Then while the bells started ringing outside the room, she fell back, shut her eyes, gasped one final loud rasping breath and let her body go totally limpid to feign death.

She heard the swish of Bart's coat when the alarm began shrieking. Instinct told her he was in two minds as to what to do. She figured he wanted to check her pulse but she prayed he had a deeper fear of being caught. At the sudden squeaking of rubber soles, Bella peeked and spied Bart's rapid flight from the room. He didn't bother to close the door behind him, which allowed her to hear cries and thumps emanating from the corridor.

She wanted to scream out but the need for Bart to think he had succeeded in murdering her kept her mouth clamped shut. She dragged herself up into a sitting position and jammed her finger over the wound she had discovered, after spotting a stream of blood down her arm, was flowing freely. God, now she was going to bleed to death.

A doctor and two nurses rushed in. 'What happened, are you all right?' yelled the doctor. Lights flashed on as a nurse reached up and flicked the switch on the wall just inside the door.

'I thought Jared said I was to have no visitors. That bastard wandered in here and tried to kill me again,' Bella shrieked, 'Get Jared.'

'Calm down, Mrs Perez.' The doctor reached for her wrist as though to take her pulse, then reeled back when he noticed her bloodied arm without the catheter. 'What happened in here?'

Gulping down a deep breath, Bella fought to control her breathing, her anger and her thoughts as she realised someone had leaked out the information about her still being alive. There was absolutely no doubt someone had told Bart Hudson where she was. Suddenly, she didn't trust anyone and especially not members of the medical staff who were supposed to be keeping her safe.

'Doctor, I don't know how, but someone informed that man I was here. How else would he know where to find me? Which means, for my safety, I can't trust any of you.'

'But,' the doctor stuttered before she interrupted him.

'It could have been anyone on this staff. Therefore, until Jared gets here, I want you all out of my room and my door locked, and that includes you. The only person I will talk to is Jared.'

'But your arm, the drip, you need the fluids. Let me put it back in?' The doctor lifted her arm to inspect it but Bella instantly dragged it out of his hands then shoved the shocked man in his chest. He tripped then fought to steady himself by grabbing a hold of the cabinet next to the bed. The jug of water rattled against the glass then there was a thump as the box of things from her office desk flew to the floor.

Ignoring the scattered items, Bella hissed, 'the last thing I need right now is for you or anyone else to be touching me. Missing out on a few hours of fluids and antibiotics is not going to kill me and the fact that you are the one insisting I need it makes me suspect you are the one who organised this.'

Bella's accusation stunned the dazed doctor as he righted himself and the jug and glass but she didn't care. Dragging her broken leg from its perch she swung it over the side of the bed, gasping at the shaft of intense pain as the raw edges of her fractured bones protested at the sudden movement. Then she slid off the side of the bed onto her one good leg, resting back as the dizziness and pain overwhelmed her for a few seconds.

She sucked in a breath to steady herself. 'I want every one of you out – now. I'll wait for Jared. Now get out!' she screamed. Gasping at the pain, she waited a few seconds for a reaction before lowering her voice to hardly more than a whisper, punctuating every single word in slow staccato. 'If you don't leave, then I will know it is you who just tried to have me killed. Now get out!'

All three stared at Bella then at each other before turning to leave, their slow progress across the room indicating their reluctance. To ensure the door was locked to prevent further entry she swung the chair around then attempted to shove it by hopping but the pain was so intense at the first feeble attempt that she gasped then sank into the chair. Lord, but it hurt.

Realising the chair had slid a fraction as she landed she shoved with her good leg. The chair moved a few centimetres. Shove followed hump as she made slow, awkward progress across the floor. Every jerk sent a wave of nauseating agony through her body but she didn't stop until she had slammed the door closed and budged the chair under the handle. Closing her eyes and swallowing down the nausea caused by the pain, she slumped back into the seat of the chair, feeling very ill, sore and plain petrified.

Chapter Nine

An interminable amount of time passed before there was a loud thumping on her door.

'Bella!'

She recognised Jared's voice yelling out her name at the same time as the door handle turned. She felt the slight shove as he tried to push the door open. A thud and bump against the wood, followed by Jared's frantic voice yelling out her name several times gave Bella the impetus to drag her aching body out of the chair, staggering as she tried to gain her balance. Standing sent the room spinning and a wave of pain induced nausea to rise so rapidly she almost wasn't able to swallow it down.

'Wait a second,' she yelled through the acidic sting in her gullet then gulped down a second wave of rising bile.

Gritting her teeth, she hopped to one side, bent and pushed the heavy chair out of the way then turned the handle of the door. Jared thrust it open in panicked haste. She screamed out at the sharp stab of pain as she was knocked off balance. As she wavered then began falling, she thrust her arms out to take the brunt of her weight. Despite doing her best to keep her cast leg straight so she didn't injure it further, the still moving chair caught then thumped against her cast. The agonising jolt robbed her of breath.

'Bella, I'm so sorry. What in heaven's name has happened here?' Jared sank down onto the floor next to her. Then taking a great deal of care he untangled her limbs then eased her into an upright position. 'Are you okay?' he asked as he squatted in front of her.

'Jared, please just hold me. I'm so scared.' When her voice cracked on every word she knew she was close to breaking down. She fought for control as a surge of relief flooded her. He had finally arrived.

Still on his haunches, Jared shuffled around and slowly lifted Bella into his arms, taking care to keep her injured leg straight, then sank down into the chair, settling her in his lap. As she tucked her head against his shoulder, his arms wrapped around her. The security she felt at that moment was indescribable. Unable to hold back any longer, hot salty tears flowed against his already wet shirt.

'Here, lift your foot a fraction,' rumbled in her ear. She straightened as Jared eased her fractured leg onto the arm of the chair for support. Even though there was instant relief of pain, she wondered if she had skewed the bones apart again for the pain had been intense. But at the moment she didn't care. She flopped back against his chest and lapped up the sensation of being safe as Jared rocked her in his arms, whispering soothing words into her ear. She knew it was ridiculous but she felt like she was a toddler again, being comforted by her father.

It was a good thirty minutes before Bella felt able to lift her head: thirty minutes during which she'd been vaguely aware of Jared sending frantic staff away from the door several times, demanding they be left alone while ensuring them Bella was upset but fine. She felt far from fine but wasn't up to letting the fact slip. Lifting the corner of his shirt, he wiped away the remnants of her tears from her eyes as she turned to face him.

'Are you up to telling me what this is all about now, or do you need more time?' he murmured in her ear.

'Please don't laugh, but first I need to pee,' she gasped between sniffs. 'Can you carry me to the bathroom and leave me there for a few minutes so I can freshen up? Then I'll tell you everything.'

She could see he tried hard not to but Jared had the temerity to laugh then grinned at the face Bella pulled in response. 'I'm getting a complex about this. My knight-in-shining armour acts are just to help a lady in distress take a pee. What a sad story to tell my grandkids. They are going to die laughing.' Jared's words were said with enough humour they elicited a small giggle from Bella as he carried her across the room to the private bathroom where he left her standing on one leg, leant up against the vanity basin before giving her the privacy she yearned.

'I'll be just outside the door in case you need help. Just yell,' he said as he pulled the door shut.

***

While he waited, Jared cast his eyes around the room. The sight of the smear of blood on the sheets and the torn out catheter still dripping its contents on a darkened damp patch, had him striding across the room for a closer inspection, his face screwing up in consternation. 'What the hell happened in here?' he muttered under his breath as he stared at the mess. Reaching up, he blocked off the flow from the drip by turning the small plastic wheel, jamming the tube closed. He spun around when he heard the bathroom door open and was at Bella's side in an instant, lifting her into his arms then depositing her back against the pillows of her bed, keeping her close to the dry side of the sheet.

'Bella, what happened?' Taking as much care as he could he eased her cast onto the pillows mounded at the bottom of the bed in order to keep her leg elevated.

She gasped at the movement then sighed. 'Bart Hudson happened.'

'Pardon?' Shocked to the core, Jared reeled back then sat of the edge of the mattress as Bella detailed the entire story, including how she had suspicions about one of the staff members revealing her whereabouts. All the while she talked, he alternated between sitting then pacing around in agitation, not wanting to believe her story but instinct telling him it was true.

'Bella, it may not have been one of the staff. It could have been someone in the Police Force.'

Bella jerked upright then paled as she sank back onto the pillows, whether from pain or shock, he couldn't tell. 'What makes you think that? They are police officers!'

'Unfortunately, not all police officers are the upright citizens they are supposed to be. I didn't particularly like Travers, the way he dismissed your claims, his shifty demeanour – the way he acted. I've been speaking to a private investigator friend of mine, and he suspects some kind of corruption. We weren't sure about police involvement but now I'm more certain than ever. How else did Hudson find you so quickly?' He paused as an idea came to him. He snorted. 'Hudson could have just rung reception to enquire about your well-being, but then how did he know you were still alive?' Frustrated, Jared ran a hand through his hair.

'My friend is making some enquiries now. Simon is one man I trust implicitly.' Jared ceased his pacing and returned to the bed where he settled onto the edge yet again and grasped one of Bella's hands. 'By the way, I went by your house and am fairly certain no one has been in there yet. I was going to retrieve your car but your call had me racing back here.'

'Jared, can you get me out of here – now? There's some kind of poison in that bag.' She pointed to the plastic bag on the stand. 'Bart knows I'm here and since someone told him where I was, it won't take long for him to find out yet again that I'm still alive. I was scared before – now I am absolutely terrified.'

'You realise you can't go back to your own home?' Jared stood then took two steps to the stand holding the fluid bag. He studied it for a moment. 'Are you sure about this poison?'

'Why else would Bart use a hypodermic needle to squirt some liquid in there? If it wasn't poison then why do that,' asked Bella with a curious twist to her mouth then added, 'why can't I go home?'

'Hudson has a key.' A tremor slithered down the entire length of Bella's body. 'Can I suggest I take you to my house until we work out somewhere else to hide you? But before you make that decision, I need to figure out how to get you out of here without being observed or followed and I'll get Simon to test this bag. I no longer trust…'

The door flew open, preventing him from finishing. The same two police officers from their earlier meeting didn't bother with knocking but barged in, striding across the room, their belligerence obvious until they noticed Bella sitting up in bed, her body rigid. A look of total shock couldn't be masked from their faces before both men attempted in vain to compose their features. Both men came to a grinding halt.

Jared's muscles tensed then he leant over Bella and whispered in her ear. 'Did you have the police called?'

Bella shook her head without moving her fixed stare from Bill Travers, her lips pulling into a tight thin line. The only other movement on her face was a twitching muscle on her jaw line, searching for release. For several seconds it was as though everyone in the room had turned into bronze statues. No one moved or spoke. The shocked looks of the two men told Jared they hadn't expected Bella to be sitting there alive, which confirmed one fact - they were in cahoots with Hudson. Unless the doctor had called in the police: which was possible given the time he had spent calming the distraught Bella.

Bella broke the impasse. 'I've got nothing else to say to you, so you might as well go away,' she called out tersely as the two men began walking hesitantly towards the bed.

'We were called in to investigate another attempt on your life, so I think you might have plenty to say to us,' stuttered Travers as he came to a halt. He then seemed to gather his wits. 'We need the details so we can track down this person and put him behind bars.'

Alarm bells shot through Jared. A quick glance in Bella's direction told him she received the same message.

'Who called you?' cried Bella. 'I certainly didn't since you dismissed my claims a few hours ago. I don't see how anything has changed. Why the sudden renewed interest?'

While Bella spoke, Jared dragged the chair back from the doorway, setting it on the opposite side of her bed, then settled his large frame into cold vinyl that was all the more frigid given the wetness of his clothes. Then he carefully observed the faces of the two men, ready to interrupt if Bella said too much or the wrong thing. He hoped his earlier warning about Travers would keep her quiet.

'Your doctor rang to inform us you had passed away.'

Jared noticed Bella stiffen an even already rigid body and prayed she was smart enough to understand what the statement meant. This put Jared on instant alert. Even if the doctor had made the phone call, which was possible given the lengthy time frame, he wouldn't have said anything about a successful murder since she'd been very much alive when she threw the hapless man out of her room. And it was a stupid thing for Travers to say since Bella was sitting up in bed. Maybe the twitch in the fingers of Travers' right hand was an indication he might have realised he'd said the wrong thing. Jared smiled inwardly at the blunder.

'Did he now?' said Bella. 'Did he happen to say how I was supposed to have met my demise?'

Jared gulped and stood to prevent Bella saying any more. His progress was brought to a halt when Travers opened his mouth.

'Something about poison in your bag of fluids here.'

Jared sent up a fervent prayer that the two men didn't put any meaning on the way Bella jolted further upright but her actions told him she understood only too well what it meant. For Travers to have said that meant the man was more stupid than Jared had at first thought. Didn't the man realise what he was saying?

'Which is why we're here, to collect it for forensic testing. Care to tell me what happened?' Travers seemed intent on doing all the talking while the other man cringed and took a step not only backwards, but also sideways as though wanting to hide behind his superior: the actions of a guilty man in Jared's estimation, or maybe one that was smarter than his boss and had understood exactly what Travers had given away.

'No, I'm in no frame of mind to be talking to anyone. I need time to calm down and right now I'm in a lot of pain and feeling incredibly nauseous. I'm sure there is quite a bit of poison in my system. In fact, Jared, I think I'm going to have to ask you to carry me to the bathroom again, my stomach isn't feeling so good.' Holding her hand across her mouth, she brushed her brow as though a cold sweat had broken out then began heaving her chest as though she was gagging.

Gaining an instant understanding of Bella's tactics and being very impressed with her quick thinking and acting skills, Jared bent to lift her from the bed while the two detectives turned and dragged the drip bag from the stand, carrying it out with them as they virtually ran across the room. Halfway to the bathroom, as soon as she knew the two men had disappeared, Bella giggled then asked Jared to take her back to bed. Once settled, she sucked in a deep breath to try to control the frenzied trembling of her body. Jared didn't know whether it was fear, pain or delayed shock causing her body's uncontrollable shaking. Then when she made a choking sound he realised she was fighting to hold back laughter.

'Well that answers one thing,' said Bella on a sucked in breath in a concerted effort to gain control. 'Travers is the mole and is in cahoots with Bart Hudson.'

'What makes you say that?' Jared ran his hands along Bella's arms. 'You're freezing.' He continued rubbing in gentle but firm strokes to put some warmth into her skin.

'Because I never mentioned anything to any of the medical staff about being poisoned or about the drip. The doctor wouldn't have said I had died when he knew I was still alive. Only Bart Hudson would have said that.' She sighed long and deep. 'I suspect we will never hear any results if the fluids are even tested.' She looked up, surprised when Jared chuckled.

'Oh, yes it will. There is a huge puddle of fluid from the drip on your sheet. We're out of here, I've thought of a way to whisk you off. I need to make one phone call then we can discuss a few ideas I have while we prepare to execute an amazing Houdini disappearing act.'

A short while later Bella was seated in a wheel chair up on the very top of the hospital building. She and Jared held hands to shade their eyes from the sun that had finally come from behind the clouds, as they watched the Air-Sea Rescue helicopter hover above the circle marked out to indicate the helipad. The moment the chopper was stationary Jared whipped the door open, lifted Bella from the chair then settled her in the rear seat of the chopper. He held open the warm jacket he'd asked King to supply then shimmied the fabric down her back after she'd slid her arms into the sleeves. Clipping the silver studs together down the front he then ensured she was strapped in securely with a box under her cast for support. The helmet he placed on her head was a little too large but he tightened the chinstrap to make it as secure as possible.

He placed the bundled up sheet next to her before stepping back to allow King to take off before a security person or medical staff came to investigate the chopper's presence without the normal radio contact. Wrapped around the sheet were the remains of Bella's tattered clothes. Her bag was over her shoulder with one badly scuffed shoe perched on its rightful place, its mate having been lost in the fall. Since Bella hadn't been really concerned about the bits and pieces retrieved from Hudson's office, apart from the two photographs, they had been left behind.

Within seconds of the chopper lifting off Jared shivered then glanced down at the reason. Clothes that had only just begun to dry were now spattered with a deluge of water whipped up from the rotors. He smiled wryly – Bella was beginning to make a habit of leaving him dusty and torn or very wet.

He wheeled the chair back inside, leaving it in the passageway parked next to two others thus making it appear as though it belonged there. Instead of wasting time waiting for the elevator he raced all the way down the stairs to Bella's room, checking to ensure he wasn't seen approaching. Waiting inside the room for a few moments he then retraced his steps, seeking out the nurses and doctor to have a few words with each, indicating he was going home but would be back later in the evening to check on Bella. He re-iterated the need for Bella to have no visitors then rode the elevator down to the front entrance where he lingered for a while so that if necessary, people would recall seeing him alone.

The sight of the helicopter was a common occurrence at the hospital and the sight of him going to his car to drive off was what was expected. He felt certain no one had seen him remove Bella from her room and there was now a sign on her door saying she didn't want to be disturbed. It would take the staff a while to figure out she had gone - at least until her next hourly observation. Then, he was sure, he would receive a call to inform him of Bella's disappearance and if he didn't, he would be back later in the evening to find out why. Either way, no one would suspect he had been the one responsible for her vanishing.

Jared paused in his car before driving off, long enough to phone Simon Adler to ask if they would be able to meet at Hudson Enterprises to pick up Bella's car and also to give him a brief update on the latest occurrences.

Simon was waiting in the street as planned when Jared drove up. The pair walked straight down the driveway to the rear of the two-storey building, not bothering to speak to anyone or seek permission. Neither man was breaking the law. Bella's car was where she had said but Jared circled around it first, studying it from all angles, certain Hudson would have tried to get into it to search for whatever it was he thought Bella had. Not surprised when he saw it, Jared pointed to the jemmied lock on the passenger side before slipping the key into the driver's door and holding the door open for Simon.

They wasted no time. Simon had the car started and had manoeuvred out of the parking bay and was almost down the driveway before a blustering well-built woman came running out to confront them. The woman was not the same one he had encountered before and was unfamiliar to Jared.

'Hey, what are you doing?' yelled the woman as she continued running towards Jared, her ridiculously high heels making the task awkward and giving her a waddling gait.

'Collecting Mrs Perez's car, as her family requested.' The woman came to a wobbling standstill when her heel keeled over. 'Do you have a problem with that?' he added as she reached down to replace the shoe. He paused while the woman thought then he continued when she failed to come up with an answer. 'I believe it is Bella's car and doesn't belong to your firm. Is that correct?'

The woman nodded then opened her mouth a few times as in imitation of a guppy, but no words ensued.

'I noticed the damaged passenger lock and will undertake to inform the authorities. I have no doubt the fingerprints will match those of your boss, so go back up to the snivelling bastard and let him know. Also tell him I saw him peering through his window a moment ago.' He waved his hand in the general direction of the second floor bank of windows.

Turning his back on the irate but stunned woman he jogged up the driveway, ignoring her half-hearted complaints. 'How dare you speak to me like that? I'm going to call the police.'

He suspected the police were probably already on their way, especially one called Detective Sergeant Bill Travers. Jared didn't care in the least. Travers already knew Jared was assisting Bella, so they were learning nothing new and he had done nothing wrong. His actions were within legal boundaries.

Once he reached his car Jared jumped in and the two cars sped away, Jared in the lead with Simon following close behind. A call came from Simon. 'I've searched for the remote control to Bella's garage. It's not where she said it would be.'

'Which means Hudson has a second means of entry to Bella's home,' replied Jared. Interesting, but not unexpected, he thought as he hung up. Having already discussed the possibility, they planned to disconnect the power to her garage door, rendering the control useless. Although Jared couldn't see the logic in stealing the remote since Hudson already had a key. Maybe they thought the garage was separate from the house. That made sense but then nothing else about this whole fiasco made much sense.

Less than a minute after driving up Bella's drive-way and parking in front of her garage door, Jared had sprinted around to the back, dug up the spare key and was walking out the garage door which he had manually opened from the inside. After driving his car inside the two men proceeded to empty the wardrobe and drawers in Bella's bedroom, placing the contents in Jared's car, along with the other few items Bella had requested, including all of her toiletries. As an afterthought Jared dismantled and carried out Bella's personal computer system. He planned on having her hard drive searched for some clue as to what Hudson was searching for. There had to be a reason and the only logical one Jared could come up with was that Bella had, or knew something very important that was incriminating.

An internal bolt on the front door was installed to render the front door key useless. The two men swapped the cars around, leaving Bella's in the garage where Jared unplugged the electric cord, thus disabling the remote control. A few more seconds and he had shut and locked the back door, but this time he slipped the key into his pocket so he could make regular inspections of the house.

Before collecting Bella, Jared drove Simon back to Hudson Enterprises so he could claim his own car, which had been parked amongst hundreds of others in a nearby shopping centre. He transferred Bella's computer into Simon's car. 'Get this over to Mario Basile. I've already spoken to him. If there's anything to be found on Bella's computer then he'll find it.'

'Does Bella know about this?' There was a surprised look on Simon's face.

'Not yet, and she doesn't really need to know. If it comes up clean I'll simply say I picked up her computer on one of my inspections of her property. If we find something untoward, then… well, I'll figure out what to do about it when that time comes.'

'What if she asks for the computer?'

'I'll ask Mario to put this search on top of his list.'

Simon shrugged his shoulders and made to get in the car. 'You're a braver man than me. I just hope she doesn't find out what you're doing.' His head disappeared from view and the motor turned over.

'So do I,' Jared muttered as he returned to his car. As he drove his mind was focussed on what they'd just done, forcing details of the computer to the back of his mind. What had been a hastily prepared plan had gone off a lot better than either man had expected but Jared figured it wouldn't take very long for those seeking Bella to add two and two together, especially since they had crooked law enforcement officers working for them - or at least one. Travers he was certain of; the other one he wasn't so sure about. His one desperate prayer was that by the time Mr Hudson and his cronies had pieced together all the parts to the jigsaw puzzle, Simon would have a few answers and they knew what the hell was going on.

Chapter Ten

Relieved to be away from the hospital Bella made the most of the flight in the helicopter, enjoying it a lot better than her previous one. King spoke to her through the headphones inside the helmet, explaining all the sights they were flying over and taking her a few extra kilometres on the way back to the base. 'We have plenty of time, for the longer we are in the air, the less time I have to keep you hidden away while waiting for Jared.'

'Won't they realise the helicopter isn't there?'

King grinned. 'As far as the authorities are concerned I have the chopper on a test flight after making a few minor repairs.'

'Oh, sounds dishonest to me.'

'Yeah, well, it was Jared's idea so I'll point the finger at him if any questions are asked.'

As they hovered to the ground, Bella noticed a silver sedan parked under a shady tree nearby. The reason was explained when she was whisked into the vehicle and driven the short distance into the maintenance shed, a place that was usually, King explained, his personal domain.

Within five minutes a wonderful aroma of brewing coffee had Bella's salivary glands working overtime. It was the best sensory experience she'd had from the time she walked out of her office – was it only yesterday? She shook her head in disbelief. So much had happened it seemed so long ago and she still didn't have a clue as to why her world had been turned upside down in such dramatic and very painful fashion.

The wooden stool she was perched on was hard and too high, making it difficult to find a way of holding her injured leg without it aching. She wriggled to get more comfortable while praying King would find her a more satisfactory seat as soon as he finished making the coffee as he had promised. To fill in time and take her mind away from the nagging ache, she glanced around the large workshop.

Walls were laden with tools and spare parts. All were hanging from wire hooks poked into small holes drilled into the plywood boards lining the walls of the shed. Neat printing on sticky labels indicated exactly what each part was, its purchase date and use by date along with its serial number. For a working garage, the floor was immaculate making it obvious King cleaned up every single oil or grease spot as soon as he completed a maintenance or repair job. It seemed he was a proud man and Bella felt sure his aircraft would never mechanically fail. King appeared to be a perfectionist and wouldn't allow neglect be the reason for his chopper to crash.

Wooden benches along one side contrasted with more modern metal benches down the far end but it was obvious by the layout of the tools, King had an affinity with working on wood, probably because it was warmer and quieter.

The other long wall consisted mainly of a large corrugated iron door that rolled aside to allow the helicopter to be wheeled inside but right now it was only partially open, just wide enough to allow natural light to stream in, showing off the empty floor-space. The other end was walled off with only one opening, a small personal door, which was presently standing wide open. Bella assumed it was an office because it was where King had disappeared into and from whence the gorgeous aroma was emanating. King had been reluctant to let Bella sit in his office chair because, he explained, 'the big picture window overlooks the main building on the base and anyone can see you. The fewer people who know your whereabouts, the better.'

A scraping noise from the direction of the office had Bella swing her eyes around towards the small door. King emerged, one hand pushing a padded office chair rolling on castors while the other carried a tray. As he neared Bella could see the tray held two mugs of coffee, a few small packets of sugar, two teaspoons and a plate of chocolate biscuits. Her stomach emitted a loud rumble at the sight of the biscuits.

King grinned at her obvious embarrassment. 'Promise you won't tell any of the others about my secret stash or they will all be down here for coffee every day, messing up my workshop and then I'll never have any peace and quiet.'

'I promise so long as you don't limit me to only one – I'm starving. I think the only things I've eaten over the past two days are the two pieces of toast Jared forced down my neck early this morning.' She sighed. 'I can't believe it was only this morning. So much has happened that it beggars belief.' Before she took a bite of the chocolate-coated biscuit, Bella lifted the mug to her nose, drawing in a long whiff of the rising aromatic steam. Absolute bliss! She brought the rim of the mug to her lips and took a tentative sip. Heaven - especially compared to the poison she'd shared with Jared at breakfast. She shuddered at the thought of poison. Maybe that wasn't the correct word to be thinking about right now.

To get her mind away from unpleasant recent happenings she took another sip. 'This is so good, King. You can make me coffee any time.'

'You're welcome. Here, let me help you into this chair.'

King pushed the chair closer then slid his hands under her armpits, lifting her with ease as he kicked the wooden stool aside by sliding it with his foot. Then he nudged the other chair under her backside before easing her down. Reaching under the bench he drew out an old plastic milk crate, gently lifted Bella's cast and placed it on the ridged surface of the crate, checking she was comfortable before settling his long, lean frame on the wooden stool, his gangly legs reaching the floor with ease.

Bella sighed with relief. 'Thank you, that's much more comfortable. Am I allowed to ask why they call you King?'

'You can ask but it doesn't mean you'll get an answer.' He grinned then partially capitulated. 'It's short for Kingman, which is my surname.'

'And I take it you aren't so happy with the Christian name you were landed with.' She grinned at his widening eyes, knowing she had guessed correctly. 'It can't be much worse than Annabella. In my younger years at school kids used to moo at me so I shortened it to Bella. I believe there was some cartoon cow called Clarabelle so it didn't take long for the kids to make a connection. To make it worse, my maiden name was Brown so I was also tormented with *Brown's cows.*'

'Yeah, kids can be cruel. I know how you feel, but my first name is definitely worse and I will only answer to AJ or King and don't push me for any more information or those chocolate biscuits will disappear in an instant.'

Bella snaked out her hand to remove two more biscuits from the plate. She polished them off as well as the coffee very quickly then held out her empty mug for a refill. 'Is there any of your yummy coffee left?'

Before King reached his office, they heard the crunch of a car pulling up on the gravel outside. King veered over to the crack in the door to check whose car it was, sliding the door further open to allow Jared entry. After switching off his engine Jared unfolded his body from the front seat, pointing to the empty mug still in King's hand.

'Is there any more of that? I could use one of your coffees, mate.'

While King went one way, Jared strode the other towards Bella, spotting the remaining two biscuits on the plate. 'How come you get special privileges? All I ever get from King are dry cracker biscuits.' He snagged both biscuits then wolfed them down, grinning at the look of disgust from King when he held out mugs of coffee to his two guests.

'Looks like your secret is out, King, but I promise I didn't tell him,' Bella chuckled as she sipped on her second coffee. 'Are you married, King? Anybody who can make coffee this good must be married.'

'Nah, I can't find a woman who can make coffee better and my cooking isn't anywhere near as good. Once they taste my cooking they run a mile. How about you marrying me?'

Jared glanced at King, looking alarmed and surprised.

'Uh,uh, if you can't cook then you're not for me. I like a man who can cook and besides, I can't make coffee anywhere near as good,' said Bella.

'I might have to tell Maree you've just asked another woman to marry you, King. I imagine she will probably be a tad jealous.' Jared smiled at his friend then turned back to Bella. 'Maree and King have been quite a serious item for a couple of years, I believe. King hasn't found the courage to pop the question.'

'Just goes to show how much you know, we've been engaged for six weeks now.' King had the grace to blush at his admission.

'You cunning old fox! Congratulations and might I add it's about time. Come on, Bella, I need to get you out of here to where nobody can find you.'

After passing on her own congratulations and hugging King in a tight embrace, Bella was bundled into Jared's car, both men keen to give her all the assistance she needed, something she wasn't used to having. Once he had the motor running, Jared swept out of the hangar, around the rear of the building, taking a back route to the long driveway to ensure his workmates in the office didn't spy his passenger. Once on the main road he turned away from the city, heading towards the hills.

He reached over to switch on the CD player. Bella was startled to hear opera arias fill the car from several speakers. 'You look surprised I would appreciate classical music,' Jared murmured as he turned the sound down a fraction.

'A little, but then I don't really know you well enough to be making any judgements. I like your choice. How far are we going?'

'Only about twenty kilometres. You can lie back, close your eyes and rest if you like.'

Feeling an overwhelming exhaustion, she did exactly as Jared suggested.

The next thing she was aware of was the sound of a dog barking, the deep woofs waking her from her slumber. Opening her eyes she peered around to see where the noise was coming from.

'Oh, how gorgeous,' she said, surprised at the scene in front of her. They had come to a standstill in front of a large house built out of cedar wood planks. A covered portico sat in the centre with double garage doors to the left. In front of the car, a large tan and black Alsatian stood wagging its tail in frantic sweeps from side to side.

Bella eyed it with trepidation. 'That's a dog.'

'It certainly is.' Jared leaned over the steering wheel while staring out of the windscreen at the animal in question.

'It's a big dog,' Bella managed to squeak out.

'I take it from the look on your face, you're not over happy about that fact.' Jared turned to see the expression on Bella's face.

'I'm not keen on big dogs. I was attacked by one of those when I was a kid. It took quite a large chunk out of my backside. Is it yours?'

'Duke belongs to me, yes, but I promise you he is extremely well trained and won't attack you, well unless I order him to.'

Bella leaned forward to get a closer look. 'That's not so very reassuring. Do I have to go out there?'

This elicited a smile from Jared. 'Unless you are planning on living in my car, you are going to have to go out there. Duke was trained as a police dog but failed his final test, so I guarantee he has had the very best training.'

'Can I ask why he failed his final test? What did he do so bad that he didn't manage to pass?'

To answer her question Jared opened his door. He was immediately covered in a large, furry, slobbery animal whose tongue flicked out and licked him all over. Jared grinned. 'He was too friendly with the crooks. Every time he went anywhere near someone he licked them to death then turned over to have his belly scratched. Down, Duke.'

The dog instantly obeyed by dropping his body across Jared's lap, his tongue lolling out one side of his mouth. Big brown eyes stared up at Bella as she cringed against the door.

Reaching over, Jared grabbed Bella's trembling hand. 'Hold out the back of your hand to let him sniff you.'

She wasn't doing anything of the kind and tried, without success, to tug her hand back. Instead she found it up against a wet, slimy, black nose. Duke sniffed then stuck his tongue right out and licked the proffered fingers. It felt like a rasp on her soft skin.

'See, he likes you. He will be your friend for life.' When Jared grinned at her she turned to stare at him fair-square in his face. 'I'm pretty particular about choosing my friends and right at this minute, neither of you are in that category. Do you mind if Duke and I keep a little bit more distance between us until my nerves get used to the idea of having a furry monster as a friend?'

'Out, Duke,' ordered Jared.

Duke instantly backed out of the car, sitting by the side of the open door waiting for his master, his tongue still lolling and his tail now thumping the ground with soft thuds. Jared followed him out then moved around to assist Bella, Duke padding along behind, much to Bella's amusement. The dog sure adored his master but it didn't mean she had to get so close.

The next thing Bella knew, she was air-borne as Jared carried her the short distance to the front door. He settled her on one leg while he retrieved the key from his pocket, slipped it in the lock then shoved the door open with his foot. Lifting Bella up again, he carried her down a wide, tiled passage leading into a large open room overlooking a man made lake. The outdoor scene was even more gorgeous than her first picture of the house. A grove of shady trees fringed three sides of the lake, creating the effect of a glorious oasis in the desert, only instead of sand all around, the paddock was covered in low verdant grass. From the veranda of the house a wide compacted gravel path curved all the way down to the water's edge where a small wooden jetty had been built. To complete the idyllic picture, a well-maintained wooden boat, the shiny paint gleaming in the sun, was tied to the end of the jetty.

After gently lowering Bella into a comfortable leather lounge Jared found a small footstool to set under her plaster cast. It took about two seconds flat for Bella to find a big head sitting in her lap, waiting, she felt sure, for a scratch behind his ears.

'Jared?' she squeaked.

'Duke, on your mat!' The dog slunk over into the corner where a large cushion had pride of place. He circled around the cushion three times them dropped down, head on his two front paws, unblinking brown eyes staring at Bella.

The rich tones of Jared's laughter rang out. 'He has his nose out of joint. He just wants you to pat him. Bella, you really have no need to be afraid. If Duke didn't like you, he would have let you know by now. I'll leave you two to become acquainted while I bring in your belongings.'

The instant Jared left, Duke started creeping along the floor on his belly, heading right for Bella. Yes, Jared, a really obedient dog, Bella thought as she sent a scornful frown and nasty thoughts towards Duke in the hope they would deter the animal. But he kept creeping forwards, only stopping when he reached her one foot planted on the ground. The long tongue came out, found the piece of skin peeking above her sole shoe and licked one big slurping lap of its tongue. It felt surprisingly warm. Encouraged by her lack of an order to go back, Duke stood then dropped his head back into her lap. She couldn't help but smile at his obvious disobedience and reached out with one shaking, tentative hand behind a pointy ear, where she nestled in amongst the long fur and scratched him. She was certain Duke grinned at her.

***

Jared returned with his first armload of clothes. He paused standing in the doorway to the room, watching the sappy smile on both his dog and the woman who was, only two minutes ago, too afraid to go anywhere near the animal. He said nothing but moved away, leaving the two to bond, knowing Duke would guard and protect Bella with his life from hereon in. He'd always maintained that Duke failed his final test because he was so smart he knew the man acting as the thug was in fact a good man.

After arranging Bella's clothes in the guest room, Jared found a plastic chair and placed it in the shower recess before returning to the vast living room where he came to a sudden standstill in front of the sofa. He'd been gone less than fifteen minutes but Bella had sunk down on the cushions and was fast asleep. Duke, who knew damned well he wasn't allowed on any of the furniture, was stretched out alongside her, his head on her stomach, watching her. There was a human hand held firmly around his neck with fingers tangled in the fur. Jared couldn't help but smile but a quick stern word was all it took for Duke to leap off and slink back to his own bed. The sound of Jared's voice and sudden movement from Duke woke Bella.

'Much as I enjoy looking at you in your very seductive hospital gown, would you like to have a shower and get changed into something more comfortable and less revealing?'

He grinned as Bella pulled the gown down as far as it would go. He enjoyed the pink flush rising up over her cheeks that had arisen because even stretched down tight, the cotton fabric only reached halfway down her thigh.

Giving up, Bella pulled herself up into a sitting position. 'How does one shower without being able to stand and without getting the plaster wet?'

'Well, we could opt for me giving you a sponge bath.' Jared laughed at the indignant look he received but thought it would be wiser to take pity on her. 'Come with me and I'll show you how it can be done.'

Without waiting for a response, he had Bella in his arms, carrying her through to the guest bathroom. In no time at all he had her plaster wrapped in plastic and sealed with tape. He settled her on the strategically placed plastic chair so her leg reached out the door of the shower recess. Soap, a flannel and a bottle of shampoo had been placed within easy reach. Checking she could manage on her own, Jared left her alone, leaving a very large fluffy towel on the side of the bench within her reach.

'Yell out if you need me for anything. Wrap your towel around your body when you have finished and I'll carry you into the bedroom so you can dress. It will take a little bit of practise to get used to things but I'm sure a tough cookie like you will manage. Tomorrow I'll find you a pair of crutches.' As he left Jared pulled the door shut.

*****

For Bella the easy part was removing the oversized jacket she still wore but it was quite a struggle to divest her underclothes and the hospital gown, but she was soon enjoying the harsh, stinging spray of hot water, soaping several times those parts of her torso she was able to reach, shampooing her hair then rinsing off before reaching for the towel. It felt so good to be shower clean, instead of the simple and highly embarrassing bowl bath she'd had to endure. She found it a little awkward standing on one leg to finish off the drying process but managed before wrapping the large towel around her body and tucking in the end. After cleaning her teeth she hopped to the door to call out for Jared, only to find Duke lying on the floor outside the bathroom door, his black nose pressed up against the crack under the door.

'Pervert,' Bella muttered as Duke stood with his tail wagging.

At the sound of her voice Jared emerged from the kitchen carrying a tray. He bypassed her then slipped into her room to place the tray on the bedside table. 'I heated some soup for you. It's been a long time between meals so you must be hungry,' he called before returning. Then he picked her up and carried her to the bed and settled her down. 'Get dressed and then eat while I take Duke out for his run. I haven't heard from the hospital so either they haven't checked on you yet or they are still searching the building. I'll settle you in bed then I'm going to pay the hospital a visit on the pretext of visiting you.' He chuckled then added, 'It should be an interesting evening.'

*****

The sight of the sleeping woman presented a dilemma for Jared when he returned from his nightly run with Duke. With an empty bowl by her side, it was obvious she'd eaten and then fallen asleep. His conscience tweaked. He couldn't leave her lying in a wet towel on top of the covers, especially in her weakened state. As he stared down, wondering how best to remove the towel, he studied her face again. She looked so fragile and delicate with dark rings of fatigue and pain around her eyes. The halo of soft damp curls around her head contrasted with the harshness of the mass of dark bruises covering the exposed parts of skin. He imagined she had similar bruising under the towel and could certainly feel his own injuries every time he moved. Running hard with the dog was the way he kept fit but this evening he'd had to let Duke run on ahead for his muscles had protested vehemently until he'd slowed to a walk.

Not hesitating any longer, Jared lifted Bella from the bed with infinite gentleness, pulled back the warm quilt then loosened off her towel before laying her back down. He had no choice but to remove it so slipped the towel from under her as he settled her back down on the sheets then pulled it from the front of her body as he dragged the quilt back over her. An act of parliament couldn't have made him not skim his eyes over her naked form. He'd seen plenty of naked women in his day but Bella was so slim, so beautiful, so bruised and battered. Not once had she complained about the constant pain she must be in. A strange stab of warmth spread through him as he tucked the quilt around her shoulders. He made a cushion of pillows to raise her fractured leg to make it more comfortable. After replacing the light quilt over her leg, he ordered Duke to stand guard, locked up his house, double-checking that it was secure then drove back into the city to visit Mrs Annabella Perez in hospital.

He hadn't reached the end of the driveway when the ringing of his mobile phone had him pulling over to answer.

Chapter Eleven

'She's what?' Jared tried hard to sound alarmed but a grin spread across his face.

'What do you mean you can't find her? She's got a plastered leg and certainly couldn't walk from her room.' He leant back against the door as he smiled into the darkness.

'Her clothes are missing? Have you called the police? … Well maybe you should…. An attempt was made on her life this morning and if you have allowed that bastard to come back in there to kidnap her from under your noses … if she has been murdered? … I realise that nurses are there to nurse and not waste time standing guard but Bella wasn't to have any visitors so how did anyone get to even know which room she was in? I'm on my way now.' Jared switched off the phone and slid it into his shirt pocket as he straightened then started the engine, grinning like some inane idiot.

As he entered the main entry of the large hospital, Jared strode towards the lift but paused mid-stride when he glimpsed the back of a man leant towards the reception desk. He could only see the man's back but the thinning blond hair look vaguely familiar. He studied the fellow, his eyes drifting down the entire length of the body, assessing details while he wondered where he had seen the man before.

The breath hissed from his lips. Hudson? Surely the man wouldn't be game enough to come back? Jared glanced around then sidled into a small florist booth to observe. Turn around, he willed. As if in answer the man straightened then headed for the elevator giving Jared only a side on view. Right hair, right height but was Hudson that lean or did he have more of a paunch? Having only seen Hudson once, Jared wasn't sure.

When the stranger entered the elevator, Jared waited until the doors closed then scooted to the receptionist. 'That man, with blond hair, I'm sure I know him as a friend of Mrs Perez. Did he ask for her room?'

At first the woman stared at him then a telltale blush rose up her face. 'You gave him her room number? Surely there's a tag on her name that she was to have no visitors!'

'Yes, but he insisted he was her husband.'

'Her husband! Her husband is dead. That's the man who tried to…' Jared turned and fled towards the stairwell, pounding up the steps two at a time until he reached the third floor. Forcing the stairwell door open he quickly glanced around then seeing the corridor empty raced in the direction of Bella's room.

A flurry of activity near the nurses' desk slowed him to a walk. Not stopping he ambled past while straining to listen to the hushed talk. It was obvious by the mumblings that Bella's disappearance was the cause of the agitation but he was more interested in tracking down a blond head than listening to the details.

He approached Bella's door, which was standing wide open. Stepping inside he was most surprised to see everything exactly as they'd left it. A scraping noise from the bathroom had him stop in his tracks before creeping nearer to the half closed door. His heart ceased beating before kick starting again when the door flew open and a woman dressed in pink cotton pants and top emerged with a tray of cleaning utensils.

'Oh,' she squealed as she jerked back a step. 'My, but you scared me,' she said as she held a hand to her chest.

'Not half as much as you scared me,' said Jared. 'Where is Mrs Perez?'

'Nobody knows. She just disappeared this afternoon.'

'Disappeared! But she's got a broken leg, she couldn't have walked!'

'That's what's so strange. Now I must go, I have five more rooms to tidy before I can get home. Excuse me.'

As the cleaner swept past him Jared turned to follow. He was halfway across the room when he heard a male voice mumble a few indistinct words then the same woman answered. Then a blond headed man appeared in the doorway, a stunned look spreading across his features when he spied Jared. It wasn't Bart Hudson but the man had a strong similarity of features.

'Err, umm, Doctor,' the man stammered. 'I umm, am looking for my wife, Bella.'

'Your wife?' Jared asked, hoping his voice didn't sound as shocked as he felt. He fought to gather his wits. 'Well, as you can see she's not here. And I'm not a doctor. But I do know one thing for sure,' Jared began moving towards the stranger, 'since Bella is a widow, my friend, you are not her husband.'

Before Jared had even completed the sentence the man spun and shot from the room, the sound of heavy footsteps echoing from the walls and Jared hot on his heels. They raced down the corridor then the man turned the corner. Jared heard a few shouts then a scuffle as he approached. Rounding the corner he was met by a trolley laden with medical supplies and implements. He grunted as he barrelled into it, sending the trolley spinning as he staggered, tripped then crashed to the ground, implements and God knows what scattering around him and making an awful ruckus. Lifting his head he saw the man disappear into the open lift. Jared scrabbled to his feet, skidding on something hard before finding solid ground and purchase to be able to chase after the man, but the doors slid closed before he reached them. He glanced up to see in which direction the lift was going. Down.

'Damn,' he hissed as he thumped a closed fist against the wall.

Turning, he raced towards the stairwell and clattered downwards, breathing hard and grabbing a hold of the railing each time he felt his feet missing a step. Reaching the bottom, he yanked the door open and raced towards the lift, only to find the car rising again. Not sure whether the man had exited on another level, was still in the lift or had already left, Jared didn't know which way to go or what to do.

He shot outside and scanned the area but with numerous buildings, hundreds of vehicles and a vast number of people, trees and bushes he realised he didn't have a hope of finding the man. There were innumerable places to hide. Knowing Bella was safe he headed for his car, his eyes skittering around searching for a blond head as he raced through the car park then along the street to where he'd parked.

As he drove off Jared caught a glimpse of a blond head from the corner of his eye. He quickly twisted his head to see the person he'd been looking for, jotting down something on a scrap of paper. He turned at the first place he was able, sped back but the man was gone. Even standing on the door sill of his car and scanning the area, he could find no trace. After swearing profusely he figured that he would be wasting precious time by hanging around.

His one stop on his way home was to visit Simon Adler, to whom he told what had occurred at the hospital as he handed over the hospital bed sheet for a private, secure analysis of what poison had been injected into Bella's fluid bag. 'I'm very doubtful the police report will show anything untoward, even guessing the bag and its contents might be completely lost in the system. If a report is made I bet my last dollar it will be a fake analysis.'

'With the things that have been going on you're probably right,' said Simon as he swapped the sheet for a sheaf of papers. 'Here's a preliminary report on the publicly known workings of Hudson Enterprises. This isn't really what we want. We are still looking for the hidden, secret workings of the numerous individual companies Hudson has set up. I've already got someone snooping around and another man looking for Hudson. Phone taps are being put in place as we talk and the business premises will be receiving a late night intruder.' Simon flicked through the paper work as he spoke.

Jared closed his ears to anything sounding illegal. 'Don't even give me an inkling of how you find your information and I'm assuming the phone taps are not quite legal. You know I have to shut my mind to it. Once we have the data we need we can work out roundabout legal ways of presenting it by tracing back from the result to the cause. You and I both know it's not entirely ethical but it usually works, as long as I'm not the one being unethical. That's why I hire you to find information. This time it is personal so I trust you to pull out all stops.'

'Personal? Bella mean something to you does she?' Simon smiled.

'She has no one else here to look after her so I'm making it personal, but not in the sense you are inferring. Strewth, Simon, I barely know the woman. I must go. I'm sure Bella is safe at my place for a while but I don't want to leave her alone for too long. This man I saw, he looked similar in build and colouring to Hudson. See if there is a brother or close relative about the same age.'

'Sure thing,' Simon said as he waved to Jared.

An inky black darkness had fallen by the time Jared pulled into the driveway of his property. The rain had ceased but dark clouds prevented even the tiniest skerrick of light from the stars and moon to show through the heavily laden sky. There were no reflections on the blackened expanse of the lake in front of his home until the beam of the car headlights swept over the water as he swung around the curve. Even the house was in darkness, which meant Bella was still asleep. He hoped she was still asleep, giving her body a chance to heal and the effects of the anaesthesia to dissipate. By the time he opened the car door in the garage Duke was standing beside him.

'Hey, boy, how's Bella?' A single, quiet whimper ceased as soon as Jared reached down to pat the dog's back. Together, man and dog entered through the communicating door. Switching on a single passage light Jared continued striding until he reached Bella's room where he paused in the doorway; one glance telling him she was as he'd hoped. Feeling exhausted, he fixed a quick cold meal, showered then dropped onto his bed, still naked, his normal sleeping attire. He was still awake when Duke left him to take up a position next to Bella's bed. Jared's last thoughts before he succumbed to sleep, was something along the lines of his best friend being a turncoat and how he was going to have severe words with both Bella and Duke in the morning.

The sound of whimpering and the feel of Duke's rasping tongue on his hand woke Jared from an unpleasant dream where he was flying wildly around on a rope, putting his hands and legs out to prevent them from hitting the side of the cliff. In the process he had just let Bella slip from his grasp. He awoke with a start, ramming his body into a sitting position before his foggy brain could ascertain what had woken him. By his side, Duke whimpered loudly again.

'What is it, boy?' Duke padded to the door, waited, then returned to the bed when Jared didn't follow. A louder whimper had Jared searching for a pair of jeans, slipping them up over lean hips and pulling the zipper closed but ignoring the stud at the waistband as he began striding to the door and trailing after the rapidly disappearing animal. The sound of quiet sobbing had Jared quicken his pace, switching on a passage light when he reached Bella's door.

'Bella? What is it?' Kneeling beside the bed, he reached out with one finger and brushed the moisture from her face. In the dim light her face looked drawn and ghostlike. She should have looked better after a good few hours sleep but instead she appeared to be worse. Hell, she hasn't been put back on antibiotics. Please don't let there be an infection. His thoughts were interrupted by a tortured groan.

'Everything hurts so much. I can't stand the pain any longer.' Bella's voice was wrung out of her as though it was agonising even to speak, causing Jared's heart to turn over in his chest.

'You should have called out to me. In hospital they would still be giving you strong painkillers. I can give you some tablets, which will take about half an hour to have any effect or I can give you a shot of pethidine, which will ease the pain much quicker. I keep an emergency kit in the house in case I get an urgent call. Which would you prefer?'

'You can give injections?'

'Yes. We often have to do it with seriously injured patients. I am a trained paramedic amongst other things.' He ran his fingers down the side of her face, brushing curls to the side and moisture from her cheeks. 'But I can only give you the one shot as it is an addictive drug. After that we'll resort to normal, over-the-counter painkillers.

'Go ahead then, but first, can you help me get to the bathroom?' Bella went to throw back her covers but Jared pressed his hand over them.

'You'd better make sure you want to get up in your state of undress before you go exposing your entire body to me.'

Bella paused while she felt over her body with one hand. 'I'm naked?'

Jared grinned. 'You are. Completely starkers.'

'I don't think I really want to know this, but I presume it was you who…?'

'I plead guilty. You fell asleep in your wet towel and I couldn't leave you like that so I unwrapped the towel and pulled the quilt over you to keep you warm. I'm not going to apologise because I'm not sorry. It was a health issue. On top of all your injuries you can't afford to become chilled. I'll find you a proper nightgown.' He unfolded his body from the floor then withdrew one of the nightgowns he had packed away in the drawer earlier. Moving back to the bed, he placed one arm under Bella's shoulders, hoisted her up then slipped the soft cotton gown over her head.

'Hands.'

Muttering under her breath about bossy men, no privacy and a few other unfavourable comments that had Jared burst out in laughter, Bella complied, shoving her outstretched fingers through the armholes then grabbing a hold of the hem she shimmied the fabric downwards.

'You are so cute when you are angry with me,' Jared commented as he carefully scooped her up into his arms and carried her into the toilet, settling her on one foot and leant up against the wall next to the porcelain commode before going to fetch the medication. He grinned at the prospect of her having to bare one cheek of her backside to him so he could jab the needle in. When he returned, armed with a filled syringe, Bella was grasping at the doorframe in obvious distress with pain etched across her face.

Jared slid the small tray onto the bedside table then returned to Bella. He lifted her off the floor and carried her the two steps along the passage then into the room where he laid her on her side in the bed. 'I promise you will start feeling better very soon but first I need to tell you this goes into your backside, so excuse me while I hoist up your nightie a fraction.'

Bella's sigh of capitulation was very audible showing she no longer cared a damn about her dignity. 'Just get it done. I ache too much to care.'

She didn't move at the feel of the cold fluid used to disinfect the area but winced when the needle went in, the substance stinging for a few seconds. With a great deal of tenderness Jared rolled Bella onto her back, lifting her leg back up onto its nest of cushions, covered her with the warm quilt then sank down on the floor beside her, his fingers brushing tendrils away from her face while his other hand held hers.

'Do you want to hear what happened at the hospital?' he asked softly. At her nod, he related all the details as he continued to gently caress her skin. 'Does Hudson have a brother?'

'I'm not sure. I wasn't close enough to Bart to be talking with such familiarity. I don't even know if he is married. Are you sure it wasn't Bart?'

'I've only seen Hudson the once but this man seemed a lot thinner. Look I can't be a hundred percent certain but the man wouldn't be stupid enough to try the same thing twice, surely.'

'I'm so confused I'm not sure about anything anymore. He's tried twice in two days. I just wish I knew what the hell was going on.' Bella sniffed then swept one hand over her eyes and pressed hard against each side at the bridge of her nose.

Guessing she was forcing tears of either frustration or pain to stay at bay, Jared gently lifted her hand away. 'You look exhausted. Try to relax. The pethidine should be kicking in soon.' As he continued calmly stroking her flesh, he carried on a soft banter. 'Simon Adler has set the ball rolling in finding out Bart Hudson's dirty little secrets and your bed-sheet is going to be analysed at a private facility to find out what charming substance they used. I'm betting the police report will come back negative. Right now we have to concentrate on you getting better and keeping you not only hidden, but safe. But there is one thing I need to know.'

'What's that?' came back in a husky voice, which indicated Bella was getting drowsy.

'If you saw them again, would you recognise any of the men in that meeting?'

She opened her eyes. 'I saw them for all of ten, fifteen, maybe twenty seconds. Maybe… if I saw them again. Why?'

'Was Sergeant Travers one of them?'

Bella's eye widened to great orbs. 'No. I'm sure. I'd never seen him before he first questioned me.'

'Can you say that with certainty?'

Bella thought for a moment. 'Yes, I'm certain.' Then she added, 'Jared, thank you for everything. Did you get these from saving me?' She ran her fingers along the dark black lines outlining his bruising. He sucked in his breath at the feel of her warm fingers on his bare chest then grabbed her hand, pulling it away from him to ease the wonderful torturous feelings her touch elicited: a touch that sent all his blood flowing south, giving him an instant hard and uncomfortable reaction. This woman was driving his emotions crazy.

'They are no worse than yours and when you consider the alternative, they don't matter. The bruising will heal but it is one of the reasons I am on leave. I can't wear a harness for a while so can't do my job properly. It's one of the hazards of the job. Looking on the positive side, it means I can keep an eye on you. Is the pain beginning to ease?'

'Slightly,' she murmured with eyes closed.

'I'll start you on a course of painkillers in the morning so you don't have to go through the indignity of exposing your backside to me any more. Plus, you should take a course of antibiotics to ward off any infection. Now, try to sleep but call me if you need me.'

Jared remained seated on the floor while caressing Bella's skin in soft, gentle strokes until he was certain she was asleep. Leaving Duke on guard he returned to his own cold bed, lying awake for hours, thinking about the wonderful, sassy, gentle natured but tough woman who was asleep a short distance down the passage. The woman who had stirred up a host of emotions and feelings he'd kept suppressed ever since his disastrous engagement to Lynne Wilson, eighteen months previous.

A flash of remembered pain hit as he visualised the scrap of paper handed to him at the altar by a complete stranger. *I can't marry you,* it read. *I've found someone else.* There hadn't even been a single word of apology or reason given and he'd never heard a word from her since. But he did know that she'd married someone else within three months. A man, he discovered, who had far more wealth than Jared. It was then that Jared knew that Lynne was nothing more than an unscrupulous gold-digger. Now, he was beyond thankful she'd found someone else to fleece. But the experience had left him in an emotional vacuum and distrustful of the female population for way too long.

Chapter Twelve

The sun was perfect. Not too hot, not too cool. After a week of constant showery and overcast weather leaving her trapped indoors, Bella lay stretched out on a sunlounge on the wooden decking outside Jared's lounge room window, basking in the glorious warmth of the sun and the serenity of her surroundings. Now that his coat had dried out after his weekly bath earlier that morning, Duke had edged his way below Bella's body and was lying sprawled underneath the lounge. She grinned at the way for the entire week, the animal had shadowed her, remaining by her side whenever she sat, rested or slept. As though sensing her injuries Duke always waited patiently when Bella struggled with the awkward crutches Jared had hired, and then padded far enough behind so he never got in her way.

At first Bella found it unnerving to constantly find Duke watching her but was now so used to him she felt a sense of loss when Jared took the dog for his exercise run each night. Her initial trepidation had turned into great respect and love for the huge animal. She smiled at the thought of Jared teasing her about stealing his dog's affections.

Then her mind turned to the week in hiding. It had done wonders restoring her health. Her cuts and bruises were well on their way to being healed with her body changing colours from deep indigo, through to green and yellow as the bruises faded. Her image reflected from the mirror earlier that morning had shown her to still be quite multi-coloured, the deeper bruises taking longer to heal. Constant tending by Jared saw her open wounds healing without becoming infected. Her ribs hardly hurt anymore and the throbbing headaches had ceased. Still in the awkward heavy plaster cast, her leg no longer had a relentless ache but torn muscles and ligaments in the flesh around the fracture gave her quite a bit of grief, especially if she moved suddenly or stayed still in the same position too long. According to Jared it would be many weeks before she would be using the leg to walk. The doctor hadn't got around to telling her those finer details before she'd fled. It had taken a couple of days, a few awkward stumbles and quite a bit of practise to master the use of crutches but she no longer depended on Jared to get her from one part of the house to another. Her latest greatest pleasure was being able to pee at her leisure and in privacy.

After a week of leave allowing his own deep bruising to heal, Jared had decided he was fit enough to return to the job he loved, leaving Duke to guard Bella. She smiled as she recalled the way he insisted she carry her mobile phone at all times so he could be contacted at a moment's notice if she felt threatened. With no sign of any strangers or Bart Hudson over the past seven days, she felt safe hidden in Jared's house.

Jared. She smiled. He was such a gentleman and gorgeous to boot. He showed infinite patience and a teasing sense of humour. He was so perfect she spent hours wondering why some woman hadn't snaffled him up. Her one broach of the subject had seen the only negative reaction. He'd answered her tersely before leaving the room. It didn't require genius status to figure he'd been hurt by some woman so she'd not asked again. After all, it wasn't her business but it didn't prevent her from being curious.

Jared's week hadn't been idle for they'd both spent many hours with Simon Adler while they discussed the findings of Adler's men. She shifted to get more comfortable as she recalled some of the things they'd discovered. There was plenty of evidence to arrest Bart Hudson for attempted murder but they wanted to keep him unaware of his close monitoring until they could find who his cohorts in high places were. After talking to a senior police officer in headquarters, a man Jared trusted, Detective Sergeant Bill Travers was placed under official surveillance. The fact he had falsified the report on the fluid test was all the convincing the Regional Inspector needed. Assuming it was a standard glucose, Bill Travers had failed to include the antibiotic, which had been added to the drip, in his falsified report. The results from Jared's testing of the sheet were being kept under wraps for the time being, but a copy of the report was in the hands of Regional Inspector, John Wright.

Bella grinned as her thoughts continued. To make things official, a missing person's report had been filed and a prominent newspaper article outlined the disappearance of one Mrs Annabella Perez with a hint of underworld connections. The article had generated quite a few frantic phone calls both to and from Bart Hudson, all of which had been taped. Hudson accused Bill Travers of kidnapping her and vice versa. It had become obvious neither man trusted the other but what was increasingly apparent was that both were seeking her whereabouts. Both men wanted her dead but the reason for this, apart from her ability to name Hudson as her attacker, had not yet been disclosed. More importantly, the calls verified a link between the two men.

Bella shielded her eyes against the glare of the sun as her thoughts returned to the man who had saved her life. She couldn't figure Jared out. He had been wonderful in tending to her every need, treating her with respect and kindness, teasing her, making her laugh. She could recall the feel of his long fingers gently caressing her when she was in pain, his arms around her and comforting her when she was distressed and the feel of her body against his bare chest when he carried her. Without a word she found her freshly laundered clothes folded in a neat pile on the end of her bed every couple of days, her meals were cooked, her bed straightened and fresh sheets appeared two days ago. What really had her concerned was that the couple of times she had reached out to touch Jared, she'd felt him physically wince and jerk away, even to the extent of grabbing her hand and dragging it away from his body. For some reason she couldn't fathom, he didn't like her touching him. Even though she knew she had no right to feel that way, deep down it hurt - really hurt.

Bella didn't know the number of times during the dark of night Jared wandered into her room to check on her, but she had woken a couple of times to find him standing by the head of her bed with his fingers running in sensuous movements through her hair. Only once had she spoken to him in the dark. The immediate withdrawal of his hand and his terse response had her mystified so she pretended she wasn't awake every other time he'd stirred her to wakefulness.

A sudden deep growl from Duke brought Bella back to the present in an instant. His rapid crawl from under the sun lounge followed by a bristling stance by her side, with a continuous rumble emanating from deep down, told Bella something was wrong. When Duke clamped his lips around her wrist, tugging her hand as he backed towards the door she became really concerned, her heart beat accelerating before her innards clenched like a vice. Searching around for fallen crutches, Bella yanked her hand free and murmured, 'what is it boy? What's wrong?'

At the sound of a vehicle coming to a standstill some distance from the house Bella clamped the metal crutches to her arms. Without waiting to see who it was she turned and hobbled inside, following the still growling dog. She hopped to the front room to peer through the translucent curtains. Sudden panic caused an onrush of adrenaline to flood through her veins when she recognised the car. With her stomach churning she turned and swung her hips between the crutches harder than she'd ever dared before as she made her awkward way to the kitchen where she grabbed the two largest sharpened kitchen knives from their wooden sheaths. Then she fled down the passage searching for a hiding place.

How the hell did he find her? Did he know she was here or was he just looking for Jared? Wasn't he supposed to be under watch? It didn't matter which for she couldn't afford to be found and needed a room where she could lock the door from the inside. Phone – she needed her mobile phone. Why didn't she listen to Jared and carry the darn thing with her at all times?

After a week of peace and harmony, complacency had set in. Bella had heard Jared's warnings but not heeded them, leaving the phone in her bedroom all day. Her crutches made a rapid plopping noise as the rubber ends hit the tiled floor while she sped down the passage to her bedroom. Grabbing the phone, she slipped it into her pocket then with both knives held between her thumb and the hand bracket on one crutch she sought a hiding place. While thinking of where the safest place would be she raced back out of her room, pulling the door shut behind her. Duke was hot on her heels, still rumbling low menacing growls.

There was only one room she could recall which had a lock. She headed straight for it. Hearing loud knocking at the front door she stepped into the cramped room of the toilet, dragging Duke in after her. She perched on the closed lid at the same time as she pulled the phone from her pocket. As she pressed the button to summon Jared she sent up a fervent prayer that he had his pager attached to him and he wasn't hanging off the side of another cliff or suspended at the end of a winch wire in the middle of the ocean. Slipping the phone back into her pocket, she stood on one leg, pressed the lock on the toilet door then jammed one crutch handle under the door knob, the other end pressed against the porcelain bowl. It wasn't much, but it was the best she could do under the circumstances. She settled the other crutch upright in the corner but within easy reach in case she needed to use it as a battering ram over Hudson's head. And she'd keep on battering until she could batter no more.

As she sat on the closed seat, Bella settled Duke on one side of the pan, his head in her lap. Running her fingers through the hair behind his ears to keep him still, she whispered, 'Quiet, boy.' She prayed instinct and excellent training would tell him to obey as she bent her left leg by her side ready to stand, even though there was absolutely nowhere she could flee. The cast rested on the angled crutch, the leg inside beginning to throb from the hasty movements. She sat rigid, not daring to move, not daring to make a sound while she listened intently for any noises from outside.

At the scrape of footsteps moving along the passage Bella gasped then turned rigid as she suddenly remembered she hadn't locked the glass sliding door when she'd fled from the veranda. She hadn't known then that it would be needed and her haste in finding her phone and then a hiding hole, she'd thrown the thought from her mind. Terror gripped her innards into a knotted coil while she followed the sounds Bart Hudson made as he searched the house. Instinct told her he wasn't here to speak to Jared. The very nature of his stealth told her exactly what he was here for. Somehow he had found out where she was hiding. She pressed the button on the mobile again and wished she had the number for the base. If she managed to get out of this alive the number would be committed to memory.

Bella listened. Bart was in the end room, Jared's large study. Cupboard doors opened then slammed shut again. She heard the contents from the top of Jared's desk being swept to the floor, a rush of papers, the breaking of glass and a tinkling of metal hitting the polished wood. Jared's bedroom and en-suite were next to be searched with drawers pulled out and upended, doors slammed and a few frustrated curses, followed by footsteps in the passage.

The unused bedroom next to Jared's room contained spare furniture and a mass of boxes, some empty, others full and taped closed. Bella heard every square centimetre of the room being searched. She pressed the button on the mobile again and wished she could call the base in case Jared was out on a call. This not knowing whether or not he was on his way was too darn hard.

Across the passage from the bedroom was a door leading into the large open-plan kitchen, dining and lounge area. Bella prayed Bart would go in there next. It would give Jared a few more minutes to arrive, if he had received her message. A sense of calm swept over her as she pressed the button on the mobile phone once again, but underneath she felt absolutely petrified. Her innards were clenched into a tight ball while her heart felt as though it was about to burst. With her stupid crippled leg she had no possible means of escape even if she attempted to flee. Her only hope was that Bart didn't have the sense to search the smallest room in the house, after all, who would be stupid enough to hide in a tiny toilet?

Because she wanted the search to take the entire length of time it would take for Jared to reach her, time seemed to fly. It seemed like only seconds before she heard Bart cross the passage from the second door of the lounge area to her own bedroom. The door creaked open then Bart exclaimed with glee at his success in finding evidence Bella was living there. She heard him gloating.

'Gotcha, bitch! This time you won't escape. You are going to pay and I'm going to enjoy watching you suffer.'

Swallowing down rising bile, Bella held her breath. Duke seemed to sense her increased fear for he became agitated but thankfully remained silent, Bella continuing the caresses to his skin in the hope of keeping him calm.

The door next to her opened. The family bathroom.

There were no hiding places in there but still she heard the banging of the glass shower door being flung against the wall, the crashing of toiletries as they hit the tiles and the slamming of the bathroom door when Bart left it. As footsteps moved towards the laundry Bella expelled her held breath in a quiet gush. There were only two rooms left, the garage on the end and this separate guest toilet. Footsteps came towards her. 'Go past, go past,' she willed. They stopped, paused. Bella sat motionless, not daring to breath. Duke stood alert, his ears pricked, his hackles high, but thank God, he still didn't make a sound.

The steps passed her by, disappearing down to the garage. She breathed then relaxed for a moment as she heard the door hit a wall as if flung open. Duke stood, his sensitive ears pricked, his tail whipping the wall but Bella was unaware as to the cause of his sudden interest and tried to settle him down again. At the return of the footsteps Bella sucked in her breath. The door handle jiggled and something heavy pushed against it.

'Got you, you bitch!' The gloating words were spat out in a ferocious hiss. Bart thumped on the door while trying to force it open. Unsuccessful, he returned to the garage. Bella heard his footsteps retreat then return a few seconds later. It took only two savage blows against the hollow sandwich, wooden door for a metal rod to crash through the panel near the handle. A few more belts made the hole large enough for Bart to reach through with one hand in an attempt to unlock the door.

'You can't escape, bitch. There's nowhere for you to go.' He laughed: a derisive snivelling chortle.

As Bella watched transfixed, Bart's hand reached inside. 'This time I am going to make damn sure you die. Slow, very slow and very, very painful.'

Bella gasped.

'And guess what, bitch? You're gonna be watching my face as I do it. Nobody gets away with besting me. You are going to suffer for not dying the first time, or the second. Third time lucky they say. Well it's going to be third time lucky for me.'

Boggle eyed, Bella stiffened as Bart's right hand reached through the hole while trying to avoid the sharp, jagged splinters of wood. Once his hand was in as far as the centre of his forearm, he spun his hand around at the wrist to grab a hold of the round doorknob.

A sudden frenzied attack of stabbing rained down on his exposed limb. Knowing her life depended on it, Bella slashed and stabbed repeatedly as hard and as fast as she could with the larger of the two knives. Blood spurted up the door and wall as she sliced savagely, the knife severing part way through his index finger, which was trapped against the wood. She gasped at the sight of the top two joints left hanging by a large flap of flesh. That she had sliced through the joint was pure luck she thought as she gagged at the gore. She certainly hadn't wasted any time with deliberate aims.

A cry of shock escaped her lips then she grinned as Duke grabbed the hanging digit, shaking his head from side to side ferociously, a loud belly growl rumbling from deep down.

'Aghhhhh! Call the mutt off!' Bart screamed out again and again as he attempted to pull his hand free, levering his body against the door. All of a sudden the finger was torn free from the hand, the release being so rapid Bart staggered backwards with the momentum but the flesh from his inner wrist caught on the sharp, jagged wood fragments, slicing through what Bella thought must have been an artery with such a ferocious stream of red liquid squirting like a small fountain.

Duke dropped the torn digit onto the floor, ignoring Bart's screams of pain.

Mesmerised, Bella stood as in desperation, Bart tried to withdraw his hand back through the hole but his flesh was caught too deep. The sight of the bloodied finger turned Bella's stomach but at the same time she smiled. 'Suffer, you bastard,' she screamed. 'If I'm going down then you are coming with me.'

Bella hovered over the hand ready to continue her vicious onslaught while watching the wrist as it tried to wriggle free of the jagged pieces of wood. Bart howled out in agony while Bella said nothing and Duke growled, a low menacing rumble. Blood increased its flow, spurting all over her clothes and hands, the walls and floor as well as the dog. Bella was momentarily transfixed as one tiny vessel spewed so much blood so rapidly. She guessed Bart's heightened heartbeat and continued struggling would be the cause. She sincerely hoped he bled to death. Tears of anger, fear and frustration flowed from of her eyes while both of her raised hands gripped the handle of the knife in a tight clench, her knuckles white. She didn't dare relax, didn't dare give him a chance to open the flimsy door. If she had to, she felt no qualms about using the knives on other parts of his body in self-defence, especially after what he'd done to her.

A sudden frantic barking from Duke along with the sound of the thrumming from the helicopter had Bart pull with an almighty jerk accompanied by a high-pitched scream, his bloodied hand finally freeing from the door where his mangled flesh had been caught on the razor-edged slivers. Pieces of raw flesh hung in a gruesome adornment from the splinters, blood soaked into the unpainted edges of the wood, turning it a deep crimson. Bella heard unsteady steps as Bart fled then she sank back onto the commode and sagged against the cistern.

Chapter Thirteen

Jared was out the chopper door before it had even landed, running full pelt towards the house. At the sight of the blood he came to a grinding halt outside the wide-open front door. Buck and King pulled up beside him. There was so much blood.

'Bella!' The haunting scream echoed across the hills.

Jared had sped to King the moment he had seen Bella's number on his pager. They had lifted off within seconds and flown as fast as possible: much faster than Jared would have been able to manage by car. But they were still too late. Together they followed the trail of blood along the ground to where it ended. The spun out gravel indicated where a vehicle had taken off at speed.

The frantic barking of Duke had the men spin around then pound towards the house, Jared calling out to the dog. 'Duke, here boy!'

The barking continued but no animal emerged. They followed the incessant noise. The blood down the passage was extensive. Fear engulfed Jared. How could anyone survive such a loss of blood? God, don't let it Bella. Jared stopped at the smashed door, Duke's nose poking out.

'Duke, quiet!' Jared commanded. 'Where's Bella, boy?' After wrenching at the door and finding it locked, he crouched down to peer through the bloodied hole. A wave of relief swept over him at the sight of Bella sitting hunched up on the closed toilet seat. Her arms were wrapped around her trembling body, rocking backwards and forwards. She was covered from head to toe in spatters of blood but he had no idea whose blood it was. Her glazed eyes stared into nothingness, her lips moving as though trying to speak but no sound came out.

'Bella, sweetheart.' Jared cried out as he tried to figure out how to get her out. He didn't care about compromising evidence. Bella needed help; nothing else mattered. Flying down the passage to his study he paused when he spied the mess then searched around the strewn items for a paper clip. Coming up triumphant he unfurled it as he tore back to the wrecked door. He knelt at the door then poked the end of the metal clip into the tiny hole in the handle, which released the locking mechanism from the outside. Standing, he tried pushing the door inwards but it moved no more that a few millimetres. Kneeling once again, he peered through the hole and noticed the wedged crutch.

'Damn, it's wedged.'

'Take the bolts out of the hinges and lift the door off. Here use this.' Buck held out an already unfurled pocketknife.

'I can't, the hinges are on the inside. I have an idea.' Jared shot down the passage into the garage. Sucking in a breath at the sight of his belongings strewn across the floor, he pulled the door of the metal cabinet open then dragged out a power saw and an extension lead. Plugging the lead in and switching the power on, Jared unwound the long electrical cord as he hurried back to the toilet door. Peering in the hole, he ordered Duke to lie down on the floor then began sawing through the thin panel, making the hole large enough for him to reach through. Buck reached up to grasp the wavering panel as Jared finished sawing. Together they pulled the panel free, ripping the last few centimetres of wood apart. Handing the machine to King, Jared reached through the hole and pulled the crutch away from under the handle then wrapped his hand around the bloodied handle to open the door.

He called Duke out before sidling his way beside Bella, jamming his back against the wall. Cradling her in his arms, he held the stricken woman against his chest knowing she was in a state of shock.

'Hell, man, what happened here?' King stood outside the door, looking horrified by the gruesome sight.

There was so much blood Jared couldn't tell whether or not Bella was injured.

'Call the police and ask for Regional Inspector John Wright. Tell him it is an emergency and give him my name. He will understand. Then give him the details of where we are. Here use this phone - his number is already punched in. Then search for Simon Adler's number and get him here as well.'

Releasing one hand from Bella, Jared slipped his mobile phone from his pocket flipped it open then held it out for King, who took one step inside the room to remove it from

Jared's hand. King walked back outside to make the calls, leaving Buck to assist Jared.

It was difficult manoeuvring his large body in the tiny room, but Jared somehow managed to lift Bella from the seat and carry her outside. He kept going until he reached the veranda where he settled down in a wooden seat with Bella still nestled in his arms. Just as he had done on the side of the mountain, Jared rocked her like a baby while whispering calming words into her ear, his warm breath fluttering against her hair. While he spoke he inspected all the parts of her body he could see without disturbing her, checking to see if any of the blood was coming from her. How much more could this woman take? He didn't need her to tell him what had happened – he had already figured it out but he wasn't sure whether it was Hudson or Travers who had found her. Both men were supposed to have been under constant surveillance and this fact worried him enormously, although, he reasoned, either man could have hired a paid killer. Or maybe it was the other blond man who he now knew was Hudson's brother.

After the phone calls, the two men sat on the veranda with Jared, who said, 'King how about making four coffees and add at least three teaspoons of sugar to Bella's. I figure she needs the glucose. She's in shock.'

'Who can blame her,' muttered King as he stepped through the door of the house.

After escaping from the confines of the toilet, Duke had fled outside with his quivering nose hovering over the trail of blood. He returned, padded over to Jared and apparently satisfied all was now well lay down in a docile heap by his master's side, brown eyes watching them both.

Two coffees in each hand, King sauntered out to the veranda, dragging a small table over towards Jared with his booted foot before setting the mugs down. 'Is Bella hurt?'

'I don't think so,' said Jared as his eyes roamed over her body once again. 'I can't see any more injuries than she had before. She's just traumatized and who can blame her. Anybody, man or woman, would be in a state of shock after all she has been through. Did you reach John Wright?'

'He's on his way with a forensics team. There's half a finger on the floor in there.'

'I noticed.' Jared turned his attention to Bella who had ceased her continuous trembling and was squirming in his arms. 'Bella?'

'Did you catch him?' she whispered, her voice tremulous.

'No, he drove away. Who was it? Hudson or Travers or someone else?'

'Hudson ... Jared, I was so scared ... I had no way of escaping ... He was bragging about making my death slow and painful ... Why, Jared? ... Why does he want me dead?'

'As to why he originally tried to kill you, I have no idea, but now it's probably because you can identify and give evidence against him. You saw him each time he made an attempt on your life. But this time he has left behind his own evidence. Apart from all the blood and bits of skin hanging off my toilet door, you cut off his finger. Finger prints are useful, but the entire finger?'

Much to his relief and thankful his attempted use of humour had sparked her up, Jared saw Bella's face twitch into a brief smile. 'I only half cut it off, Duke pulled it the rest of the way and then spat it on the floor. Duke was so good. He warned me someone was coming and was so quiet when we were locked in the room. I was so scared you were out on a call and wouldn't get my message.'

'You are one very smart and extremely brave lady. I would love to be able to let you have a shower but the forensics team are going to need to photograph you.' Jared turned to Buck. 'Buck, could you fetch the blanket on the end of the lounge, we can at least cover her up for a few minutes?'

Before Buck was able to return, his beeper sounded. All three beepers hanging from the men's belts began an orchestrated tune. Buck paused to answer the call. 'We have to go, Jared. We have a callout. You stay here. King and I can manage. It's a one person car accident not far away.' Handing Jared the blanket, Buck left, following King out to the still idling chopper, which lifted off as soon as the door slammed shut.

Every time Jared tried to release Bella she begged him to keep a hold of her. So he stayed in the seat, instinct telling him Bella had reached the end of her tether, which in his eyes was more than understandable. He continued comforting until the police arrived when he settled her in the chair, leaving Duke standing by her side and her hand on the dog's head.

Jared insisted the photographer take all the shots he needed of Bella first, then he assisted her down to his own en-suite so she could shower. After wrapping her blood spattered cast in plastic he settled the plastic chair in his shower recess then found her a clean change of clothes from the strewn garments on her floor. He left her to shower at her leisure while he joined the group of police officers crammed in his passage and toilet, collecting the evidence they needed. He couldn't help but grin at the thought of the association with toilets and Bella needing to pee in the most awkward of situations.

During the proceedings Jared had a call from King; a call that elicited a huge grin and one he would enjoy relating to Bella.

After Bella emerged she winced at the sight of her crutches.

'I've washed off the blood,' said Jared as he held them out.

'Thank you.' She snapped the hooks around her arms then made her own way down the passage to the lounge room where three men were waiting to interview her. Bella paused as she neared the bloody mess on the passage floor. Shrugging as though dismissing her memories, she turned into the door leading into the kitchen. She eyed the three men who were standing waiting for her.

Noting her hesitation Jared moved up behind her and nudged her elbow. 'Come on, I'll help you through this and I have something to tell you that might make it a whole lot easier. Come and sit down.'

Following Bella into the room, Jared waited until she was settled before he began. 'Bella, gentlemen, you will be interested in this little piece of information. The callout King and Buck went to was an accident where a car went off the side of the road. The driver had passed out from loss of blood and was missing part of a finger. Bart Hudson is alive in hospital under the care of an armed guard.' He turned to face Bella. 'He has been arrested for attempted murder and won't be bothering you again. Unless he pleads guilty to all the charges, there will be a trial and you will have to testify but I think with all the evidence we have, he won't stand a chance.'

Jared turned to face John Wright. 'John, I'm curious about something – what happened to Hudson's tail?'

'I'm not sure but I'll certainly be asking questions as soon as I get back to headquarters. Could be Hudson gave them the slip, especially if he was tipped off by someone on the inside, which, sadly, given what I know now, is more than possible.'

The news appeared to boost Bella's confidence as she had no hesitation in answering all the questions, even though she shivered whilst relating the lurid details. She also repeated all the facts of the other attempts on her life after Jared had assured her John Wright was one police officer she could trust to do the right thing by her. The sky had darkened before the last man left the house.

With Bella too jittery to move out of his sight, Jared shoved frozen pizza into the oven. They ate in the lounge room whilst listening to quiet background music, appreciating the peace and quiet. Jared insisted Bella sleep in his bed for the night so that she had easy access to his bathroom.

After spending a couple of hours cleaning all the blood and gore from his house and fixing a temporary patch on the battered door, Jared went to check on Bella, sighing when he spied Duke had found where she was sleeping. He was curled up on his old rug in the corner of the room, the rug he had always slept on until Bella's arrival. Jared shook his head in disgust. The dog had become devoted to Bella. Never before had Duke swapped his allegiance to any person other than Jared, and he had done it so quickly. Jared recalled his ex-fiancée. With Lynne, Duke had been the opposite, growling every time she came, barely tolerating her and sulking outside until Lynne had gone home again. Jared snorted in derision at the memory. Duke had been right about that woman and after being jilted so callously at the altar Jared was still wearing the emotional scars: scars that had prevented him from forming any long standing attachment to any other woman since.

As he had done every night Jared stood staring down at Bella, his heart turning over in his chest. 'What secrets are you holding so tight, little one?' he whispered. 'There has to be something you know or have.' When she moved he stilled until certain she hadn't awoken. As he looked down he thought how her dogged determination, stoicism and calm composure had seen her through shocking experiences. Yet at the most dastardly times, Bella managed to crack a wry smile, see the positive side of the situations and shake negative thoughts from her mind. Before leaving her side Jared knew without a doubt, he had fallen for the inimitable Bella. The thought pleased him as he loped down the passage, collapsed into Bella's bed, exhausted, but at peace with the world. His last thoughts before he fell asleep were about Bella.

'Sweet, intriguing, beautiful Bella Perez, much as I don't believe in love at first sight, I'm in love with you, desire you, want you, admire you and will do everything in my power to help and protect you. But until this is all over, little one, I'm going to have to keep my feelings for you on a tight rein,' he whispered into the darkness. His deep sense of propriety and innate sense of correct protocol prevented him from taking advantage of her. It was so hard to continually pull back his hand from exploring her soft delicate skin, so hard to keep his rampaging hormones under control every time he caught sight of her, so hard to fight back his awakened emotions, so hard to deny to himself that Bella had crept into his heart.

He felt as though he had only just gone to sleep when a piercing scream echoed through the dark stillness, jarring Jared upright.

Chapter Fourteen

Jared flew out of bed then stumbled around in the grey light of dawn as he tried to gather his bearings and figure out where the hell he was after running smack bang into a wall and finding the door wasn't where it was supposed to be. The unfamiliarity of the room temporarily fazed him despite the continual penetrating noise that was closely followed by a loud bark from Duke, who flew into the room almost bowling Jared over. The screams continued while Jared dragged on a pair of jeans, hopping and scrambling to get through the door, which he finally found after realising he wasn't sleeping in his own room. Duke was no help, yapping for him to hurry while bounding around his legs.

'Heel, Duke, and for heaven's sake shut that noise.' Freed from the hindrance of the madly frolicking dog, Jared fled down the passage. There was enough light from the first rays of the morning sun to see Bella's thrashing body moving from side to side in his bed. Becoming aware that she was still asleep, Jared knelt on the side of the bed, gathering her up into his arms to soothe her.

'Bella, wake up, you're dreaming.'

She woke suddenly, her eyes wide with fright, a band of sweat across her brow. Flinging her arms around Jared's neck she began sobbing while clinging to him like ivy tendrils on a wall, desperate to get away from what ever was that had been taunting her.

'Oh, Jared, it was ghastly. He was chasing me with an axe, chopping off bits of my body every time he caught me.'

'Shush, sweetheart, it was only a bad dream. You're safe here.' Jared continued holding her close while his own pounding heart settled down to a more normal pace and Duke returned to his mat, as though satisfied all was now well. Once happy that Bella had calmed, Jared returned to his hastily vacated bed in an attempt to catch another couple of hours of much needed sleep. Life with Bella had certainly turned his routine and his house into turmoil, he thought as he pulled the quilt over his shoulders.

The smell of eggs cooking drew Jared from his bed, mainly to investigate what the devil Bella was doing in the kitchen when she could barely move around on her crutches. He stood in awe, staring at the neatly set table and Bella perched on one leg while deftly turning bacon with a pair of tongs.

'You don't have to do this you know, Bella?' He strode over to the gas cook top and attempted to remove the tongs from her hand.

'I know I don't have to but I want to. It's boring doing nothing and besides I was too terrified to go back to sleep. I've been sitting on the settee just staring and trying to block the memories, without success I might add. So I had to occupy my mind by doing something. Now sit down, breakfast is ready.' Tugging the tongs back, she placed two slices of warm toast on each plate, topped them with fried eggs then draped perfectly fried rashers of bacon alongside the eggs. She did allow Jared to carry the plates to the table.

'How did you manage to carry all these items to the table?' Jared asked while trying his best to look as though he was serious in reprimanding Bella. In truth he was relieved she was carrying out normal everyday duties but then wondered if her actions were covering up a deeper mental trauma.

'One at a time,' Bella broke his reverie by answering. 'Now eat and enjoy. It's not very often I cook breakfast so make the most of it and Jared…?'

He paused, fork held in the air, suspicious of the sly look on Bella's face and the sugary sweet tone of her voice. 'Why do I get the impression I'm not going to like what you have to say?'

'I want to go to work with you today. I'll sit in the office, make the coffee, tidy up, anything … just as long as I don't have to stay here by myself all day. I know I've got Duke and he is a wonderful guard. I know Bart is under armed guard but after yesterday … well, I'm kind of spooked and right now I … well … I just don't think I can handle staying here all day by myself.'

Bella sat in meek submission, head bowed, hands twisting in her lap and looking as though she were fully expecting him to say no. She didn't see the look of deep compassion and understanding he sent her way. Her words and actions confirmed his earlier thoughts that she was traumatized and doing her utmost to hide it.

'I think we might be able to accommodate you. I understand how you feel. I had planned to send you to Simon's place for the day but another thought has just come to me. You said you were an accountant?' Jared grinned at the surprised look on Bella's face. 'I have just the right job for you. We all hate doing the monthly reconciliation of our outlays and costs for the Government. Being a Government-funded organization we have to account for every single cent we spend. We fight over who gets to do the tedious job and it takes us hours. How about you doing it for us?'

Jared laughed out loud at Bella's eager agreement. 'I'm looking forward to seeing everyone's faces when I tell them what you will be doing. I personally, will keep you supplied with coffee and will even take my life in my hands and dare to go and raid King's office for his hidden stash of chocolate biscuits. Mind you, he might be willing to hand them over since it is his turn to tackle the books, although he has an uncanny knack of getting out of it by insisting the chopper needs some kind of repair. Yes, Bella, you are more than welcome to come.'

***

Bella grinned at the speed in which a fresh packet of chocolate-coated biscuits was produced after Jared had teased King, before letting on that she was going to do the books for him. All five present members of the staff bowed and scraped to make her comfortable before piling an untidy heap of papers in front of her.

'I see you have a very workable, efficient filing system in here.' Sarcasm dripped from her tongue as Bella began to rifle her way through the scraps of paper while trying to ascertain whether or not there was actually any order in the pile. 'It reminds me of one of my first customers; a farmer who led me into his home office, unlocked the roller door on his desk then ran, as two years supply of papers spilled out onto the floor. It took me a week to sort them before I could even begin to tackle his books. I understand now why none of you like doing the monthly accounts.' Bella knew all eyes were staring at her but she refused to look up, hoping they were all feeling equally embarrassed and guilty.

Happy to have something to do, Bella worked without a break, sorting, writing and computing without comment. King, Jared and Buck went out on a call to a three-car accident soon after she started. When they arrived back not long before lunch, Bella was sitting back in the office chair with her cast leaning on the edge of the desk, her other foot draped over it, mainly because the elevation eased the throbbing but she knew what impression she was giving. Not a paper was in sight. Without looking up she casually pointed at the next desk. Sitting on Jared's desk, in a prominent position was the monthly reconciliation report, all neatly typed out and printed off in triplicate. Underneath, was a pile of newly labelled files; all empty. She thoroughly enjoyed the sight of Jared's mouth gape.

'You've finished?'

'Piece of cake. If you all file away your papers in the correct file from now on it will make your life much easier in the future.' Dropping her legs to the ground she turned to face the men. 'Now, is there anything else that needs doing? If not, I could set up your computer system to a much easier way of doing this than the one you already have. It will only take me a couple of hours.'

As if carefully orchestrated every single one of them stood, offering Bella their seat and computer.

By the time Jared was ready to drive Bella home, all five staff present had collectively been given a short tutorial on the easier and far more efficient way of undertaking the monthly account as well as instructions on which papers to put in each of the files she had created.

A detour to a large hardware store on the drive home saw Jared slipping a new wooden door into the rear of his four-wheel drive after he had lowered the two back seats. After a dinner he went all out to prepare as a thank you, he removed the remains of the old toilet door and hung the new one. It was obvious by the way he handled the tools and the efficiency in how he cut in the hinges and door handle that Jared was more than comfortable in working with his hands.

'You've done this before,' Bella commented as she stood leant against the wall while observing his skilful hands. She was unable to shake the deep uncomfortable feeling of anxiety besetting her body at the sight of the door-less room.

'I built the house. I enjoy working with tools. Dad is a carpenter so I've been doing this sort of thing all my life.'

'I'm impressed, a handyman as well as a great cook, is there anything you can't do?'

He grinned. 'Financial paperwork. You are certainly capable in that area as well as very computer literate. Your work today will be much appreciated. How about a glass of wine before we call it a day? I think we both deserve a treat. It's not often I drink alcohol when I have to work the next day but I think maybe one glass of icy cold white would go down rather well and won't put me over the limit.'

Work completed, tools put away and shavings swept up, they lounged on the settee in silence, watching the moonlight flicker on the gentle ripples of the lake. The grey of the wooden pier shone silver, giving the whole vista a magical appearance. Soft classical music wafted around the room, interrupted only by the occasional snuffle from the sleeping Duke who was curled up on his cushion in the corner. When Bella began yawning Jared shooed her to bed, muttering under his breath at his not so faithful best friend when Duke followed.

With all evidence of Bart Hudson's little interlude now gone, Bella assured Jared she was happy to stay at home the following day to recover from her ordeal. Jared had strong misgivings about leaving her alone but accepted her word. Before he left he again wrote down the base phone number as well as his mobile number, insisting she call even if she had the slightest feelings of unease during the day.

Bella refused to mention the shiver of fear whenever she paused at the toilet door and waited until Jared had left before sneaking through to his personal en-suite to use his facilities.

After struggling with a couple of loads of laundry, her efforts frustrated by having to have crutches in her hands all the time, Bella clicked her way down to the lake to take a breather, being careful not to slip on the compacted gravel pathway. The effort from her first extended walk on crutches made her arms ache so she hobbled to the end of the pier, wedging her backside on top of one of the large wooden pylons to rest while she surveyed her magnificent surroundings. Jared had found an idyllic spot to build his home. She knew from an earlier conversation that the property consisted of ten acres and the sloping hillock behind the lake was all a part of his land. The three-metre firebreak around the edge had a double purpose. Jared used it as his running track, making several circuits each night with Duke. Bella winced at the thought. One lap would be more than she could handle and she thought she was reasonably fit – well pre being dropped over a cliff she'd been fit. She shook her head at the thought of how her life had become nothing more than terror in the past week. It was so darn ridiculous especially when she'd done nothing all her life but mind her own business and work her butt off. She wasn't one to make waves in any situation, especially at work and now look how she was being repaid.

Bella sighed then continued her exploration by moving slowly through the shady grove of trees around the edge of the lake, the light dappling through the leaves giving a rippling effect on the ground. Duke seemed to love the fact that she had taken him for a walk and after galloping over the hill at a full run, he returned to sniff around under the bushes of the low underbrush, his tail wagging to and fro non-stop.

After investigating all the way around the lake while enjoying the warmth from the sun and the intermittent sounds of cicadas and birds, Bella was almost back at the little jetty when Duke stopped dead in his tracks and rumbled a low warning growl. The hair on the back of his neck bristled up, his erect ears stiffened. Bella turned to see what he was staring at.

Two men were walking towards them: one in uniform, the other dressed in a crumpled suit and oh, Lord! They both had guns drawn. What was going on? A shiver snaked down her spine but what really scared her the most was that she recognised both men and she wished she didn't. Slowing, she scrambled in her brain on how best to handle the situation, cursing under her breath about not remembering to carry the darn mobile phone with her. Relief swamped her when both men holstered their weapons as they neared but her senses remained very wary and on full alert, a sliver of unease continually stabbing at her innards.

'Mrs Perez, a few words please.'

'Sergeant Travers, I don't believe I've met your new partner.' She hadn't met the man but she definitely recognised him as one of the men who had been at the meeting in Bart Hudson's office. Some innate feeling told her it would be very unwise, in fact probably suicidal, to show any signs of recognition, especially since both were armed. Far better to pretend total ignorance, she figured as she straightened her back.

'You don't recall ever seeing Sergeant Walker?'

Bella needed no more hints. With that simple question there were no doubts why these two men were here. They were on a fishing expedition to find out exactly how much she knew and if she recognised the people at the meeting. Now one hundred percent certain these men were working for Hudson, she shivered at what her knowledge could mean. She was also fairly confident they were here on an unofficial basis. Why else would they approach with weapons drawn? This was Australia, not America and she was well aware of the rules pertaining to police use of firearms and she hadn't broken any laws. How stupid did they think she was?

After staring at the man in question, Bella shook her head in slow denial. 'No, I am absolutely certain. I don't get to personally meet many members of the Police Force and I'm sure if I had met him I would remember.' She swung her line of vision back to Travers. 'Now, how can I help you gentlemen? Do you mind if we walk while you talk, I'm getting rather tired and need to get back to the house to rest?' She hoped she sounded a lot calmer than she was feeling for her heart was thrumming in her chest and her innards were doing strange things, none of them in the least calming.

'We'd like you to come down to the station. We have a few questions we need to ask you concerning the alleged attacks on your life.'

Dropping her head as if to be concentrating on each step she continued her ungainly progress up the path, finding it hard to negotiate the gravel on the slight rise, but determined to keep moving towards the house, towards her phone. The niggle of unease she'd started with was turning into continual stabbing thrusts and there was no way she was going to stop walking.

'I'd prefer to answer them here since this leg hampers things a bit. Would you mind?'

There was a slight pause before Travers spoke again. Bella hadn't missed the two quiet gasps of displeasure. 'Yes we would mind. It would help if you agree to come in peacefully but we can insist, if you know what I mean?'

Startled by the innuendo of a threat, Bella's fear heightened, especially when both men moved behind and to one side of her as if to herd her away from the house towards their car. A really sick feeling settled in her gut, accompanied by another strong surge of adrenaline. Her heart began hammering against her ribs and she fought to sound as though she were calm and not fussed. 'If you insist, but I need to get back to the house, lock the dog in and visit the bathroom before I go. I've been out here far too long and am a little desperate to relieve my bursting bladder.' She paused then added, 'Unless you don't mind me having an accident in your car.'

Not waiting for a response she continued on with her awkward gait, increasing both her speed and her breathing rate to give the impression she was being co-operative and yet was tiring. The brushing against her by Travers eased off so she took that action as consent. While she moved she wracked her brain on how to contact Jared. She took her time to clomp up the stairs onto the veranda, taking one slow step at a time. It was something she hadn't mastered so well yet, but she made it without stumbling. Asking the two men to wait outside, but knowing they wouldn't, she slipped inside, calling Duke after her. She finally remembered the phone was on the settee and headed that way. Slumping down next to it she splayed her skirt over the instrument as she sank into the cushions, deliberately panting, making out she needed to rest.

'I'm sorry. I need a moment to catch my breath. That was hard work. Here boy?'

To hide what she was doing she made a fuss of Duke, rubbing him with both hands then dropped her right hand down by her side, scooping the phone up and slipping it into her pocket while keeping her other hand scratching Duke's head, which she had deliberately pulled closer to hide her actions. With a big sigh, she struggled back up onto her crutches then headed straight down the passage to Jared's bedroom, shutting the door behind her.

The door opened. In a deliberately slow movement Bella turned then stared at Bill Travers who stood filling the doorway, hands on hips, feet astride in what she knew to be an attempt at intimidation. It was working but Bella returned his icy stare, her eyes unmoving. There was no way in this world she was going to be the first to drop her eyes. 'If you don't mind, I'd like a little privacy when I'm on the loo. As you can see, there is no door to this bathroom. So please leave and shut the door.'

Bella remained still, waiting, not moving a muscle until Bill Travers relented and took a step backwards while peering at the contents on the room before shutting the door with a resounding bang. She didn't know what he was searching for but didn't really care. She scooted into the bathroom, slipped her briefs down then perched on the seat while withdrawing the phone from her pocket. She punched in the base number she had memorised earlier, knowing that if she needed Jared in a hurry, she wasn't going to have time to search for a scrap of paper. She'd learnt her harsh lesson at the last unwelcome intrusion.

Chapter Fifteen

It took two rings before Jared answered the phone she knew was at his desk.

'Air and Sea Rescue, Jared Mann here.'

Bella whispered over the noise from the flushing toilet. 'Travers is here with a Sergeant Walker who was one of the men at the meeting. They are insisting I go to the station with them for questioning. They had their guns drawn. What do I do?'

Hearing his expressive expletive, Bella knew Jared was as shocked as she. She heard his seat roll backwards and a rustle of papers as she clomped her way slowly along the tiles with the phone held in place by her ear against her shoulder. She turned on the tap as she heard Jared answer.

'Go with them. I'll call John Wright and will meet you at the station. Is it a marked police car?'

'Yes.'

'Good, I'll get King to see if he can pick it up and follow from the air. He, Buck and Jim Piggot are in the air now on their way back from a call and are not far away. Play along with them. Keep strong but see if you can stall for time. As soon as I hang up I'm on my way.'

Keep strong, she thought as she slipped the closed phone into her pocket and moved towards the door. She felt like just crawling up into a ball and letting these thugs shoot her. What further torment did they have planned for her? She wasted as much time as she could, waiting just inside the door.

An insistent thumping close to her ear jerked her up straight as Travers yelled, 'Hurry up, we need to go.'

'I'm coming,' Bella called back as she twisted the door handle. She'd just taken thirty seconds of the thirty minutes required for Jared to reach the house. It would take longer for him to reach the city. Just how slow could she go before these two either hustled her to the car or shot her? She was tailed by Travers as she put out food for the dog, even though it was not time for him to be fed. But Duke made no complaints about getting an extra meal, tucking in as though he hadn't eaten for at least a week.

The time she took to check the washing machine and drier, switching the power off then gathered an armload of dry washing by draping the items over her shoulder was almost unbearable even to her. She could sense the two men shadowing her were getting edgy, further unnerving her. Then she checked to ensure all the doors were locked, all the time feigning awkwardness with her crutches she really no longer had, wasting a few more precious seconds. She searched for, and found her bag, taking her time to slip it over her shoulder before clipping the metal arms of her crutches back into place.

It wasn't just fear enveloping her the moment she began to slip into the rear seat of the police car - it was abject terror. Her mind was beyond frantic. What if these two drove her to some unknown destination to do her in? Should she let them know she had told Jared where she was going? In case they decided to shoot her on the spot, she decided against disclosing any information for the moment, better to keep it quiet until she knew for sure what was going to happen. Her fingers closed over the phone still hidden in her skirt pocket at the same time as a message came over the two-way radio. 'Travers, you need to report back to base immediately. The boss has a special job for you.'

Bella noticed the glance passing between the two men before Travers slowly lifted the transmitter to his mouth, looking as though he was searching for a suitable response. 'Travers here, tell the boss I'm on the tail of a suspect and will be in as soon as possible. Is everything I asked for in place, Jennings?'

'It's all ready, Sarge, but don't you need a court order for this?'

There was another sharp glance between the two men before Travers replied. 'That's all sorted so don't worry. I'll be there within the hour.'

Staring out of the side window Bella pretended a deep interest in the scenery by following objects in her view, although her eyes were unseeing and her brain not absorbing any of them. "Within the hour" had her concern levels rising. If they were going straight to the station they'd be there a lot sooner than an hour. Glancing upwards she noticed a tiny dot high in the sky. Recognising the shape as a chopper, she sent up a silent prayer of thanks. King was flying higher than normal but she guessed it was to not arouse suspicion about him following the car.

When Travers leant forwards Bella wondered what he was up to. For a moment she thought he was about to pick up the gun he had drawn earlier. The sudden noise from the sirens and flashing red and blue emergency lights jolted her. She jerked forwards and was then thrown backwards against the back seat when Travers planted his foot on the accelerator. Taking a quick glance in the rear vision mirror, Bella caught Travers' eye in a very brief glance before she dragged her eyes away. It was obvious he was enjoying her discomfort.

***

Speeding, Jared turned into the road, heading home. With his mobile switched on to speaker he was in constant contact with King who was trailing the police car. The moment he reached home Jared raced inside, ripping off his clothes as he evaded a jubilant Duke going down the passage. Minutes later he emerged from his bedroom dressed in a tailored suit, fine cotton shirt and smart silk tie, well polished shoes on his feet and a well worn leather briefcase under his arm. By his timing he was fifteen minutes behind Bella and it worried him. A lot could happen in so short a time. Bella could disappear off the face of the earth or even worse – die. At least she'd had the good sense to name the men she was with. He raced down the steps to his car and slid in, driving off before buckling his safety belt. He hadn't reached the end of the drive before he heard crackling from the still open line of his mobile phone.

'Jared, are you still there?' yelled Buck.

'Yes, I'm on my way into town.'

'You'd better hurry, mate, they've turned off the highway; I think it is into Ridge Road. It's a gravel road, which looks as though it goes for miles into the bush. They've turned off the strobe lights and have sped up a fraction.'

'I know the place. Are you still in contact with Wright?'

'Yes, King is keeping him informed. Keep your line open so we can keep you in the loop.'

***

Bella's breathing almost ceased when the car skidded around the corner and fishtailed on loose gravel until Travers regained control of the speeding vehicle. What was she supposed to do now? Indecision gnawed at her innards. Should she tell them about her phone call and the helicopter above them or not? Daring another glance skywards she felt an adrenaline surge when she was unable to see the dark spot above. Not wanting to be caught searching the heavens Bella tried to keep her head sideways pretending to study the thickening bush, but her eyes kept shooting upwards. Relief flooded her body when the helicopter came into view once more. It registered that King was deliberately keeping behind the car.

What she figured had been several kilometres later the car turned into an overgrown driveway and pulled up in front of a derelict homestead. Her head held low, Bella studied her surroundings as Travers and Walker alighted from the car. A wooden veranda adorned the front of an asbestos and weatherboard house. Rusted corrugated iron covered the roof. The wild garden looked as though it had been gone over with a mower or whipper snipper sometime in the past week. A shadow at her window prevented her from seeing anything else. Her door opened.

'Get out, Mrs Perez.' Walker's voice was terse and demanding.

'This doesn't look like the station to me so I think I'll stay put until we reach headquarters.' Even though she figured she would pay for her stubbornness in the long run, Bella was determined to delay as long as she could. She was no genius but smart enough to know that this was intended to be the place she was to meet her maker.

'No games. Get out.'

How slow could she do this? As she reached down for her crutches a sly grin crept across her face as an idea settled into her brain. Making out her crutch was jammed she tugged hard, aiming directly for the paunched midriff standing in the open doorway of the car. Her aim was not so accurate, hitting lower than she intended but the effect brought a wicked smile to her face as the man doubled over in agony and clutching his groin.

'Bitch!' The hissed word gushed out of Walker's mouth.

'Oops, sorry,' Bella meekly apologised as the man knelt on the ground gasping for breath, moisture rushing across his eyes.

The door behind her opened. Travers was a little more polite in his request. 'Please climb out?' His words sounded weird but when Bella glanced towards him, his face was contorted due to a suppressed laugh.

Figuring a second attempt would not be seen as accidental, Bella obliged. She figured now was the time to talk. 'What are we doing here?' she asked as she wriggled out, stood then clamped the arm braces around her forearms.

'We want to ask you a few questions.'

'Oh, please! At least treat me as the intelligent human being I am. If you were going to ask me questions about the attempts on my life you wouldn't be doing it out in the middle of nowhere. I've already told you everything I know exactly as it happened. I wish I knew more, especially why

Bart Hudson is so hell bent on killing me. Jared knows where I am by the way. I rang him while I was in the bathroom. I told him both your names so if anything happens to me you will be the ones answering questions and you left your fingerprints on his bedroom door.'

There was an audible hiss of sucked in breath from Travers. Glancing at him she saw his face tighten into an angry scowl. Then the scowl eased off. 'There was no phone in his bedroom, I looked.'

Pulling one arm free of a crutch Bella removed her mobile phone from her pocket, holding it high in the air and waving it to and fro. 'Ever heard of mobiles? Jared insisted I carry it with me at all times. This little button here …' She pressed the button. 'It's a direct line to Jared's pager, but I dialled in his office number and spoke to him. I believe you can scroll down for recently called numbers. You want to check?'

'He won't find you out here and we only want to ask you questions.' Travers moved behind Bella and began shoving her in the small of her back.

'Suit your self,' Bella commented as she slid the phone back into her pocket then took her time to ease her arm into the crutch then made her slow, awkward way towards the house, sending up fervent prayers that Jared was nearby. Surely it was over half an hour. Somehow her gut feeling told her that after the questions the intention was to ensure she was never seen alive again. She wondered why she felt nothing more than an icy cold numbness.

Chapter Sixteen

When she was shoved into a chair without any regard for her leg or any other part of her body, Bella fought back by flinging her arms around wildly and kicking with her one good leg. She didn't flinch when her limbs connected with hard muscle or bone but kept on with the onslaught. With two beefy men fighting back it didn't take long for her to be subdued and held down. Her crutches were dragged from her arms and sent flying across the floor, hitting the far wall with a clang. Clouds of dust eddied up into the air shimmering in the sunbeams slanting through the openings. She also struggled for freedom when both of her arms were grabbed at the same time and tied to the arms of the chair with leather straps.

Finally secured and despite feeling very apprehensive, Bella was determined to not let her anxiety show through.

Stubbornness lifted her chin; defiance turned her eyes to a glassy, unblinking glare.

It intrigued her to see the look of doubt crossing over Travers' face when he neared her carrying a covered tray. When both men pulled chairs towards her and sat, one on each side of her knees, staring at her, she figured they were trying their best to intimidate her. They were succeeding but she didn't dare show it. As Travers settled the tray onto the floor next to him, Bella gave him her undivided attention by staring into his eyes. She felt a shiver of pleasure that gave her an inner feeling of triumph when Travers looked away first.

'Mrs Perez.' Bella turned to Walker. 'We have studied your testimony about all your allegations and no one believes a word of what you said. You are hiding something and we intend finding out the truth. How about you start from the beginning and tell us everything as it really happened?'

In turn, Bella eyed both men with long, hard stares, wondering what they were up to and knowing she still needed to stall for time. Jared said he would be here. How much time did he need? Knowing damn well this wasn't the real reason she was sitting trussed up in a wobbly chair, she gulped down a couple of deep breaths then in an excruciating slow monologue began relating everything, exactly as she had told it all before and adding minute details of embellishment. She knew by their frustrated faces these two men were losing patience but she had no idea what she was supposed to know. All she could tell them was the truth.

Halfway through her testament Walker grabbed the top of her arm, squeezing hard, the acute burning sting sending her the message that all patience was gone. Was now the time they were going to shoot her, for she knew that was the final intention. The only glimmer of positivity she had was that the scumbags would get caught.

'You are wasting our time. You have in your possession some stolen property and we want it back and we do have another way of getting the truth out of you. I have a court order here to allow us to use Sodium Pentothal but I would prefer your permission.'

She couldn't mask the alarm she knew shot across her face. 'I've never stolen anything in my life. I have no idea what you are talking about.'

'Papers stolen from Hudson's office. He lodged a complaint and wants them back.'

For a moment Bella sat silent, wracking her brain in a vain attempt to figure out to what papers they were referring, knowing she had never taken any papers home. 'I've never taken any papers home. You can search my house if you like.'

'We've already done that.'

Bella jerked back as far as she could causing the rickety wooden chair to rock. 'Excuse me? You've been in my home?' She glared at Travers as his hand shot out to steady the chair. 'I trust you had a search warrant.' There was a palpable pause during which the two men passed a guilty glance at each other. 'I bet you didn't find any stolen papers.'

'That's why we are here. Where are they?' Travers squatted in front of her, his fingers none too gentle as they grasped her chin and forced her face to look at him.

Anger suffusing her Bella yanked her face free, his touch feeling like a slimy aberration to her senses. 'I truly have no idea what you are talking about. I've never taken any work home from the office.'

'No, but your husband did.'

Stunned by the accusation, Bella writhed in her seat, the blood dropping from her face at the mention of Raoul. 'My husband? He's been dead for over four years and he sure as hell never had anything to do with Hudson.'

'We know he's dead. He stole the papers two days before he died and we want them back.'

A picture of Raoul's emaciated, cancer ridden body lying in agony in his bed shot into Bella's mind causing a rush of tears to sweep across her eyes. Two days before he found release from the torture of his illness she had sat by his side constantly, tending to his every need while her heart broke into a thousand pieces. Even the regular doses of morphine had little effect against the continuous pain. Raoul spent most of the time comatose, his few moments of lucidity an unbearable agony for them both as they tried to hide their pain from each other. Having been completely bed-ridden for weeks, Bella knew these men were lying. Her voice, when she managed to get a few words out, sounded anguished.

'Now I know you are lying. There is no way in this world my husband stole anything from anybody two days before he passed away. I was with him every second of the day and night.'

Much as she fought them back, Bella wasn't able to prevent a few salty tears from escaping and rolling down her cheeks. With her hands bound to the arms of the chair she had no choice but to let them flow unabated. From then on she acted dumb, asking in an almost inaudible voice what the chemical was, what it was for, what it did, any side effects – as many questions as she could in order to waste more precious seconds. She already knew what the chemical was and her greatest fear was that she would unwittingly in her subconscious state, let on about recognising Sergeant

Walker. She had a strong suspicion it was what they wanted so refused permission then demanded to see the court order.

The glance between the two men told her plenty, either they didn't have a court order or if they did it was fake. A piece of paper was unfolded then wafted in front of her face, giving her no time to make out any of the words. It was refolded in haste then slid into the top pocket of Sgt Walker's shirt while Travers retrieved the tray and removed the cover. A quick glance told Bella the syringe he held up in the air was already filled. Awful memories of another syringe flooded her brain. Travers lifted a rubber strap, turned towards Bella then wrapped it around the top of her arm, pulling it tight to force a vein to the surface. It was so tight she worried it would completely stop the flow of blood into her lower arm. Travers then turned, held the syringe into the light, squeezing a small amount of liquid from the thin needle, spurting it into the air.

The door flew open with a resounding bang as it hit the wall behind it. 'I don't think so, gentlemen.'

Bella's eyes flew open, staring at the immaculate suited Jared. He looked so different, so handsome. Travers spun around to face the intruder, flinging his hand behind his back to hide the evidence.

Taking one step into the room Jared continued. 'What you are doing here is highly illegal. My client was not given the opportunity to ring me, her lawyer. She has committed no crime and you brought her here under false pretences. The fact that you are in such a remote location tells me your intentions are illegal. The insidious six-foot hole out the back tells me exactly what those intentions are. I believe you both had your guns drawn when you visited Mrs Perez before bringing her here against her will.'

At the mention of guns Jared stepped in front of Bella. As he spun around there was a loud blast at the same time as he jerked. The force of the blast sent him off balance, tumbling over the seated Bella.

'Jared! No!" Bella screamed as she fell backwards still attached to the chair. As her head cracked against the floor the breath was knocked from her lungs when at the same time, Jared landed on top of her, his elbow punching into her ribs.

He lay so still Bella knew he was dead. She screamed.

'Damn but that hurt,' was gasped into her ear, confusing Bella. She ceased screaming and twisted her head to see who else was on the floor.

A second blast had Bella jerk under Jared's weight. There was an almighty thud as something hit the floor then a scrabble of feet. Thinking Jared had been shot again Bella sucked in a lungful of air and released a high-pitched squeal. 'Stop it. Can't you see he's already hurt?' She wriggled and squirmed until a pair of hands landed on her frenzied arms and a voice whispered in her ear.

'Calm down, Bella, I'm not hurt.'

Before she could say a thing, what seemed like a mass of legs crowded around her head and then arms swept down lifting Jared from her moments before she was lifted holus bolus, chair and all and settled upright on the floor. It took a moment for her head to cease its dizzying spin.

Jared was standing in front of her with an enigmatic smile on his face but one hand was rubbing fiercely at his side. 'Christ but that hurt,' he muttered as another man inspected his side for signs of blood.

'The bullet just grazed the side and ricocheted off,' said the stranger as he straightened. 'Now are you glad we made you put the vest on?'

'I wasn't so keen on being the guinea pig to test out its worthiness at close range,' said Jared. 'I didn't realise it would hurt so much.'

'You'll have quite a bruise for a while.'

'Can somebody tell me what's going on?' piped up Bella over the ruckus.

Jared stepped aside then squatted in front of her giving her a clear view of exactly what was going on. Travers was sitting on the floor with a stream of blood pouring from his upper arm. His arms were behind his back and an armed man wearing black clothes with a large assortment of shapes attached to various belts was standing guard over Travers. Bella recalled seeing television news snippets of the tactical response group in action. The guard's getup looked remarkably similar. Walker was standing to one side also with his arms behind his back. She turned questioning eyes to Jared.

'I was wearing a bullet-proof vest just in case things went pear shaped.'

'I gather it was a humungous pear,' Bella replied with as much sarcasm as she could muster. She couldn't begin to describe how she was feeling. There was a sense of great relief but at the same time she felt rising anger and frustration.

'You could say that, now are you up to answering a few formal questions so these guys can get a few details about what happened to you?'

She nodded then Jared stood and turned around to face the two men while calling to Bella over his shoulder. 'Were you formally arrested, Mrs Perez? By that I mean, did these men tell you that you were under arrest, elucidate the exact crime you had committed and read you your rights? Did they tell you that you had a right to call your lawyer?'

Bella was too stunned to talk so shook her head from side to side even though Jared couldn't see her. Arrest? Crime? Lawyer? A glance up and Bella noticed even more men with guns aimed into the room standing at each window and door. 'I told these two punks that you knew where I was. I didn't expect the entire cavalry to come with you.'

Ignoring her jibe Jared continued on with his questions that were demanding a verbal answer. 'Mrs Perez, did these two officers let you know you were entitled to a lawyer and that you didn't have to answer any questions until you had one present? Did they give you the opportunity to ring me?'

Still beyond speech, Bella shook her head again.

'Have you answered any of their questions?' As he turned to face her Jared gave her the briefest of smiles, his voice, although still business like, had softened.

Bella forced air into her lungs then found her voice, which was a bit squeaky at first but became stronger as she gained confidence. 'They said they had studied the details of my previous interviews and nobody believed a word of what I said. They accused me of having some stolen papers, which they said my husband stole just before he died. He didn't, it's impossible, he was so ill … in so much pain.'

Bella's voice faded away as her eyes stared blankly into space. She shook her head then began speaking again. 'They wanted me to tell the truth, to tell them everything in detail. So I did. I repeated everything exactly as I had told before. I repeated it very slowly just to make sure they understood every single word.' She smiled as she relayed these words as slow as she had retold them. She noticed the small grin tugging at the corners of Jared's mouth. 'They had their guns drawn when they approached me at the lake and I wasn't given any choice about coming here. In fact they threatened me. If I didn't come quietly they had ways of making me come. They said they had a court order to use this drug on me. I asked to see it but even though they waved a piece of paper in front of my eyes I wasn't given the opportunity to read it. It's in his top pocket.' Bella pointed with her chin towards Mike Walker. 'Is it possible for someone to untie me?' Her last question was quiet, her voice sounding frustrated.

Jared stared at Travers then turned to Walker. 'The court order please?'

When Walker didn't move and realising the man was handcuffed, Jared stepped forward, removed the paper from his pocket, opened it out, glanced at it then slipped it into his own pocket, ignoring the look of fear on Walker's face. Since no one moved towards untying Bella, Jared squatted in front of her and undid the catches on the leather binds, rubbing each wrist as it was released to allow her blood to flow. Bella stretched out her hands then reached up to ease off the still tightened rubber around her arm, rubbing to ease the stinging soreness.

Jared grimaced when he noticed the reddened marks from Walker's hand. He glanced up to her face then ran a gentle finger along the imprint. Bella could see the tenderness in his eyes change to anger as he turned towards the other two men.

'Gentlemen, I'm not going to bother asking what you thought you were doing with my client, I'll leave that to your superiors. But believe me, she will be pressing charges for every single illegal act you carried out against her today. The list forming in my brain is quite extensive. Inspector, you can have them now.'

The two men paled as their Regional Inspector stepped inside the door and snapped the switch of what looked like to be some kind of recorder. 'Travers, Walker, you are both under arrest. I've seen and heard more than enough. Mrs Perez, once again you have my humble apologies for the terrible treatment you have received from officers under my command. We will get to the bottom of this but in the meantime I sincerely thank you for keeping a cool head under such duress and for helping weed out corrupt officers. Unfortunately, I suspect these are not the only two.'

As he spoke, Travers was hoisted to his feet then both men were shoved outside, giving Bella a view of their handcuffed wrists. She couldn't help but think how two people couldn't be more deserving to be arrested than those two. She heard rights being read as man after man left the room.

John Wright turned to Jared. 'Jed, it's good to have you back in the legal system. I hate saying this but I don't think Bella is safe yet. We'll probably need to interview her some time soon but in the meantime you take good care of her.'

He swung towards Bella. 'Bella, Jed mentioned Walker was one of the men at the meeting in Hudson's office, are you certain about this?'

'One hundred percent sure. And … I was asked in a round about way if I recognised Walker. To them I denied ever having met him before, which is true – I had never actually met him before today, but I had seen him. He was definitely one of the men in that meeting.'

'That fact concerns me a great deal. Thank you once again.' He turned and strode across the room then outside.

The moment Inspector Wright left, Bella turned to Jared, her lips in a thin line of determination. 'I think you have some explaining to do Mr Jared Mann, or whoever you are. Client? Jed? Care to tell me exactly what is going on?'

Dragging one of the chairs around, Jared sat in front of Bella, a grin spread across his face. He held out his business card. Snatching it from his grasp she scanned the printed words. *Jed Manning. Barrister and Solicitor.* Underneath the prominent words was a whole row of letters for which Bella had no understanding of their meanings, but she figured there was more than one degree in law listed there.

'Well this explains some of it, what about the rest and why didn't you tell me?'

'Okay. My real name is Jared Manning but I use Jed in the legal profession. It was a name I grew up with and has always stuck, although my certificates have Jared since it is my given name. I am a senior partner in a law firm but became jaded with my work about a year ago so took a year off to do something entirely different. I've always been an outdoors type and have climbed mountains, abseiled and enjoyed other such sports all my life so when the job with Air and Sea Rescue came up I pounced on it. I am a trained Paramedic. I learnt first aid years ago as an adjunct to my rather risky sporting activities. One never knows when one is going to need medical skills beyond sticking on a bandaid when you are stuck on the top of a mountain with an injured climbing partner, so I did extensive first aid training and became a paramedic. It was a necessity with this job so I did a refresher course. I love the work but my year is coming to an end and I was going back to my legal practice in a couple of months. You have brought me back a little sooner than I expected.'

'I don't recall ever asking you to take my case on? Do I need a lawyer?'

'I'm sorry, I was a bit presumptuous there but those two louts turning up meant you were in deep trouble and yes, you definitely need a lawyer and to answer your next question, I'm doing this case pro-bono, which means …'

'I know what it means.' She paused in thought. 'Jared, why am I in deep trouble? I've never done anything illegal and Raoul was incapable of moving let alone stealing papers. Is this why they want me dead – because they think Raoul had some stolen papers?'

'I'm certain they want you silenced because they think you can recognise those men who were at the meeting in Hudson's office and by the determined and unrelenting way they have gone after you, we are sure something very big and very illegal was going down that day. We'll try to find out through tough questioning why they believe your husband stole papers. Simon has done a bit of research. Hudson was not only running his legitimate businesses but they are a front for his more seedy dealings. He is quite a nasty piece of work. We have legally taken possession of all his computers and they are being gone through by a couple of experts now. What started off as me hiring Simon to help you has turned into the Police Force, plus other Government departments, footing the bill for a much larger inquiry.' He paused as he glanced around the room. 'Do you want to get out of here? I'd much rather explain things in far more conducive surroundings. This room gives me the creeps.'

'Gives *you* the creeps?' Bella shuddered then glanced back at Jared. 'Yes please. But before we go, I heard you say something about a six-foot hole. Does that mean what I think it means?'

'Sorry you had to hear that but I'm fairly certain the hole was dug as a grave. Without you ringing me these two would probably have gotten away with…' He glanced at her but didn't finish.

Bella shuddered. 'I get the picture. I was already well aware of the outcome if you didn't get here on time.' Not wanting to dwell on her fourth near death experience Bella changed the subject. 'Can you pass me those blasted crutches? Sheesh, but I'm looking forward to the day when I can get around on my own two feet again.' As she stood, she let fly with a clenched fist and punched Jared on his arm.

He yelped then recoiled. 'What was that for?'

'That's for scaring me half to death by getting shot at.' She punched him again. 'And that's for putting yourself in the line of fire. This one...' The third punch was caught mid-air. 'Is for lying to me.'

Since it was obvious, by a loud and highly embarrassing sniff that she was on the verge of tears, Jared drew her into an embrace. 'I didn't lie, Bella.'

She sniffed hard to prevent embarrassing herself – again. The scent of him had her leaning into his chest, then, remembering how he didn't like her touching him, she jerked out of his arms. He looked surprised. 'You didn't tell me you were a lawyer.'

She could have sworn there was a look of hurt in his eyes before he turned away and retrieved her crutches.

'Not telling isn't the same as lying.' He handed the hated aluminium walking aids over. 'And I wasn't practising law all the time I've known you, until a few minutes ago. I was on a sabbatical.'

She jammed them into place. 'It's still keeping things from me.' She stalked outside.

Chapter Seventeen

After formally quitting his position, Jared was required to work out a week's notice with Air and Sea Rescue while they found a replacement. Not daring to leave Bella home alone again he insisted she go to work with him where she carried out a variety of small jobs each day. The evenings were spent poring over reports Simon kept faxing through or delivering in person. So far there was no link between Bella and Hudson Enterprises apart from her being an employee and inadvertently walking in on a meeting at which she was present for all of about ten seconds. Nobody could figure out why they thought Raoul had stolen any papers.

After a leisurely lunch at Simon's home on Sunday, Bella, Simon and Jared were throwing ideas around the table to see if they could come up with a reason Bella was being pursued with such zealousness.

'Bella, your house, how did you come by it?' Startled at the personal question from Simon, Bella sat back in her cane chair, her body at ease but her mind on alert.

'I bought it after Raoul died. I was left a share of his inheritance. It wasn't a huge amount and the members of his family all received an equal sum. Before marrying Raoul I sold my previous home, which I had been paying off and those two amounts together, along with my savings, gave me enough to pay for my present home outright. It left me pretty well skint but I had a well paying job in an accounting firm so I was able to afford it. It was all above board. I have all the paperwork as proof.'

'I'm not insinuating anything untoward, only searching for some clue.' Simon sounded apologetic as he leant forwards and tapped her on the knee.

At the same time Jared placed a hand on Bella's opposite arm giving it a gentle squeeze. 'If we get too personal let us know but somewhere there has to be a link. You said you were working for an accounting firm. How did you come to be working for Hudson?'

'I was headhunted, offered a remuneration package too good to refuse, so took them up on their offer.'

'Now I'm interested. How long ago?' Simon spoke as both men leant even further forward in their chairs, their eyes focussed on Bella, which felt uncomfortable, causing an involuntary shudder to wind across her body.

'Almost three months ago, and this is interesting – *why?*'

'Apart from the fact that you are very good at what you do, why did they headhunt you? What was their interest in you?' asked Jared.

'I never thought about the reasons at the time and have no idea. I liked the pay and the fact that I was my own boss in my own section.' She steadied her gaze on Simon. 'You're scaring me. I had never met any of these people before, never even heard of them and had no association with them, so why me?' She swung her eyes in Jared's direction.' And why so long after Raoul died?'

'We will pursue that line to find out exactly why they are so interested in you. Do you have a problem with us tracing back both your and Raoul's financial trails?' Simon asked.

Bella was beginning to feel like a yo-yo the way her head was waving between the two men. Thank goodness, she thought as Jared finally sat back in his chair, picking up his coffee mug to take a sip as though the response wasn't all that important to him but he looked mighty curious.

Slumping right back into the chair to gain some space, Bella sighed. 'Sure, but I can assure you I have nothing to hide. I met Raoul about six months before we married so I can't vouch for his past but there certainly wasn't an unusual amount of cash left in his will. It was less than two hundred thousand dollars after his home had been sold and the bank loan paid out. Raoul was twenty-eight when he died so I don't consider the amount to be unreasonable given he had worked since he was about fifteen. My share was fifty thousand.'

'Was there any acrimony from the family about you receiving a share?' asked Simon.

Feeling affronted, Bella glared at Simon. 'Definitely not, in fact they wanted me to have more since they are quite wealthy but I insisted Raoul's will go the way he wished. We all got on really well. They are a really lovely family. Both his brother and sister received the same amount as me and his parents the remainder between them.'

All the while they spoke, Simon jotted down notes. He dropped his pen then settled back into his chair, fingers splayed out tip to tip. 'I think we might go down the Perez line to see if there is anything. We have to find a link somewhere. It is interesting they head-hunted you, Bella, and I would like to know why. There may be a clue in the computer files so I'll get Mario to look for anything along those lines.'

'What about your old job, Bella? Did you have any unusual clients?' Bella turned her head to stare at Jared. This was starting to feel like a serious inquisition.

'Come on, fellas, you know I can't discuss clients' names or their finances but on a general level, I was one accountant in a firm of twenty. I simply processed the customers as they came in and were assigned to me. I didn't come across anyone or any set of books that made me sit up and think something wasn't really right. Sure there are always questions I have to ask to verify facts and figures, you get that with most customers, but nothing worrisome – not the way I think you are inferring.'

Bella was thankful when the probe into her personal life ceased while the three wound up their chat and packed up their respective bits and pieces.

***

At the jarring jangle from his phone Jared reached out and lifted the receiver to his ear. He yawned. 'Jed Manning', he muttered as he glanced at the digital number on his bedside clock. Dear, God. This had better be important. It was only two in the morning.

'We found a link. Open your door and let me in.'

Simon let out a hearty laugh at the mouthful of abuse he received before Jared slammed the phone down, but he had the front door open and was leant against the doorjamb wearing only a pair of hastily pulled on jeans when Simon drew to a halt in front of his house. Duke stood by his side, far more alert than his master. Simon was ushered into the lounge room while Jared checked on Bella, closing her bedroom door, plus the two doors leading into the vast living room from the passage.

'This had better be good, waking me at this hour.' He swept a hand through his tousled hair in an attempt to look less dishevelled as he dropped into a padded lounge chair, one denim clad leg draped over the arm. Simon smiled as Jared shivered at the contact of the cool leather rubbing against his warm, bare torso.

'At least you've had some sleep. Mario and I haven't seen our beds yet, but I'm sure you will find this worthwhile. It seems your Bella is not quite the innocent she is making out to be. I think you have been duped.'

These words had Jared fully awake in a split second. Jerking upright, he planted both feet firmly on the ground. 'That's a pretty harsh statement to be making. I sincerely hope you have some concrete evidence to back up your accusation.'

As a response Simon handed over printed sheets then sat back in his chair, studying Jared's face for a reaction as the pages were scanned. They outlined a trust account in the name of Juan and Bella Perez. For the past four years numerous amounts had been deposited and withdrawn. Each deposit was under the ten thousand dollar "reportable to the authorities" mark, meaning the banking institution didn't have to notify the Taxation Department of the transactions.

'Bella's husband's name was Raoul, not Juan and this is a Trust account. Who's to say Bella knew anything about this?'

'Would you mind telling me why my name is being bandied around at this ungodly hour of the morning?'

Both men started at the voice and stared at Bella who was dressed in nothing more than a fine cotton and very short nightie. The outline of every part of her body was very visible. Strong desire welled up in Jared as his eyes roamed from her toes all the way up to her face as he tried to find his voice. He was forced to turn away in a bid to dampen down a strong yearning.

'Simon seems to think you have been lying to me all along,' he managed to squeak out as his eyes swung around again and fixated on hers and not daring to stray lower. He held out the papers but didn't move from his upright position in the seat.

Bella eyed his face then her glance strayed over to Simon as she began the journey across the room. Reaching the outstretched hand, she removed the papers from Jared's grasp, straightened them out then scanned the details.

'Izzy?' The word was nothing more than a harsh whisper of shock. Both men stared at Bella, waiting for more explanation from the startled face but all they saw was a clamping of lips and her face suffuse with anger. Looking furious she turned on Jared.

'This whole mess is like some ghastly never-ending nightmare and I wish I could wake up from it and know it has all been a bad dream. I might as well admit to the world that I actually did hit myself over the head with a dead branch, fling myself off a cliff, inject poison into my own fluids bag, invited Bart Hudson here to kill me because no judge or jury is ever going to believe otherwise when my own lawyer thinks I am as guilty as hell.' She waved the papers around in the air, her hands shaking.

'I mean are they really going to believe Travers came here with his gun drawn, forced me into his car and tied my wrists to a chair. They are police officers. Who is going to believe little old me against members of the Force? Look at these pieces of paper – damning evidence that you,' she pointed an accusing finger to both men in turn, pausing on each, 'both believe is about me. I can see in your faces that you believe the conclusions you have drawn, that a regular amount of money has gone into my account and I have just as regularly withdrawn a similar amount.'

She spun around using only her crutches to pivot on then when she had steadied her swaying body by planting one foot on the ground, tossed the papers on the floor before speeding out of the room, down the passage and out the still open front door, slamming it shut behind her.

As soon as he could get his body to move from its stunned position Jared raced after her, flung the door open and called out to her. 'Bella, wait.'

'Don't you dare come anywhere near me, Jared Manning,' Bella screamed over her shoulder.

He stopped dead, feeling guilty as hell, knowing for sure he deserved her harsh words. For a short while he had doubted her honesty, was stunned at her reaction but was now certain she had never lied to him. 'Duke, go with Bella.' The dog shot out of the door and sped after the rapidly disappearing woman who, at the rate she was going, would do justice to any race in the disabled games.

Figuring Bella needed time alone to cool her ire he returned to Simon to see if he could fathom out what the papers and the word *Izzy* meant. Duke would see to it she came to no harm. Jared joined Simon at the closed French doors. Both men studied the rapidly diminishing, scantily clad woman as she headed towards the lake.

'I think I might have just made a monumental mistake and I need to apologise to Bella,' murmured Simon.

'You and me both.' Retrieving the scattered papers Jared studied them with intense concentration. 'What is going on here? There has to be a lot more to this than what is written down here. Is this the only Trust Account?'

'No, there are one hundred of them. Mario was printing them all when I left. I think it might be wise for me to leave while you try to make peace with Bella. I'm sorry, mate. I'm going to catch a bit of shuteye but I'll be in touch tomorrow.'

After seeing Simon off Jared went in search of warmer clothes then collected a thick jacket for Bella before jogging down the path to find her.

***

Bypassing the lake, Bella slowed as she entered the grove of trees searching for somewhere to rest and think. She found an old gnarled tree and leant up against the trunk, feeling the rough bark against her back through the thin cotton of her nightie. At her feet Duke dropped on the carpet of moss where, during the day, the sun's rays were unable to penetrate through the thick cover of leaves. Bella's anger had cooled to a bitter disappointment in Jared. How could he not believe her? Why did he doubt her word? Feeling the whip against her leg from Duke's tail as it began its steady side-to-side buffeting, told Bella that Jared was approaching. She straightened her back ready to take flight again, watching as he emerged from the darkness then stood motionless in front of her holding out a jacket.

'Put this around you, it's cold out here.' Neither moved until Jared took one very tentative step towards her, his eyes not moving from her face. 'I'm sorry, Bella, truly sorry for doubting you, even for one second.' Another two steps and Jared reached out with both hands and gently pulled Bella towards him then wrapped the warm jacket around her slim shoulders, pulling it closed over her chest then allowing her to rest back against the tree as he dropped his arms to his side.

'Who, or what is, Izzy?'

'Izzy was Juan's wife. You thought my marriage was brief. Their union lasted for only one very tragic week.'

'One week! I'm sure that's what Hudson said about your marriage. So who is Juan Perez?'

'Raoul's cousin. I only met him a few times but mainly before his wedding two months before Raoul was diagnosed. Juan is Brazilian and was here on a study visa at university. His father and Raoul's father are brothers. Raoul's mother is Australian and Raoul was born here. Juan met Izzy at university. She is Colombian and was also on a study visa but living here with her grandmother. They were married in a small ceremony on a Saturday. Izzy's grandmother died very suddenly two days later. It was the strangest thing. I sat next to Senora Duarte at the wedding. She was a vibrant, healthy woman in her early sixties. Two days later she was dead. There was an inquest into her sudden death because she had no health problems but I don't know what the results were. Juan and Izzy had to return from their honeymoon for the funeral and then Juan was killed in a car accident a few days later. Some mechanical failure, I believe. Juan's funeral was so awful. Izzy was devastated and fell apart emotionally. The day after the funeral she flew back to Colombia to live with her parents.'

'So the account Simon showed me was in Juan's name, but why did it have your name on it as well?'

'It didn't.'

'Huh? It says Bella.'

'So you jumped to conclusions.' Her glance was definitely accusatory before she looked away. She knew she sounded very bitter but heck why shouldn't she? 'Izzy is short for Isabel, which is the English version of Isabella. Her friends here called her Izzy, her family called her Bella.'

Straightening up once again Bella grasped the handles of her crutches and began traipsing back towards the house. It was only when she stumbled catching her bare foot on the side of a rough stone that Jared touched her. Following close behind, he grabbed her as she began sinking towards the ground. In one foul swoop he lifted her up into his arms and carried her the rest of the way, ignoring her struggles and protests. After depositing Bella onto her rumpled bed Jared bathed her muddy foot then stood beside her bed.

'Bella, there are quite a few things I have regretted doing in my life but I think the worst was doubting your word. Sorry is nowhere near adequate enough to explain the remorse I feel. If you can find it in your heart to forgive me, I promise you it will never happen again. Now try to get back to sleep, we can work on figuring out what those accounts are in the morning.' Without waiting for a response, Jared left the room.

Chapter Eighteen

It was while carting a critically injured woman from a serious car accident that Jared remembered a small detail both Bart Hudson and Bella had let slip. Until now he hadn't connected the two comments. His second last day in the job had been more harrowing than usual. This was the third call out for the rescue team, an unusually high number for any single day. The first call had been just after dawn when emergency services had scrambled the team from their beds to attend an isolated property where a woman had been thrown from her horse and then trampled by the rearing animal after an early morning exercise gallop.

When the phone rang early to call Jared into work he had not long gone back to sleep after tossing and turning, his rampaging thoughts of Bella preventing his brain from relaxing enough to sleep. Too afraid for her welfare to leave her home alone, he dragged Bella from bed, drove to base then left her to fend for herself in the office while the three men flew off.

Before they had even landed on the hospital roof with the woman they were called out to an upturned dinghy off the coast. Two men were returning from a dawn fishing trip when they had been swamped by a freak king wave. Despite their best efforts after Jared had been lowered on the winch to rescue the two men, one elderly man had died from his injuries. After an extended time treading water in the choppy ocean, holding the dead man afloat while his companion was winched to safety, Jared returned to base soaked through and frozen. He was still trying to thaw out under the hot shower when this latest call came through.

A car had run off the road into a ravine in the hills. The male driver was killed instantly and his wife, the woman now secured in the papoose Jared and Buck were carrying up the side of a ditch, was in a bad way. It was the accident that had jolted Jared's memory, although until they were back at base, there was not a lot he could do about pursuing it.

Once in the chopper all thoughts of Hudson were tossed from his mind as they fought hard to stabilise the badly injured woman. They were very relieved to hand her over to the emergency team of doctors and nurses at the hospital. Exhaustion from lack of sleep and extended hours of activity had set in by the time they were back at base. After completing the mandatory cleaning of the chopper and replacing medical items they had used, readying the aircraft for an immediate take-off, Jared sought out the small bunk bed set up in a tiny room at one end of the base for this type of situation. He was asleep within seconds of his head hitting the pillow.

***

Even after the others had gone home at the end of the day, Bella let Jared sleep. She had scrounged around in cupboards all day, tidying, cleaning, sorting, tossing and had come across an old novel. While she waited her head was immersed in the pages of the macabre thriller. It was not her favourite genre of reading material but it helped pass the time. It wasn't until she had read the last page she decided that unless they were going to spend the entire night at the base, it was time to wake Jared.

The small room was dark and appeared empty until Bella's eyes adjusted to the gloom and she was able to discern the dark shape sprawled on the narrow bunk. Jared's dark head was lying to one side while one hand hung down to the floor. Bella clipped over, bent, and then reached out with one hand to shake Jared's shoulder.

'Jared, wake up.'

He stirred then rolled over.

'Jared.' Her voice was louder, her shove harder.

Jared flung one arm over his head, smacking it against the wall and it was this thump that caused him to open his eyes.

'Jared.' He sat up and wobbled till he found his balance.

'Where … Bella?'

'It's time to go home. You've been asleep for ages. Come on, I'm starving.' As she brushed her fingers against Jared's face she felt the immediate pulling back of his body. She sucked in her breath at his automatic reaction. He'd done it again – winced then rapidly withdrawn at her touch. Feeling utterly disheartened by his action, Bella straightened, turned and left the room, unable to figure out why he hated her touching him so much. She determined she would never make the same mistake again but was unable to rid her heart of the hurt she felt at his physical rejection, for deep down she knew she was falling for him. She'd had similar feelings for Raoul and even though she missed her husband, she knew to pine for him was fruitless. When she'd married him she'd already accepted that their marriage would be no more than a few months.

Footsteps told Bella that Jared was following.

'Bella, why didn't you wake me earlier?'

'You've had a tough day and needed the rest but I would really like something to eat. We didn't get breakfast this morning.' She kept walking, headed towards the door.

'Are you telling me you've eaten nothing all day?' His footfalls told her he was following.

'Well, we didn't exactly have any time to prepare any food this morning and its not as if I can drive to the local shops during the day like every one else does to spend their lunch hour. Besides I haven't seen you overindulge in food during the day. Can we go?'

Reaching her he grasped her shoulder, pulling her to an ungainly halt. 'We have a stash of high-energy food on the chopper. Why didn't you ask someone to get you something?'

Bella felt the heat of a blush rise up her cheeks and pulled away, hoping Jared hadn't noticed but as she headed for his car he caught up to her again.

'You haven't got your bag, which means you didn't have any cash with you today. Damn it, Bella, why didn't you say something?'

Bella didn't miss hearing him curse under his breath as she slid into the passenger seat and she couldn't help but grin when he detoured to his favourite Thai Take-away on their way home, ensuring there was more than enough food to fill both empty stomachs. 'You've got so much food here we're going to be eating cold leftovers for an entire week.'

'I'm guessing you are starved. I'm really sorry, Bella.' He reached over and grasped her clenched fist.

All Bella could think was why did he have no hesitation in touching her like this yet if it were her touching him, he withdrew so dramatically?

'If I'm ever this inconsiderate again, please don't be afraid to say something.' Bella ignored his comment and stared out the side window for the rest of the journey home. She wasn't in the mood for inane chitchat.

The flashing red light on his answering machine had them listening to the messages while setting out plates and food on the kitchen table. All three messages were from Simon urging Jared to call him back as soon as possible. Hunger pangs meant they ate first. Bella insisted on cleaning up after the meal so Jared took the opportunity to return Simon's call. He was back in the kitchen within seconds.

'Bella, how would you like to spend the day with Simon tomorrow, going through all those accounts and trying to make head or tail of them? Simon has found a few other interesting bits and pieces that he would like to discuss with you. It saves you from having to spend the day at the base and I've insisted he feed you non-stop if you agree.'

The tender smile on Jared's face caused Bella to blush. Feeling self-conscious, she turned away and busied herself at the sink, calling out her agreement over her shoulder. 'It beats hanging around the base all day and I refuse to stay here alone.'

The change the following day was pleasant in the sense that Bella had plenty to do, familiar accounting things, challenging her brain to sort out the list of trust accounts. Being of an organised nature she spread out all one hundred accounts in alphabetical order on a row of tables. After totalling amounts of deposits and debits for each account, she then turned to dates of each transaction. It was then she discovered a regular pattern.

'Simon, I think there may be something here.' With her finger resting on the first date on one of the accounts she waited until Simon unwound his body from its crouched position over a computer keyboard to join her.

'It looks as though on any one day ten or so different accounts were chosen to deposit large sums of money evenly between them so that no one account showed more than the ten thousand limit. See this date, the fifth of June. Fourteen accounts each received eight thousand, four hundred and twenty two dollars. A different range of accounts, sixteen I think it was, was used ten days later. This has been occurring on a regular basis for over six years. Each time the money has been allowed to sit there for two weeks and then most, but not all of each deposit has then been withdrawn. I think you need to start looking for business transactions having the totals for each of these daily deposits. Then start tracing details of the signatories for these accounts. I'm betting only a few people, probably ten, own ten accounts each.'

Simon plonked into the nearest chair to study the figures Bella had already calculated, a look of amazement spreading across his features. There was silence as he read more. 'You're right.' He glanced up and grinned. 'Bella, you are a genius.'

'This particular account really interests me.' Withdrawing the three sheets pertaining to one separate account, Bella placed them in front of Simon then pointed to the name on top. 'This is Parkin Industries as trustee for Senora Duarte, who was Izzy's grandmother. She is dead, so is Juan. What is particularly interesting is that these two accounts were opened only a few days before each person died. You are a private investigator, Simon, what does that tell you?' She turned to stare into Simon's startled eyes, which were only centimetres from hers.

'It tells me that their deaths are suspicious, that there is a reason why the accounts were opened in their names. I'd better look through the records to match other deceased persons whose names are probably on these accounts. Then I have to trace down the trustee companies for each which will in turn lead me to the actual signatories on every single one of these accounts since dead people can't sign papers. Along with that I need to investigate the totals of the daily transactions so I can match them up with dealings in Hudson's records having the same total. Hell, this is going to take forever but at least we now have something to look for.'

Straightening out the paperwork they'd pulled out, Bella kept talking over her shoulder. 'I can give you another hint. Bart Hudson used twenty different banking institutions, five accounts in each. They never used the same institution on any single day. The accounts are spread out so they didn't have to. There is something else I have just remembered. Senora Duarte sold her house a few weeks before she passed away. There was a bit of an uproar in the family because no one knew about the sale and it was still listed in her will as an asset. I recall Raoul telling me Juan was trying to investigate the sale. He had been on the phone one evening after Senora Duarte's funeral for quite a long time discussing it with Juan.'

'I think you deserve my special lunch for your brilliant detective skills. I'll call Mario so we can fill him in then give me thirty minutes and you will have the best pasta dish you have ever tasted.'

Spinning his seat backwards, Simon stood then deposited a kiss of appreciation fair-square on Bella's lips before reaching over his own desk to phone Mario. Surprised at his actions Bella felt rather pleased as she sat back in her chair enjoying the tingling of her lips. A man hadn't kissed her since Raoul's death and it felt… she thought hard. It was better than good. Then another thought struck her. How would it feel to be kissed by Jared? Her stomach muscles tightened then she relaxed and dismissed the idea since Jared couldn't bare her touching him so being kissed by Jared was never going to happen, much as she'd really like it to.

With Simon ensconced in his kitchen, Bella enjoyed the luscious aromas from his cooking while she sat with her calculator in one hand, a pen in the other, toting up the daily deposits from all the accounts then writing small neat numbers on a separate piece of paper.

A knock on the door as Simon was ushering Bella into the dining room, heralded Mario's arrival. The food was indeed delicious. Bella found it difficult to put her fork down between mouthfuls but somehow she managed to describe her findings to Mario while she scoffed down every last skerrick of pasta then scraped the dish with the edge of her fork and licked it clean. Over the equally good coffee, Bella showed the two men the page containing all the amounts she had so far totalled.

Mario sat back in his chair, coffee in hand. 'I'm going to start with Senora Duarte and the sale of her house. Simon, could I suggest you investigate these two deaths. See if there were any autopsy reports, police investigations etcetera, with the authorities.'

He turned to Bella. 'You did say you thought there was an investigation in to the grandmother's death, didn't you, Bella?'

'Yes, I'm certain.'

'While Simon looks into that are you able to complete these account audits?'

'Not a problem.'

'We also need to subpoena the banks for the signatories to these accounts. That can be Jared's job. I'm also going to search the names on these accounts to see if they match up with death certificates,' Simon said as he collected the coffee mugs for refills while Bella returned to her calculator after being shooed from the room by Simon when she attempted to clear the table.

Bella had only just begun working when Mario approached her. He looked hesitant. 'What's wrong?' asked Bella.

'You know you gave us permission to search your records.'

'Yes.' Bella felt a frisson of fear skitter across her shoulders.

'I was just wondering why you used different names on various documents.'

Now she was mystified. 'What do you mean?'

'Well, your driver's licence and passport have Annabella Brown while your most recent bank account is Perez.'

Bella couldn't help the sigh of relief that escaped in a whoosh. 'My licence and passport were issued before I married. I never changed them to Perez especially since I knew Raoul didn't have long to live. It didn't seem worth the hassle. When my licence came due two years ago, I continued to go by my maiden name since Raoul had died. Why, what does it matter? A lot of women keep their maiden name.'

'Well I was thinking it could be the reason it took so long for Hudson to come after you. From the name on the account we found, I'm assuming that he only knew of Juan's wife being Bella Perez. I'm only guessing here but maybe he had been searching all that time for that name. Even his police cronies wouldn't have been able to match Annabella Brown to Bella Perez. With the other Bella leaving the country so soon, they wouldn't have had a clue how to find her – especially if her passport was Colombian and printed in Spanish.'

'But my bank account has been in that name since I married. What made him come after me after four years?'

'It could have been this,' said Mario as he withdrew a folded piece of paper from a file. He opened it out then turned it so Bella could see. She knew instantly what it was. A reporter at a charity function to raise funds for the Cancer Foundation had caught her unawares: a charity she had been involved in since Raoul's diagnosis.

'Where did you get that?' she asked.

'I did a name search for Bella Perez on the Internet and this newspaper article showed up. It was published about four weeks before...'

'Before Hudson came to me with the job offer,' she squeaked. Since all the air had left her lungs with a vice-like cramp squeezing them empty, it took a moment before she was able to say anymore. 'So that's how he knew where to find me?'

'I'm guessing so for it makes sense. I'll let you get back to your calculations.'

'Gee, thanks! You really think I'll be able to concentrate now?'

Mario laughed as he strode away.

When Jared arrived to collect Bella, Mario had returned home to renew his search on the Hudson Enterprise records. Simon had several people searching through various records and Bella, despite her mind continually returning to Mario's words, had completed jotting down everything she could find relating to the Trust accounts and was sitting back in a very comfortable leather recliner rocker, her eyes closed, trying to ease the steady thrumming of a headache caused by the intense concentration on numbers all afternoon. Jared's comment, when he saw Bella relaxing, about her having had an easy day doing nothing earned him a withering look from Bella as well as very loud protest from Simon.

'The precious lady is a genius,' Simon commented as he reached out with one hand to assist Bella from her chair, handing her both crutches, one at a time, then walking with her to the door with one arm slung around her waist.

***

An incredible stab of jealousy surged through Jared as he observed the solicitous way Simon touched Bella. He wasn't too wrapped on the way he used the word *precious* either. Feeling taken aback by the strength of his feelings, it took a few moments for him to gather his wits before stepping forward to stand in front of Bella. 'You'd better spell out the details of your brilliance while we're driving home.'

As he reached out to take over from Simon he felt really disappointed when Bella deftly evaded his touch. At the door, she turned to thank Simon for the day, the delicious lunch and his company then edged around Jared, heading straight for his car.

Perplexed by her evasive behaviour, Jared stared after her.

'Jared, before you go, we need you to organise subpoenas for twenty banking institutions. You will understand more after Bella has told you what she discovered today but I'll ring you later this evening with more details,' called Simon.

Jared turned back to Simon. 'That's fine. I'll have to return to my office tomorrow some time but I need you to keep an eye on Bella for a couple of hours in the morning first. I want to visit Hudson in jail to ask him a few questions. I'm not keen on leaving Bella alone until we find out the names of those other men in the meeting. I can't help but have a gut feeling someone still wants her dead.'

'I'd love to have her here.' At Simon's overzealous tone, Jared's thoughts were pensive as he followed after Bella, a slight frown creasing his brow as he wondered exactly what sort of a relationship was forming between the two.

Chapter Nineteen

Even though Jared had been back to his office on a number of occasions over the past ten months, it felt strange, eerily strange, to be walking towards his old familiar haunt dressed in suit and tie, his much loved battered leather briefcase in his hand. He paused outside *Joeys* where he had purchased a take-away latte. The small café restaurant had always been his favourite nearby eatery and was also popular with his workplace peers.

He stared at the building on the opposite side of the road. The cream painted concrete building was not tall in comparison to those offices around it, only four storeys, and was not remarkable to look at but coming back, Jared saw features he'd never noticed before. He'd never perceived the four, rectangular decorative insets in each panel up near the roofline to be significant, but now, after studying the darker painted area, he could see how they reflected the shapes of the windows, which in turn were the same shape as the wall panels. Maybe because everything was of similar ratio it looked harmonious and therefore didn't grate on the senses, as did some other nearby buildings. Seen with a fresh aspect, his office complex was quite attractive.

Stepping from the kerb, he waited for two cars to pass then sprinted across the road towards the main door of the building he had been studying with such intensity. Was he glad to be back? He stepped into the foyer, paused and gave the inside the same scrutiny he'd given the outside. It felt comfortable, like his favourite old knock-a-round sweater. Also a bit like the feel of the leather on his briefcase when he'd run his fingers over it before he'd left his bedroom earlier. The briefcase had been a gift from his mother when he'd graduated with his first law degree. The gold pen tucked inside had been his father's gift on the same day. Both items meant a great deal to him.

Everything seemed the same, making it hard to believe he'd been away for so long. Josie was still on the front desk. Jared strode towards her, his long legs making short work of the distance, a bright smile of recognition lighting up her face. Jared gave her a cheeky salute with one finger while the others remained wrapped around the filled cardboard cup. Striding past her he mounted the stairs to the side of the foyer, two at a time. He didn't often use the elevator, only if he was with a client, preferring the exercise of running up and down the stairway. It was a lonely walk; it always had been since very few of his colleagues had the same propensity for favouring the use of physical energy in accessing the higher floors. Most preferred the lift, especially when carrying thick wads of legal papers.

He paused at the closed door on the top floor before stepping out onto the carpeted corridor. As a senior partner in the firm, his office was one of the larger ones at the far end of the passage. A deep breath, a shove at the stairwell door, Jared stepped over the thresh-hold, paused then zigzagged towards his office, stopping for a brief moment at every open door, peeking in and acknowledging each occupant as he went but not pausing long enough to talk.

Was he glad to be back? Most definitely! He loved his legal work but he had loved his time with Air and Sea Rescue just as much. The time away had given him a renewed energy, a vitality and zeal that had been sadly lacking when he had made the decision to take time out. Deep down he knew it hadn't been the legal work that had driven him away. It had been the emotional aftermath of Lynne's betrayal. The six months it had taken to wind up and clear away cases had been a period of emotional darkness. He snorted at the irony; a woman had sent him away and now a woman had brought him back.

His desk had never looked so barren. He stood in front of it before easing into his well-worn but comfy chair. It was another item he doubted he would ever replace unless it fell apart. He ran his fingers over the glorious patina of the huge antique oak desk, pulled out each drawer to check the contents then slapped his briefcase on top and unlocked the catches. All the paperwork pertaining to Bella Perez was soon gracing the wooden desktop in neat piles.

Jed Manning, Barrister and Solicitor had an appointment at the police station lock-up a few blocks down the road but he leant back in his chair, linked his fingers together behind his head and swung around, taking in every single detail of his office. A sudden feeling of peace gushed through his body. He was home and it felt so damn good.

A quick glance at his clock told Jared he needed to hurry. Picking up the file he had organised the night before, he slipped it into his case then snapped the catches closed. Picking up his untouched coffee, he strode out of the office.

Bart Hudson was still being held in the holding cells at the central police station while police collected evidence and lawyers prepared arguments. It had taken quite a few phone calls for Jared to arrange this interview at such short notice. He was well aware Hudson's lawyer was unhappy about having to turn up so early this morning.

Jared had met Peter Marshall before but didn't particularly like the man and liked him even less when he kept Jared waiting for half an hour.

'Jed Manning?' Marshall rushed in whilst still buttoning his jacket with one hand. Then the hand shot out in formal greeting. 'Sorry I'm late but at such short notice it was a bit difficult to re-arrange my appointments.'

Jared shook the proffered hand while scrutinising the cheap suit, less than pristine white shirt and a seriously outdated tie that looked like it had never been dry-cleaned. It was a dangerous mistake to pass judgement on first appearances but Jared had an uneasy feeling something was not quite right. Hudson should be able to afford the very best legal representation and Peter Marshall was not giving the impression of being in that category. As alarm bells began ringing Jared set it into his mind to make a few enquiries about Marshall's background.

'Peter, I appreciate you coming. I know it was short notice and there really wasn't any need for you to be here as I only have a few questions to ask your client but Hudson deserves to have you here. Shall we go in? I believe your client is waiting.'

The drab grey interview room had a single table in the centre. One hard wooden chair was occupied by Bart Hudson dressed in standard prison garb. Jared smiled when he thought how well the colour suited the man. There were two other chairs set up for them, one next to Hudson and the other opposite. Peter Marshall pulled out the chair next to his client, leaning over to whisper in Hudson's ear as he settled down. Jared lifted then slowly placed the chair opposite then took his time in lowering his tall frame, determined to unsettle the two men opposite by taking his time.

'Hudson, I appreciate the opportunity to clarify a few points.' With deliberate actions, Jared wasted time in withdrawing a blank pad and pen from his briefcase, prolonging the agony by taking meticulous care to lock the two catches, one at a time, then placed the case on the floor by his feet, all the time keeping his eyes firmly planted on Hudson. He prolonged the sip he took from the cooling cup then settled it with careful deliberation.

'I recall you telling me Bella Perez's husband, Juan, died in a car crash. Is that correct?'

'That's what I said.' Bart sounded smug and relieved at the line of questioning.

'Are you able to tell me how long ago it happened?' Jared made out he was writing notes, keeping his eyes focussed on the paper.

'About four years ago, maybe six months longer, why is this important?'

Lifting his eyes, Jared paused a moment. 'Well it's probably not important but I need to clarify things in my mind. Do you have any idea as to how long Juan and Bella were married?' He made a point of using the name Juan because if his hunch was correct, it could be very significant and the man wasn't to know to which Bella he was referring.

'Not long. I think Bella mentioned they were only married for about a week or two.'

'And she told you this after she started working for you?' Jared's eyes lifted, glancing at both Hudson and his lawyer. Both men had mystified looks on their faces indicating neither was sure where the line of questioning was leading.

'I think it was during her interview when I asked about her marital status. I don't really recall. It could have been later.'

Jared perceived sudden anxiety in Hudson's voice. He stared into Hudson's eyes noting how they were flicking in nervous twitches and unable to look back at him. Well practised in reading body language, Jared felt certain Hudson was lying.

'Surely you would know when since she'd only worked for you for a matter of months?'

'I'm a busy man. Those details are not important enough to remember.'

Cunning answer. 'How did you come to employ Bella Perez? She says you headhunted her from her previous firm, why her? Why Bella?'

There was a definite shifting of the eyes. Hudson's arms crossed over his chest. Jared eyed the twitching of Hudson's fingers on his left hand, the other still very heavily bandaged after a stint in hospital to repair the damage. He'd heard that it had been too late to re-attach the finger.

'My head accountant heard about her. We wanted someone who was good at their work so he made enquiries to a number of firms. We offered her a package substantially better than what she was already receiving.'

'Were you happy with your choice? Did Bella live up to your expectations?'

'Yes, she was very good at her work. Why?'

Surprised at such a positive response, Jared jumped in with his next question. 'So what happened?'

'What do you mean?'

'What happened that you suddenly tried to get rid of her by dropping her over the edge of a cliff?' Jared knew he was going for the jugular and was out of line. He also knew he was throwing in a question meant to skew both Hudson and Marshall's demeanour. He expected a quick response from Peter Marshall.

'My client is not answering that question or any more questions along the same vein or you will find this interview is over.' Peter Marshall made as though he was about to stand, slamming his own briefcase shut, the noise like a bullet echoing around the room and slashing the intense silence.

'Okay. I'm intrigued as to how you know so much about the death of Juan Perez since according to my client, Bella never told you about her husband's demise. I'm also interested as to the reason why you don't want Juan's wife to talk. Good day gentlemen, this interview has been very enlightening.'

Shoving his chair backwards with his legs, Jared stood, grabbing his belongings as he rose. He ignored the cold coffee, leaving it on the desk as he turned and departed feeling delighted at the look of complete shock on Hudson's face and the outraged face of his lawyer. It convinced him Hudson only knew there was a wife called Bella and that he'd had no idea where she was or what she looked like. Hudson had also tried to prevent her from talking. All Jared had to do now was figure out why. More important was the fact that his Bella had never lied to him and held no secrets. She was simply a naïve pawn caught in a very dangerous game.

There was an extra spring to Jared's step as he made his way back towards his office but instead of walking down the footpath to give him access to the building, he crossed over the road and headed towards his car. He had another appointment in the same police complex later in the morning but first he needed to collect Bella.

Regional Inspector John Wright had rung him earlier with a request to bring Bella in for an interview regarding Walker and Travers. With the phone call arriving after he had dropped Bella off at Simon's place, she was as yet, unaware of the request. There was no choice about Bella being interviewed but he was fairly certain she wouldn't be too keen on the idea. Jared felt delighted he was picking Bella up sooner than he had originally stated. He hadn't liked the warm embrace and greeting Simon had bestowed upon her when he had dropped Bella off. Simon was a single man and was well known for his short-term female conquests. Jared was not too keen on Bella being the next one. In fact, the thought downright terrified him.

Unanswered questions and methods of finding the answers buzzed around his inquisitive, logical brain while he drove. It was becoming blatantly obvious Izzy was one of the major keys to solving the mysteries and somehow he was going to have to track her down. His thoughts consumed him so much it seemed like just a mere couple of short minutes before he was pulling up outside Simon Adler's home.

Hearing voices and laughter coming from the back yard, Jared refrained from knocking on the front door. Instead he crept down the side pathway, the warm lilt of

Bella's laughter sending waves of pleasure pulsating through his body. He was afraid of turning the corner: afraid in case Bella and Simon would be standing or sitting close to each other, even touching. His body gave an involuntary shiver at the thought of the two touching. He shook his head to rid himself of the visions. He had no rights to Bella and no right to feel jealous. What was he thinking? He also had no right to be sneaking up on them. With this thought in mind, Jared called out to make his presence known then strode more boldly.

'Simon, are you around here? I heard voices.' Despite his resolve of a second ago, he couldn't help listening to see if there was a hurried whispering or movement as he turned the corner.

'We're both here.'

Bella's voice from just beside him startled Jared. He looked up to see Bella lounging back in a cushioned deck chair studying a small pile of stapled sheets of paper, her face less than a metre from his. One knee was bent while her broken leg was stretched out. The colour of her plaster gave him another small jolt. Someone had painted it bright red in order to hide the darkened splotches of dried blood. Simon was on the other side of the patio sitting in a chair pulled up against the wooden outdoor table with a stack of files and papers in front of him. Jared tried to hide the guilt and relief he felt by taking his time to walk the last few metres and mount the wood steps.

'Looks like you two have been very busy. Has our super sleuth found any more amazing discoveries?' Jared gave Bella an impudent smile as he settled into the chair next to Simon.

'We've hardly had time, you're back early,' Simon murmured. 'Coffee? I was about to brew a fresh pot.'

'Please, but before you go I have interesting news.' Jared turned to look at Bella. 'I've just been to visit Hudson. It appears he had no idea there were two different Bella Perez's. He was, and still is, under the impression you were Juan's wife.'

The silence was deafening while Jared's words were absorbed and processed.

'So it's true, all of this torture and agony I have been through is because he thought I was Izzy?' Bella's voice was very quiet. She dropped the papers she had been holding, sat up and swung both legs onto the floor.

'You already suspected this?' Jared felt stunned.

'Yes. Oh, I forgot to tell you that Mario hinted that maybe Hudson had been looking for Izzy.' She sat back down again. 'Does this mean I'm now safe?'

'You might have told me. As to being safe?' Jared thought about her last question before answering. He started to open his mouth but Simon interrupted him.

'It probably means you are less safe. You are the key and only witness who saw Hudson when he shoved you over the cliff, saw him when he came to Jared's house and saw him inject the poison. You recognised Mike Walker and also can testify against Bill Travers. You also saw all the men at the meeting in Hudson's office. I believe you are in as much danger now as ever. But now, so is Izzy. If they discover there are two of you, they'll be searching for her unless we can find her first and also the information they are looking for. We need to find those papers I presume Juan stole.' Simon slung his last words over his shoulder as he entered the house through the back door to make the promised coffee.

Bella dropped her crutches on the ground with a clatter, a look of desolation sweeping across her face.

Feeling perturbed at Bella's' reaction, Jared fought to find words to ease her concern. 'I didn't let on about there being two Bellas so Hudson won't be searching for Izzy, but Simon's right.' Jared stood then squatted at her feet. He reached out and placed one hand on Bella's clenched fist. 'We are going to have to be extra vigilant at all times but right now, the reason I'm back early is because John Wright wants you to come into the station before lunch to give a statement about Travers and Walker.'

At her look of alarm, Jared was convinced Bella was more afraid than she let on. 'I'll be there with you and won't let them harass you. John has promised he will be the one asking the questions but he wants another man, Superintendent Jack Watson to be present. This is an internal police matter as well and at the moment you are the only witness to a covert meeting between Hudson and a member of the Force. We don't even know what the meeting was about, or even if it was illegal. The only hint of it having been untoward is the way Travers tried to use illegal means to gain information from you.'

'Why am I suddenly so very afraid?' Bella's voice was nothing more than a hesitant whisper. 'He was going to kill me.'

'I'm not going to pretend you have nothing to be afraid of. If I were in your shoes I would probably feel the same. Simon and I will do our utmost to keep you safe. John Wright is doing the same. Even though one of us is with you at all times, John has men watching from the outside twenty-four hours a day. There is an armed minder parked outside here when you are here, also outside my place – sort of like an early warning system.'

'So I can't go home?'

Jared hesitated, unsure what to say. 'You can but we'd prefer you didn't. One of us would have to stay with you and I never carry a firearm, although I am licensed.' He thought it better not to inform her he was probably the worst shot ever to have handled a gun. The only times he carried a firearm was on his more adventurous expeditions in case he came across a savage wild animal. 'If there is anything you need we can stop by your place to pick it up but you won't be safe living there alone. Which reminds me, I checked out your place. They've certainly been there and didn't care how they went about their search. The place looks like a tip. I'll organise someone to clean it up.'

At the appearance of the first tear escaping from Bella's eye, Jared leant forward to embrace her, holding her tight until her distress eased. For once she didn't pull away, which pleased him immensely.

Chapter Twenty

Bella felt apprehensive as she made her awkward way into the front entrance of the Central Police Station, even with Jared keeping pace by her side. After showing his card to the desk officer Jared stood with his hip leant up against the counter, his eyes on her making her feel even more nervous so she glanced around the room.

Scanning the room she settled on two scruffy teenagers accompanied by harried looking adults. She figured, from the occasional snigger between them, that the lads had enjoyed their prank and the only thing they were sorry for was actually getting caught in the act. Their minders looked resigned and angry.

Not far away, an irate customer who wasn't appreciative of receiving a parking ticket was browbeating a desk clerk. The way he was acting, he had obviously deserved the parking ticket and like the two teenagers his only problem was he had been caught.

Her mind went back to her old job at the accounting firm. For some reason it was mostly the male half of the population who tried their best to not have to pay their taxes. Her female customers were more concerned about making some mistake in their calculations and bringing down the wrath of the Tax Department. Her job. She didn't even have a job any more and she wondered if all this hassle would be a blight on her career. She'd done nothing wrong and yet was embroiled in such an unholy mess. Would it count as a black mark on her resume? She began to think of the normal questions prospective employees would ask. Why did you leave your last job? Because my employer wanted to get rid of me so much, he dropped me over a cliff. Yes, it will go down really well. Bella giggled at the thought of the horrified face her interviewer would have.

'You find something amusing?' Jared's voice penetrated her thoughts, startling her.

'Sorry?'

'You were laughing, care to share the joke?'

'Oh, sorry, I was thinking about how I was going to explain in a job interview, why I left my last job, wondering how I would explain why my boss threw me over the edge of a cliff.' Her sheepish grin elicited a loud shout of laughter from Jared.

'Or how you are going to explain cutting off his finger and shredded his hand into mincemeat. I'd love to be there to hear your explanations. Hudson's hand is still very heavily bandaged by the way.'

'Knowing what I know now he got nothing less than he deserved.'

'Going to jail for a very long time is what he deserves and your testimony is what will send him there. Are you ready? Here comes John.' Jared stood straight and shook hands with his old friend before the two were shown into the small elevator.

Before they entered the private interview room on the third floor, John paused outside the door. 'Bella, including me, there will be four police officers present. I will field all the questions. Our Superintendent has asked to sit in and there will be two high-ranking plainclothes officers from internal affairs, one of whom will be taking notes. Remember, you are not a prisoner who is under arrest and you are in no way obligated to answer anything you don't want to. This is simply an internal interview to get your version of what went down with Walker and Travers. Neither man is talking so we need your help. You have nothing to be afraid of. Ready?'

Bella nodded but felt unable to calm her racing heart. John Wright opened the door then stood back to allow Bella entry. She kept her eyes down to the floor to seek out any uneven surfaces as she made the first few steps inside, Jared right behind her. She paused and looked up, then came to a grinding halt causing Jared to walk into her, almost knocking her over. Both his hands reached out to steady her. As quick as she could Bella turned to face Jared. Feeling the blood flow from her face she knew she had to hide from prying eyes.

'I'm sorry, Bella. Hey, are you okay? Did I hurt your leg?'

Too shocked to speak she shook her head from side to side. Her nerves felt as though they had shattered and were sending shock waves to the very extremities of her body. She needed to bring her face back to a neutral look or find an excuse to leave. 'I was wondering if it was all right for me to visit the ladies' room before we started.' The request came out strangled. Bella was finding it hard to breathe. She stared up at Jared, pleading with her eyes.

He gazed back as though trying to fathom what she was trying to tell him. 'Of course.' He glanced over her head to the silent men who were all staring at them. 'Gentlemen, I'm sure you won't mind? John, can you tell me where Bella can find the rest room?'

'Certainly, go straight to the end of the corridor, last door on the right. I'll organise refreshments while you're gone.' As John lifted the receiver for the inter-office phone system, Jared moved behind Bella and ushered her towards the door where he followed her out.

Panic stricken, Bella sped down the passage, paused and then turned to check Jared was following. He was still standing outside the door, holding it open. Bella released one hand from her crutch and beckoned him to come with her then raced off again.

She was relieved to hear Jared stride after her. Catching up, he whispered harshly in her ear. 'What the devil has gotten into you? What is wrong?'

Without ceasing the pace of her rapid escape, Bella whispered so she wouldn't be overheard. 'You have to get me out of here. The man in there with the crew cut, greying hair – he was at the meeting with Bart.'

She felt Jared place one hand in a firm grip on her shoulder, pulling her to a standstill. 'Are you sure? They are all high ranking officers.'

'I don't give a hoot if they are all the King of England. He was at that meeting. Now let me go in case they look out the door. Just think of a way of getting me out of here. I'll wait in here for five minutes then come and see what is taking me so long. I can feign illness but I'm telling you straight - I am not going back in there. Period.' Dragging her shoulder from Jared's grip she shoved the door to the ladies' room open with her elbow before galloping inside, allowing the door to slam shut with a resounding echo.

***

Wondering what he could do Jared spun around to retrace his steps. As he looked up he noticed the person in question was standing in the open doorway watching them. Damnation! Did the man suspect Bella had recognised him? Who was he? Jared needed to find out. Thinking on his feet he kept his eyes up, forcing a smile to his face as he neared the interview room.

'Sorry but Bella hasn't been feeling very well these past few days. She's had a stomach upset and I needed to see if she was all right. She says she feels a bit nauseous again and to give her a few minutes.'

To ensure the man entered the room, Jared stood in the middle of the corridor and ushered the man inside as though being a gentleman then followed on his heels before pulling the door closed behind him. Once inside the room he positioned himself closest to the door.

'Bella needs a few minutes, her nausea has returned. John, care to introduce us while we are waiting?'

'Certainly, Jed Manning is Bella's solicitor. Jed, this is Superintendent Jack Watson, Senior Sergeants Ian Shaw and Keith Guthrie, both from Internal Affairs. They will be carrying out the investigation into Travers and Walker. Now I need to see what has happened to our refreshments.'

John Wright headed for the door with Jared hot on his heels.

'I'll give you a hand and I can check on Bella at the same time.' His voice was deliberately loud, inferring he had a genuine reason for following the Inspector. Halfway down the corridor Jared dragged John Wright into an open doorway then swept his eyes around the room to ensure it was unoccupied.

'John, we have a major problem.' This time his voice was no more than a harsh whisper.

'What do you mean?'

'Shh, keep your voice down. Bella recognised one of your men in there as being at the meeting with Hudson. She is refusing to go back into the room or to answer any questions and I need an excuse to get her out of here, fast.'

It took a few seconds for Jared's words to register. John turned and stared at him in. 'Are you sure? Which one?'

'I hate to tell you this but she recognised the Super.'

'Bloody hell! Is she certain?'

'Absolutely. With Bella disappearing and refusing to talk, he will probably guess he has been recognised. With her staying and going through with this meeting then saying she recognised Walker then he is still going to suspect she has recognised him as well. Thinking on my feet right now, I'm suggesting you go back into the room, stall for time to let me get Bella out of here. Tell them she has started vomiting again and I've taken her to a doctor. Lay it on thick about her frail health after all she has been through. How you handle Jack Watson is your problem but I'm guessing that all of a sudden, Bella's life is a lot more fragile than we thought. I'm going to put her in hiding somewhere other than my place. Your men at my place may be giving information to the Super. Just give me time to get her out of here and don't let him make any phone calls.' Racing out of the room he headed towards the ladies' rest room and knocked on the door.

Jared didn't need to hurry Bella out of the Police Station, she belted out of the place so fast he was the one finding it difficult to keep up. He needed to find somewhere safe to hide her, instinct telling him the Superintendent's cohorts would stake out both his home and his office in the search for her. The moment they drove away he was on the phone to Simon explaining what had happened and asking for help.

'Bring her here for the rest of the day while you return to work as you would normally do. I'll bring in another armed man and tonight we will spirit the lovely Bella away.' Jared stared at the phone for a moment as a too familiar stab of jealousy hit him again when he heard Simon's description of Bella. It was time to find out how Bella felt about Simon.

'What do you think of Simon, Bella?'

Looking stunned at the question, Bella glanced at Jared. 'I've found him to be friendly and helpful. Why? Is there something I should be worried about?'

'No, I trust him implicitly, I was just wondering how you found him as a person?' He tried to keep the nonchalance in his voice to not show how curious he actually was. Sure he trusted Simon – professionally but he was having serious doubts when it came to Bella.

'I quite like him. He's funny, easy to talk to and he sure can cook. I think I mentioned I like a man who can cook.'

He winced. Her words in no way alleviated his fears; in fact they did exactly the opposite.

Chapter Twenty One

Catching glimpses of revolvers in the shoulder holsters Simon and Dan Mason were wearing under their jackets did nothing to ease the tension Bella felt building up. All three were ploughing through reams of paper Mario had supplied from Hudson's files. As far as Bella could work out, they had at least six years of paper trails to follow.

Dan was seated at a small desk in one of the front rooms where he had a clear view of the front garden and roadway and was able to observe any car or person who came within cooee of the house. His papers were spread out on a single bed resting against the wall under the window. He was correlating property sales to any of the list of names they had.

Simon had piles of paper scattered over the large wooden dining-room table, his chair positioned so he could see the entire backyard, which was largish for a suburban block but had very little in the way of neat flowerbeds. According to him, Simon had little interest or time for gardening so his backyard consisted of an expanse of lawn and a few large shady trees along the grey picket fence-line. He was matching up account names with the long list of deceased persons for the entire state over the past six years.

Even though she could just see both men from her position, Bella was tucked out of sight in the far corner of the lounge room, the curtains drawn across the picture windows to keep her hidden from view. She was searching for amounts resembling those of the daily entries into each account.

Their tasks were different and they sounded simple but to Bella it was a mind numbing, tedious and back breaking exercise.

Back in his office, Bella knew Jared was working on subpoenas for twenty financial institutions to release all details of owners and signatories as well as signed credit and debit forms for each of the one hundred accounts. At the same time he was trying to track down Isabella Perez, hoping to be able to speak to her over the phone. Bella had no idea where she lived except that she had gone back to Columbia after Juan's funeral. Bella had phoned Raoul's parents to see if they had a contact number for Izzy. She'd already told Jared how the thirteen-hour time difference was going to make it difficult to follow up on the possible numbers she had passed on to him earlier.

As the long shadows of nightfall began to ease across the garden, Simon started putting into place the plans he had made in order to secrete Bella away to a safe house. Not daring to take any chances, the assumption was made that both Dan and he could be followed. Jared was to call in on his way home from work so they had three cars leaving at the same time to confuse any would-be onlookers.

As planned, Jared phoned to say he was almost there. At the call Bella was hustled into Simon's car, lying as well as she could across the back seat, her plastered leg being a painful and cumbersome hindrance. With old clothes tossed in a careless heap over her, Simon reversed his car out of the garage, parking it on the lawn only a few metres in front of his house, still far enough away from the road and neighbouring properties that any onlookers wouldn't be able to make out Bella's prostrate form in the back.

From her position, Bella heard Jared drive straight into the open garage then the door was closed only halfway down. Having been a part of the discussion whilst the plans were being made, Bella was able to follow the sounds and visualise what was happening as the three men then hustled about in the garage, opening and closing the doors to Jared's car.

When the garage door opened up Jared reversed out then waited on the driveway, his car still idling while Dan climbed into his car. Both men waited for Simon to jump into his vehicle, the garage door to close remotely and then together all three cars drove off, following each other down the road then all three going in different directions once they hit the crossroads. There may have been one car waiting to follow them but they were fairly certain there wouldn't be three and it would take Bella's pursuers some time to scramble two other tails. By then they hoped Bella would be well hidden.

Bella heard Simon's mobile phone ring twice then there was a pause before it jangled three more times: the signal that one of the others had picked up a tail. 'Who is it?' she called to Simon.

She watched Simon glance down to read the screen on his phone. 'Jared has the tail, which is what we suspected would happen.' He then called Dan who now had to wind his way through a maze of back streets until he pulled up at the side of a road a few metres back from the corner and wait until Jared, who was to deliberately drive slow, passed him. Jared was to hold up a number of fingers indicating how many cars back the tail was. Dan would pull in behind the car to get a description and number plate.

Jared was then to take the unknown man on a long, wild goose chase through the suburbs, ending up back at the Central Police Station where he would alight from his car alone, walk inside and watch. Regional Inspector John Wright would also be watching from his upstairs office window to see just who the Superintendent had doing his dirty work.

To ensure Bella's escape went unnoticed, Simon drove into a multi-storey car park in the city, two blocks away from where Jared would end up. 'I would love to go up top and watch what is happening,' said Simon over his shoulder.

'Can you see from here?' asked Bella from her horizontal position.

'Yes, but we need to keep to plan. I see Mario's wife.'

'Anyone suspicious following or hanging around?' asked Bella.

'No one followed us in here.' The car slowed then turned into a parking bay. 'Janet's car is on your right. Give me ten seconds to move out of sight then transfer over. I'll see you later. Good luck.'

After counting to ten, Bella shoved off the mound of clothes then carefully rose and almost jumped out of her skin when the door on her right opened. She was about to scream out for Simon when a quiet female voice spoke.

'You must be Bella. I'm Janet, Mario's wife.'

Sucking in a breath to calm her racing heart, Bella turned to the woman. She was middle aged with salt and pepper shoulder length hair. 'You scared me half to death. Hi.'

'Sorry. We need to hurry before any cars come.' Janet opened the door wider at the same time as she opened the door to the car beside them.

Without sitting, Bella wriggled to the edge of the seat, dropped her good leg to the ground then used the door handles to lean on as she swung from one car to the other. Lying prostrate immediately, she shimmied her back along the seat until her cast cleared the edge of the seat. In less than twenty seconds, Bella had transferred from one car to the other, her hated crutches were nestled in the foot-well and the door was closed. It only took another few seconds and they were driving down the circuitous concrete exit route.

'I see Simon. He's nodding,' said Janet as she waited at the bottom to pull out onto the road.

'Which means he hasn't spotted anyone suspicious. I can't believe we got away with this.' Bella squirmed to find a more comfortable position knowing she would remain prostrate until they reached the safety of Janet's home.

***

Hidden behind a large, dusty, artificial palm tree standing inside the entrance of the police station, Jared grinned as he observed his tail pull up in the nearest available parking bay to his own car. The driver, a tall gangly man with a balding head, stepped out of his car, glanced around furtively then ambled along the path, peering into the windows of Jared's car as he went past.

It didn't take much imagination to figure out the mouthful of obscenities being uttered by the furious man standing by Jared's car. The stranger turned on his heels and raced back to his car with a mobile phone plastered to his ear. In a very short space of time, Jared was certain, Simon and Dan's car would be under very close scrutiny, if they could find them. By the time each car was picked up Bella would be gone.

While the man was still on his phone, leaning against the bonnet of his car, Jared exited from the foyer of the station and jogged towards his car, doing his best to keep a straight face as he took in the features of the man while he scanned up and down the road on the pretence of looking out for oncoming vehicles. The man looked vaguely familiar but Jared couldn't put a name to the face but with the number plate now memorised he wasn't concerned. Before he pulled out onto the road Jared glanced up towards the window where he knew John Wright was standing hidden from view.

***

Within minutes of Janet leaving the central city car park, she was pulling into the garage on the side of her house: an old, but beautifully renovated home situated on a large fenced block. The moment Bella spied the house she fell in love with it. As with most of the older style houses there was no direct doorway leading from the garage into the house. Instead, Bella was ushered through a rear door into the large backyard and then through the wide French doors leading into a magnificent large family room, which, by the looks of things, had been a recent addition to the back of the home.

Highly polished, hardwood floorboards echoed the sound of Bella's crutches as she was shown through every room then into the bedroom that was hers for the time being.

Janet handed her the four shopping bags she had been carrying earlier. 'Courtesy of Jared: a few items of clothing to see you through until we can get some of your own things here. Your bathroom is through this door.'

Janet pushed the white gloss door open to reveal a modernised bathroom, which had been renovated using period fittings to suit the colonial style of the house. A brand new claw bath sat along one wall with a separate large, glass shower recess at the end of it, the tiles and fixtures tying the modern appliances to the old style. Next to the shower sat a colonial style toilet suite. A basin and vanity unit had been fitted snugly on the end wall next to the bath. The pristine white towels and mats offset primrose painted walls with a darker yellow trim.

Left alone to freshen up before dinner Bella perched on the end of the chintz covered double bed, her eyes absorbing her new surroundings. Painted to match the adjoining bathroom, the large room had a fresh, sunshiny feel. The walk-in wardrobe on the side had mirror doors, which reflected the cheery colours and gave the impression of a room much larger than it was. A small antique desk sat snug under the window, the curtains of which matched the bedcover. Between the heavier pulled back curtains hung old-fashioned lace. A comfortable cushioned cane chair sat in one corner and a dressing table was central to the other wall. On either side of the bed, matching bedside tables held period styled reading lamps. Bella fell in love with the décor, which was simple yet elegant.

Curious as to what clothes Jared had provided, Bella yanked the shopping bags to her side and tipped out the garments of the first bag. Her cheeks heated at the sight of two sets of gorgeous, lacy underwear and a beautiful silk and lace nightgown. Staring in awe, she thought the word *negligee* would have been a more apt description. Checking the labels for sizes caused her face to heat even further, feeling as though she were on fire. How on earth did he know her size so accurately? Then she remembered him having done her laundry while she was incapacitated. Feeling mortified that he had scrutinised the labels of her intimate apparel she held the soft blue nightie up against her body, entranced by the slinky feel of the silken fabric, its soft folds falling in graceful arcs to the ground. Never before had she owned such a luxurious garment. Nightwear to her was practical and comfortable but this item was slinky, seductive and exquisite.

The second bag contained two outfits consisting of skirts and matching tops. Jared had even considered her inability to drag jeans or slacks over her thick cast. Both outfits were practical for everyday wear but were of the very best in design and quality. A warm jacket fell out of the third bag while the fourth had every item she would need in the bathroom including a quality hairbrush. Stunned, Bella sat with everything scattered around her. Jared had chosen with care and had even considered what colours and styles suited her. She recognised expensive brand names and almost choked when she thought of what the few items must have cost. She had never been one to splurge on luxurious items, not that she didn't like them; she could never justify spending so much when less expensive, practical items would suffice.

Leaving the clothes draped on the bed, Bella scooped up the toiletries into the bag and carried them into the bathroom where she set them out on the cabinet bench. A quick freshen up and she went in search of Janet, following her nose towards the kitchen from whence delicious aromas were wafting through the air.

'Did you buy those things for me or did Jared?' Bella asked in a nonchalant voice, hoping to hide the depth of her curiosity. She wasn't sure if she wanted it to be Jared. That he knew her tastes and colouring so well delighted her. That he knew her sizes, and the intimacy of the items, was mortifying.

'Jared did. I met him in the shop opposite the car park before he drove over to Simon's house. He'd purchased them earlier in the day. Why? Do they fit? I'm sure we will be able to change them if they don't.' Janet smiled at Bella. 'I couldn't resist peeking. Jared has excellent taste. How I wish Mario would shop for me the same way but he wouldn't be caught dead in the ladies underwear section. It is never going to happen.'

Her shrug of resignation had Bella reach out and place a hand on Janet's arm. 'Maybe you should drop a couple of not so subtle hints. The clothes are perfect, I was just wondering how he knew my size ... can I help you with dinner?'

Janet laughed at Bella's embarrassment. 'It's amazing how men know these things about the woman they care for.'

'I don't think Jared even likes me.' Bella could feel the intense heat rising up her neck and cheeks all over again.

'I wouldn't be so sure of that. He cares. Now, dinner's all ready, just a few more minutes in the oven. Go into the lounge while I call Mario and we'll have a pre-dinner drink. You relax.'

With her mind racing at an incredible speed tossing all the, what ifs and impossibilities, around and around, Bella found it impossible to relax. After the meal the three settled back in comfy chairs chatting. Quiet background music from the sensational sound system Mario had set up in the room created a soothing atmosphere. Finally, unable to keep her eyes open any longer, Bella made her excuses and clicked her way back to her bedroom.

Jared had thought of everything. There was even a folded piece of plastic and a roll of tape for her leg so she could shower, after which she slipped the silk nightgown over her head then stood staring at her image in the long mirrors on the wardrobe door. The garment felt like gossamer against her skin and looked so … she couldn't think of a word to describe the way she looked but she felt downright seductive and sexy. She had no idea such a simple nightgown could make one feel so wonderful. After slipping into bed Bella lay awake for quite a while, images of Jared flitting through her brain. She felt an incredible loneliness, missing the presence of both Jared and Duke.

***

Back home after an overbusy day, Jared lounged on his sun deck gazing over the dark waters of the lake, feeling desolate. The evening had been busy, taking Duke for a run, cooking and eating a lonely meal then spending a great deal of time on the telephone trying to track down Isabella Perez. It had taken several phone calls but he had finally succeeded. Izzy had remarried and was the mother of a young baby. She had a story to tell but she wasn't prepared to tell it over the phone and she also had some papers to show him. Because of her reluctance to divulge the facts he was flying to South America in two days time to meet her. Phone calls to airline companies after his conversation with Izzy had gained him a seat on the first flight available.

Never before had he felt lonely living by himself but with Bella gone the solitude hit him like a sledgehammer. Duke wasn't making him feel any better. The dog was mooching around, padding to Bella's room and then coming back to Jared with big doleful eyes as if to say, 'well, what have you done with her?' Duke wouldn't settle on his rug but stood beside Jared staring into his eyes. Jared reached out to run his fingers through the dog's mane.

'I know, boy. I miss her like crazy too. I wish she was here but it's not safe. We have to look after her, boy. I promise, when all this is over, I'll try to convince Bella this is where she belongs and I can assure you, fella, when she comes back she won't be sleeping in the spare room.'

The two walked together down the passage, pausing at Bella's door to stare at the empty bed before moving on towards Jared's room. Duke was ordered to his bed but he didn't stay there long. Jared was still awake thinking about Bella when Duke left. Jared followed a few minutes later and found his dog lying on the mat by Bella's empty bed. Jared climbed into the bed and sunk his face into the pillow, absorbing the sweet aroma that was exclusively Bella. He felt like some crass broken-hearted teenager but what the hell – there was nobody there to observe his actions.

Chapter Twenty Two

Feeling far more refreshed than he thought he would, Jared spent the next day having his subpoena's formalised urgently and then traipsing around the twenty financial institutions to seek the required vital information. Knowing it would take time for each institution to collate the lengthy requests, he ended the day with only a few pieces of paper to peruse. A cursory glance at the trustee and owners names on each account had him worried for none of the names were of those expected, and to make matters worse, most were female. To complicate matters, many had company names listed as the trustees, which meant more mind numbing searches, so he rang around and organised a meeting in his office with Mario later in the afternoon.

'How's Bella?' asked Jared the moment Mario arrived.

'She's fine. Rather quiet, but fine. I left her browsing through Hudson's files. What have you got for us?'

'Not what I had hoped. I have the details of signatories to a few accounts. The rest I won't get until tomorrow or the next day but since I won't be here, I've authorised for Simon to collect the paperwork.'

'Where will you be?'

Jared smiled. 'Colombia.' He grinned at Mario's surprised glance. 'Bella was right about the account details, but most of those with individuals as trustees indicate mostly women and none of them have the name of Hudson, Travers, Walker or Watson. The others have companies named as trustees.'

'What has this got to do with Columbia?'

'I managed to track Isabella Perez down, which is why I'm flying to Colombia early tomorrow morning. She says she has some important papers to show me. Can you look after Duke? He's driving me nuts at the moment, moping around with that hangdog look, always searching for Bella. Being with her might perk him up. I'll drive my car and park it behind the office, then catch a taxi to your place. I have some of Bella's clothes with me today and I'll bring the rest tonight.'

'Forget about the taxi, I'll get Janet to pick you up, same car park as before. Make sure you keep your eyes open for a tail and ring me if you think you have one. Let me have this lot but leave Bella's other clothes in your car tonight and I can pick them up tomorrow; but leave me your keys.'

***

Mario carted in two large cardboard boxes and dumped them on the floor in Bella's room. 'Jared says to say hi.' He dropped the paperwork from the banks onto the desk in front of her. 'We have a problem. Even though we only have some of the account details, most of the accounts are in women's names or are held by companies.'

Bella picked up the paperwork and studied it without saying a word. Her heart was thrumming. The mention of Jared's name had set it off pounding around in her chest. 'I don't think these female names are a problem at all. All you need to do is find out the maiden names of either the men's wives or their mothers. It's an old ruse. What is the password for your bank accounts?' Bella turned around to look up into Mario's stunned face.

'Hell, both Janet's and my accounts use our mother's maiden surnames as a password. I can get into those records from here. Let me at the computer.'

'I suspect most of these companies may be fake,' Bella called out, causing Mario to pause and backtrack.

'We'll have to do some company searches. Not too difficult but time consuming.'

'As if we haven't got enough paperwork to plough through,' said Bella as Mario once again headed for his computer.

Thankful for the rest away from the constant flickering of an electronic screen, Bella went in search of Janet and insisted on helping with the evening meal. They were about to serve it up when Mario joined them with a triumphant smile on his face.

'We have Hudson and Watson. Both are married and have used their wives' maiden names as the passwords on ten accounts each but they've used different trustee names on each account. Twenty accounts accounted for – eighty to go. I'm assuming we'll find Travers and Walker and there has to be the other faces from the meeting. Then we have to figure out where all the money came from.'

'I don't think it has all come from real estate deals, there's too much money. Bart had financial concerns as well. My gut tells us to look at loans he may have made at exorbitant interest rates and then calling in loans when the payments can't be made or … maybe foreclosure … or taking back goods or property; something along those lines. Also look up his chief accountant's name, James Carthew. There is no way James would not notice what was going on. I've studied Bart's accounts today and there has been a lot of skulduggery going on. If I can see it then James Carthew must know. I suspect he owns ten of those accounts. A lot of those financial workings never showed up on the computer I used but I bet they were on James' computer. I guess I was probably only privy to the workings of the legal companies. And what about Hudson's brother?'

***

Not long after midnight Janet arrived with Duke and Jared. While Duke was left free to roam and explore the backyard, Jared and Mario discussed Bella's findings but the entire time they talked Jared kept glancing towards the passage, hoping Bella would waken and come out. Mario gave up trying to keep Jared's attention, grabbed him by the elbow and led him towards Bella's room, leaving him at the door.

Jared's hand reached out, his fingers curling around the brass knob then turning it until he heard the quiet click of the lock as it released and then giving the door a gentle shove until it came ajar. Moonlight streamed in through the lace-covered window and Jared could make out Bella asleep on the bed. He felt concerned that she hadn't drawn across the heavier drapes and determined to mention it to Mario. He trod silently as he walked to the side of her bed and peered down.

Bella lay on her back with her head turned to one side. One hand was curled above her head, the other across the edge of the sheet lying across her stomach, exposing all from her chest upwards. Raw emotion forced its way up from the very core of Jared's soul as his eyes soaked in the vision. He knew the nightie was all Bella when he chose it and seeing its silky folds barely covering her breasts his thoughts shot to how much he wanted to slip the slinky fabric from her and explore what was underneath, both with his hands and his mouth. This woman touched him like no other had and in places never stirred before.

Unable to hold them back, his fingers found their way to her hair. Jared had no control as they ran through her thick curls, his sensitive nerve endings soaking in the softness before they traced a line down her cheek and stopped on her lips, barely caressing. Bella stirred then a smile spread across her face. Afraid of being caught Jared jerked his hand back. He was acting like some love-starved fool but what the heck he now knew how much she meant to him. He was a love-starved fool.

He turned back to the door and opened it only to be shoved back by an exuberant Duke who pushed past and lolloped over to the bed. There was no stopping the animal - not even the harsh whispered command to sit. Duke planted his front two feet on the side of the bed, flicked out his tongue and gave Bella an almighty lick across her face. Jared swore the dopey dog was smiling.

Bella sat up with a start. 'Duke, what are you doing here? Did you bring Jared with you?' She swung her legs over the side of the bed and stood on one leg then reached over to the wall to find her crutches.

Jared remained still in the doorway watching, his hammering heart jammed in his throat at her words, rendering him unable to speak for a moment. Without hesitation she had asked if he was there. Did it mean she cared for him? She looked so exquisite with the moonlight shimmering on the silk folds of her nightdress, just as he had imagined she would look. The outline of her slender body showed off every single curve, every hollow. Oh, how he wanted to be caressing her skin like the fine fabric was, how he wanted to be skimming his fingers along every curve, how he wanted his lips to be brushing against hers.

He swallowed, almost choking on his emotion. 'Duke has come to stay with you for a couple of days.'

Bella spun around as he coughed to clear the huskiness from his throat.

'Jared?' She stood stock-still as though unable to believe he was standing there.

He watched as she fought to control her emotions and wondering why his appearance had caused such a meltdown. 'Am I allowed to tell you how beautiful you look?'

His words had Bella glancing down at her body and suddenly realising how little she was wearing, she grabbed for her gown and flung it around her shoulders. She shot a quick glance at the bedside clock.

'What are you doing here at this time of the night?' she asked as she began making her hesitant way across the room.

'Mario is driving me to the airport. I've found Izzy and am flying to Colombia to meet with her. Hence Duke. He misses you.'

Bella stopped in front of Jared's face staring as though she were trying to read his guarded expression. He wished he could read her mind. He longed to reach out to touch her but knew that if he started he wouldn't be able to stop. Nothing short of devouring her sweet mouth would do.

When she indicated with her head for him to go outside he turned away but heard her follow as she clicked along the passage. The sensation of Duke's hot breath down the back of his legs told him the dog was now content walking along her side.

'Traitor,' he muttered to himself.

Upon reaching the kitchen where Mario and his wife stood sipping coffee, Bella stopped and then moved to a stool against which she perched her backside with her head downcast.

Jared pulled out a kitchen chair and sat on it backwards, his arms leaning on the backrest, as close as he could get without crowding Bella. If he wanted to, he could reach out and touch her. And he wanted to. Strong willpower and the fear that she would pull away from his touch were the only things preventing him from doing so. 'Mario tells me you have used your brilliance again to solve our mysteries. Well done, Bella.'

'It wasn't hard. Using maiden names is a lot more common than you think. Did you speak with Izzy? How is she?'

'Izzy has remarried and has a young baby. She also has some papers she wants to show me but wouldn't entrust them to mail services. Maybe this is what Hudson and his cronies were looking for. There's something else Simon discovered tonight - there was an inquest into both Senora Duarte and Juan's deaths and guess who signed off on the results?'

'Either Bill Travers or Mike Walker.'

'Uh,uh. Superintendent Watson. He found no unusual cause of death for Mrs Duarte and accidental death for Juan. Or at least those are the findings written in his reports. John Wright is re-opening both cases on the quiet. He's going to do the investigation himself and not even let any other officer know what he is doing. He has also gone to the Commissioner and relayed all the facts to him. Watson is now being watched and his phones tapped. Now, Bella, do you have any messages for Izzy?'

'Do you have time for me to write her a letter?'

'Go ahead, I've still got a few minutes before we need to leave.' Jared kept smouldering eyes on her until she retreated into Mario's study then sat quietly contemplating while sipping on his drink until she returned and held out a sealed letter.

'Jared, please don't let Izzy know what happened to me because of our names. She's had a terrible time as it is.'

'How am I going to let her know how we found out about this then?'

'Maybe you could say I was working for Bart and found something on his computer. I'm sure you'll be able to think of some reason. She doesn't deserve to be hurt any more.'

'And what about you, Bella?' Jared's had trouble keeping his voice even and low. 'You deserve none of this and yet you are in hiding just to keep alive. You take care and don't dare leave this house, not even to go out the back. We're pretty sure nobody knows where you are at the moment but we can never be certain. King mentioned that he thought someone had been watching the base – probably waiting for me to turn up to work. Can't figure out why since they know I've returned to my legal practice. And they certainly know where I live.' He frowned at the shiver that shimmied along Bella's arms, regretting he'd brought back unpleasant memories.

'I'll be back before the week is out. Talk some sense into that turncoat of a dog. Let him know it wasn't my fault you left him. He's been moping around like a wet mop.' Jared pocketed Bella's letter and led the way out of the house, suddenly wishing he wasn't making this journey. What if they found Bella while he was away? What if she were harmed? Damn it, he'd never forgive himself. But he had to go. He had to find out what Izzy had.

They'd only been driving a few seconds when Mario said, 'When are you going to stop lying to yourself, Jared?'

'What do you mean?' Jared twisted in the seat to stare at his friend who was watching the road ahead.

'You're in love with the woman.'

A huge sigh escaped from Jared's throat. 'She's my client, Mario. And I'm not lying to myself. I know exactly how I feel about Bella. She pulls my heartstrings pretty tight but if I am going to represent her I can't be seen to be having even an inkling of a relationship with her. Hudson's lawyer would have a field day if he thought there was any fraternization.' He straightened and stared at the passing scenery. 'Is it so obvious?'

'It is to me, but only because I know you so well. Bella cares about you too but there's something holding her back and I can't quite put my finger on what it is.'

'You think she cares?' He turned back to Mario. 'Bella has been through some very traumatic experiences. She has nightmares some nights but doesn't wake from them. So if she screams the house down in the middle of the night you'll know what it is. Having Duke with her should help. You look after her for me. I hate going away but I have a feeling Izzy's information is of vital importance. By the way, have you checked out the driver of the car that was following me? Could he be the owner of some of those accounts or was he just one of the Super's minions.'

'I haven't had time yet. That's first on my list in the morning. I'll also find his marital status.'

Chapter Twenty Three

The cool night air was a welcome surprise when Jared stepped into the arrivals lounge at the Eldorado Airport, Bogota, Colombia. He'd been in the air for almost twenty-eight hours. Waiting around inside the airports at Johannesburg and Sao Paulo for another seven hours attributed to his crumpled, aching and weary state. Even the luxury of Business Class and being able to stretch out to sleep palled after so many hours. He wasn't the only traveller shifting impatient, tired legs from foot to foot while the queue passing through customs shortened. Glancing around behind him, he was thankful he was one of the first to alight and that he carried his only luggage with him and hadn't had to go to the carousel to wait for the plane to be unloaded but it seemed he wasn't the only one.

Once through customs things moved far quicker. Striding from the customs hall Jared searched for the local transport guide who should be holding up a placard with his name. A sense of unease beset him when he had the feeling he was being watched. Had he been followed from home? He glanced around with his eyes settling on any Caucasian then studying each for any signs of familiarity or guilt. Spotting his name in the crowd he smiled at the small Amerindian man as they approached each other then shook hands. It had to have been this person staring at him. Just in case, he gave another cursory sweep of his surroundings but didn't catch any person taking an express interest in him.

Even close to midnight the traffic on the roads as they headed towards his hotel was thick and chaotic. With exhaustion dragging down his normal enthusiasm for a new destination, Jared didn't much care what his accommodation was like, as long as it had a clean bed. He was pleasantly surprised with the modern, upmarket hotel he had been booked into by the travel agent. Not that he would be there long. Another internal flight awaited him at lunchtime the following day.

Refreshed after a deep sleep, Jared tucked into an early hearty breakfast before wandering around the local streets. He always enjoyed tasting local fare whenever he had the opportunity and this time he popped a few of the more unusual items on his plate, avoiding the bacon and eggs. He had read how it was normal for rain to fall in the early morning and late afternoon and he wasn't disappointed; the rain sheeted down minutes after he departed the hotel. Dressed in denim jeans and a casual cotton shirt, Jared blended in well with the locals as he ran between buildings, hiding under protective eaves and then ambled through the shops, stopping at a local, well patronized café mid morning to taste local coffee. The coffee was strong and rich, giving him a delicious but strong caffeine hit before returning to his hotel where the same private taxi driver was waiting for him.

The local Varig Airlines flight flew to the north coastal city of Cartagena, an old sixteenth century imperial Spanish stronghold. This time a very attractive Mestizos woman, who was similar to Bella in build, held up his name. But there the similarity between the two Bellas ended. Isabella Perez had long straight black hair, pulled back into a knot on the nape of her neck.

'Senor Manning?' The quiet, accented voice tripped off Jared's name as he neared Izzy.

'Isabella Perez? Thank you for meeting me. I really appreciate you taking the time.'

'You are welcome and it's Rodriguez now. I'm sorry you had to come so far. The journey is not an easy one. Come, I have a car waiting outside.' Turning, Isabella led the way through the throng, most of them locals. Jared's build and good looks had him being the centre of attention as they wove their way through the crowd. Once in the car and away from the airport, Isabella drove them through the narrow streets where huge seventeenth and eighteenth century walls surrounded them with an abundance of palaces, monasteries, plazas and churches indicating the colourful history of the city. Along the channel leading to the Bay of Cartagena were several impressive forts. A pleasant drive along the water's edge ended when Izzy pulled into the open iron gates of a large old house.

The circular driveway swept up and ended at the base of a set of wide stone steps. Down each side of the stairway were large white pots filled with ornamental trees. It was obvious the house was old and looked to be in need of some renovation work from the outside but when he stepped into the main entry, Jared was amazed to see the well maintained modernised rooms. Thick, natural stone walls kept the inside at a moderate temperature, which negated the need for noisy air-conditioners. He was ushered up a second flight of plush carpeted stairs then along a passage to an enormous, luxuriously decorated guest room.

'Please feel free to freshen up before you come downstairs. My husband will be home soon. We eat late here, around eight-thirty. Dinner will be in the dining room. When you come down, follow the passage right through the house to the back patio. We can talk there while we have some refreshment.' Izzy's quietly spoken, serene manner indicated a quiet and gentle nature.

After being left to his own devices Jared unpacked his meagre belongings then hung his few shirts and single pair of trousers in the very capacious wardrobe. Venturing into the en-suite bathroom he showered, shaved and changed into a pair of casual cotton trousers and long sleeved fine cotton shirt, leaving it open at the neck. Thankful he'd had the forethought to bring light cotton clothing, he felt very much refreshed when he ventured out to the large back patio surrounded by fresh mown lawns and shadowed by large, mature trees. It looked and felt like a tropical paradise, with a balmy light breeze keeping the evening pleasantly cool.

On one side of the patio Isabella sat back in a cushioned wooden chair, a baby snuggled in her arms. Jared loped over to her and reaching out with one finger he brushed it gently against the soft, downy cheek of the baby. Dressed in pink, he presumed the baby was female.

'She's beautiful, how old?'

'Four months. We called her Inez, after my grandmother. I guess you know about her?' The look on Izzy's face showed sadness.

'Only what Bella told me but she didn't know a great deal. It's one of the reasons I am here. Both your Grandmother and Juan's cases have been reopened. It is quite a long story but we suspect their deaths may not have been as reported.' Jared's careful words were interrupted by the arrival of a dark haired man who was only a couple of inches shorter than Jared, although he didn't have the same muscular build. Black haired like his wife, he was tall and lean and had the same dark brown eyes, as did most of the population.

'Senor Manning, I am Isabella's husband, Alvaro. Welcome to our home.' The accented English was clearly enunciated and flowed easily.

Jared shook the proffered hand. 'I appreciate your hospitality. Your home is lovely and please call me Jared.'

'An old family home that was in need of repair. We have only recently completed the inside and hope to start outside in a few months. Please sit and join us in a glass of wine. Red or white?'

'I drink either so will trust your judgement, thank you.' Before Jared sat, he slipped Bella's letter out of his shirt pocket and handed it to Izzy. 'A letter from Bella.'

'I only met her a few times before our wedding and then at Juan's funeral but I heard how she devoted her time to making Raoul's last days quite wonderful. She is a very special lady. It wasn't an easy time for her. Raoul's parents think a lot of her and I can see in your eyes that you do as well. That is good. Alvaro understands I will always hold a special place in my heart for Juan, but Juan is gone and

I have been very fortunate to find love again. Annabella deserves a good man.'

Izzy smiled knowingly at Jared who was amazed at her perception. She then opened out Bella's letter to scan the two pages. After reading them a second time, she sat in silence then brushed away a few tears.

After handing Jared his glass of icy cold white wine, Alvarez noticed his wife's distress. Kneeling by her side he held his wife and baby in a light embrace, planting a kiss on both of their heads.

Jared sipped on the wine while observing the tender actions of the man. Yes, Isabella had found love again. The thought and the sight warmed his heart while his mind saw a vision of the curly headed, feistier Bella and he had a sudden yearning for the time when he could hold her the same way. If she would let him. Mario's words had heartened him, given him hope but he still had doubts since Bella often kept her distance as though she were avoiding any accidental touching. Somehow, he didn't think his feelings for Bella were reciprocated - at least not to the same depth.

The three sat enjoying the atmosphere, a couple of glasses of good wine and desultory conversation until dinner. Jared waited until the table had been cleared and they were seated in comfy lounge chairs, enjoying coffee made from the beans of the Rodriguez family estates before heading the conversation back to the reason he was there.

'Isabella, I know it isn't easy for you, but tell me about your grandmother. Bella said there was an inquest into her death. What happened?'

'That she died so suddenly was a great shock to everyone because she had no illness. That she had sold her house only weeks before her death was an even bigger shock. She had said nothing to anyone and that was very unusual. When we cleaned out her house we found a copy of the Offer and Acceptance form, which I have to show you. An autopsy was done to ascertain the cause of death but the report that came back said she had died of natural causes.'

'It didn't say heart attack or anything similar?'

'No and we thought it unusual, besides, she didn't have a heart condition and she wasn't really very old, only sixty-one. She enjoyed excellent health.'

'The police have reopened her file and will be investigating further.'

'Why? What happened that the police are now investigating?' Alvaro was standing at Jared's shoulder, refilling his coffee mug as he spoke.

'It's quite an involved story, one Bella didn't want me to tell you all the facts of, but I personally, believe you have a right to know about.'

'Please don't hide anything from us? Bella wrote in her letter that we could trust you. You can trust us as well. Anything you say will remain only in this house. We can promise you that.' Isabella reached out her delicate fingers and placed them on Jared's arm, her dark eyes pleading.

'Bella was head-hunted by Bart Hudson's company to work for them.' Jared heard a loud hiss of an indrawn breath and stopped, turning his head to look at Isabella. 'You know of him?'

'Evil man. His name is on the paper I told you about. Juan tracked him down and I believe there were very harsh words spoken. Why did he seek out Bella?'

'We didn't know at first but we now believe he thought Bella was you. We think he was unaware there were two Bella Perez's. Isabella, Bart Hudson has attempted to murder Bella on three occasions now and at the moment she is in hiding at a safe house.' Jared stopped when he heard the shocked cry of alarm from both Isabella and her husband.

'How?' The question was a hoarse whisper. 'What did he do to her? Is she all right?' asked Izzy in a choked voice.

'First he dropped her over a cliff but she landed on a ledge. It is a miracle she is still alive. Her leg is broken and she had many cuts and bruises but they have healed now. When he discovered she was in hospital and had survived the fall, he attempted to poison her by injecting a substance into her drip bag. It was very fortunate she spied him and very cleverly removed the catheter under the blankets then pressed the alarm button. I managed to secrete her out of the hospital unseen and had her hidden in my home, but he found her again. Once again through her resourcefulness, she was able to escape him. Not without her doing him a ghastly injury.'

'But how did he keep finding her?'

'We have arrested two corrupt police officers who revealed her whereabouts. Does the name Sergeant Bill Travers mean anything to you?'

Flashing eyes and an angry mouth stared up at Jared. 'He investigated Juan's accident.' She paused then added quietly, 'It wasn't an accident was it? He was murdered.' A fiercely determined look settled on her face. 'I'll get you those papers and show you what Juan found. Please excuse me.'

Isabella stood on shaking legs, taking a few moments to find her balance. She then moved away but not before Jared saw the rush of moisture which had sprung to her eyes. Alvaro followed his wife. It was several minutes before they returned arm in arm but Jared could see her reddened eyes. She had been crying. Two sheets of paper were handed to him. Jared perused both but was mystified when he saw they were duplicates of each other. His face must have looked puzzled because Isabella's hand reached out and pointed to the figures written on the first paper.

'This was the copy I found hidden in a book in my grandmother's drawer. The house was sold for five hundred and forty six thousand dollars. Have a look at the other sheet, which Juan stole from your Mr Hudson's office. The numbers five and four have been reversed and Nona's account only received four hundred and fifty six thousand dollars. Mr Hudson swore it was the correct amount. Both sheets have original signatures on and we don't know how that happened.' Mr Hudson signed as the agent. Juan wasn't able to track down the name of the buyer.' A sob escaped from Isabella's throat. 'Juan died before he had a chance.'

Jared peered at the names on the form, assuming the second scrawled signature of the buyer was a false name, but then thought again. As the selling agent and witness, Hudson signed his real name so logic told Jared the other must be genuine. 'So that's how he did it? Can I have these papers? I think this will crack this case right open. Hudson set up a series of trust accounts in false names and used them to dispose of large sums of money. One of those accounts is in your grandmother's name and was opened only days before she passed away. There is another account in the name of Juan and Bella Perez, which was opened two days before Juan died. All the accounts are Trust accounts with other people and businesses being the signatories and owners. I'm fairly certain these two pieces of paper are what Hudson thought Bella had and are the reason he tried to kill her. I believe it was to prevent her from revealing these.'

'If it helps to put him away in jail for what he did, take them, but can I copy them first in case they become lost or damaged?'

'Most definitely and to make doubly sure, I will make several copies and post them to the investigators who are working on this case. You don't know how important these are. What we do know is that your grandmother's house was resold less than a month later for close to the original price. It was these profits being credited into those false accounts. If you are lucky we may be able to find the missing money for you. I know it isn't much; it doesn't replace your Grandmother or Juan. I have a suspicion that you leaving to come home so soon after Juan's death may have saved your life. I think Hudson may have been searching for you and that's how he mistook Bella for you. He had never seen you had he?'

All Jared received as a response was a slow shaking of Isabella's head; her tears had started again.

'I feel so guilty, poor Bella.'

Jared reached out and placed his hands on Isabella's upper arms and gripped lightly. 'That's exactly what Bella didn't want you to feel. For now she is safe and I intend to make sure she remains safe. Bella is a remarkably strong woman and the last thing she would want is for you to feel guilty. You have done nothing wrong. It is because of her we have discovered all that has been going on and we have been able to stop this man. Now, enough of the unpleasant stuff for tonight, I feel like taking a walk around your charming city before I retire to bed.' He smiled at her and felt pleased when he received a wavering smile in return.

'Colombia is not a very safe place to wander around alone at night, especially the city. I will come with you and we will take a Chiva ride through the streets. I think you might enjoy it.' Alvaro stood and made his way to the phone.

After a brief call the two men waited at the gate for a taxi to take them into Cartagena Centro. Once there, they boarded an open sided bus with a non-stop playing band on top, the music playing while they drove through the Plazas. Drinks were handed out to each passenger. Jared eyed the fruity concoction then sniffed, reeling back at the strong smell of alcohol and cinnamon. When he sipped it he was pleasantly surprised to find the mixture was warm and quite delicious. A second woman handed around snacks on a platter.

The Chiva drove through the historical centre where Jared was enthralled by the unique architecture. Balconies overflowed with an abundance of rich exotic blooms: the heady fragrance stronger than other interesting aromas. The nightlife concentrated around the Plaza de Los Coche where he spied an interesting variety of entertainment. Alvaro pointed out places of interest as they continued on their journey. Right in the heart of the city there was the Gold Museum; a building of the Colonial era. Several unusual statues brought a smile to all the tourist's faces. There was a statue of a giant crab on Aveninda Santandor, a statue of a flock of pelicans in front of Hotel Santa Clara and a bronze casting of a pair of old boots behind the Fort of San Felipe.

The mediaeval square on the Plaza Santo Domingo was steeped in history and Jared was particularly taken by the red brick cobbles. Traditional street sellers were offering their wares of salads, horse carriage rides, cigars, shoeshine and a wide variety of other items. Quiet words in Jared's ear by Alvaro described what the shifty looking men were doing on each corner.

'They are touting contraband, mostly cocaine. You will notice they stand on the corner in order that when a policeman comes along, they can disappear down the other road. Look, see that one.' Alvaro gripped Jared's shoulder and pointed to their right. 'He is pulling small white packets from his shirt and exchanging them for money. Pure cocaine. Every one knows what is going on – even the police but it is almost impossible to stop. There are not so many sellers at night. This is why it is not safe for strangers to wander around the streets alone. Wallets get snatched even in broad daylight. You will certainly be ripped off if you attempt to exchange money in the street. Cartagena is a beautiful city but unfortunately has many security pitfalls.'

Their journey finished, Alvaro hailed a taxi, bartered the price and the two men were driven back to the house. Jared felt exhilarated and found it difficult to relax into sleep. What kept going through his mind was the conversation he'd had earlier.

Flights back to Bogota didn't occur everyday so Jared spent another day and night with Alvaro and Isabella, something he enjoyed immensely. A drive along the Caribbean beaches the next day was delightful. Jared, Isabella and baby Inez wandered along the golden sands then stopped in a beachside café for lunch, absorbing the atmosphere and enjoying watching the rich blue waters of the Caribbean Sea. Turning to the East, Jared felt a strong yearning as he stared at the Pico Cristobel Colon in the distance. The tallest mountain in Colombia, at five thousand, eight hundred metres, was snow capped and he would have loved to spend time climbing it, even part of the way. Maybe, one day, he could come back, he thought as Isabella drove them for a private showing of emeralds in a family friend's emerald shop.

'Half the world's emeralds are mined in Colombia,' said Isabella as Jared inspected the displays. He felt overawed by the size and deep colour of some of the best. A visit to the Gold Museum and then dinner in the Hotel Santa Clara completed the day's wonderful activities.

Chapter Twenty Four

Midnight, and the coolness of the air after the tropical heat of Colombia sent whispering shivers along his skin as Jared queued for a taxi. A bone wearying tiredness from his journey had his eyes close almost as soon as he gave Mario's address to the driver. He had to be nudged awake upon arrival. The door was opened before he had the chance to knock. Duke rushed out to greet his long lost master with an exuberance that had Jared tangled up and almost falling to the ground.

'Down, Duke,' he commanded tersely then waited for the dog to calm before he knelt and rubbed Duke briskly. 'How are you, boy? Have you been looking after Bella for me?'

'It beats me how you are ever going to get him to leave her. Talk about a shadow. He never leaves her side and it's been almost impossible to take him out for a walk. He drags his tail wanting to return home then almost drags me along the path on the way back. How was your trip?' Mario stood leaning against the wooden doorjamb, smiling at the way the huge dog greeted Jared.

'Very tiring but fruitful. I posted you a copy of the papers Isabella gave me, just in case these got lost.' He tapped the top of his bag. 'We now know how to look for all those amounts of money. How is Bella?' Mario dared to grin at the catch in Jared's voice, but he couldn't help it.

'She's asleep. I didn't tell her you were coming back tonight. She will never admit it but she's missed you a great deal. She keeps surreptitiously asking if I have heard from you and looks so forlorn every time I've had to say no. You could have rung.'

'I spent two thirds of the time in the air and yes I could have rung from Cartagena but thought better of it. I need to see her and then we can talk.'

Without waiting Jared edged his way past the still amused Mario and headed straight down the passage, stopping only when he reached Bella's half open door. The moment he spied Bella in the moonlight his heart somersaulted around his chest and he realised just how much he had missed her. He also realised he had forgotten to mention about drawing the drapes closed each night. Closing the door on a whining Duke he crept towards the bed then knelt by her side. For a few moments he absorbed the sight. One finger caressed her silken curls before running along her lips. He wasn't sure whether it was his touch or the frantic scrabbling at the door from Duke that woke her but suddenly Bella's brown eyes were staring at him and a wide smile spread across her face.

'Jared?'

Resisting the very strong urge to fling his arms around her neck, he watched as she pulled herself up to a sitting position and drew the covers up to her neck.

'Good morning, I didn't mean to wake you.' He laughed as he turned towards the door. 'I guess I had better let Duke in or I'll have to replace another door.'

Unfolding his long body from the floor, he unlatched the door only to find it shoved open by Duke, who gambolled across the room to stand by Bella's bedside, his tail waving frantically and beating against the side of the bed with regular whumps and looking from one to the other.

'You're a traitor, Duke,' Jared grumbled.

'He missed you.'

'So I heard. He hasn't left your side since I left. And what about you? Did you miss me?'

Bella's eyes dropped. He wasn't sure whether he was deeply hurt or delighted. What was she hiding? Was that a yes or a no? Not daring to ask again in case he was disappointed he turned and left the room, calling out as he sped back down to the passage. 'If you want to hear about Isabella, I'll be in the kitchen.'

***

Flinging back the bed covers Bella swung her legs over the side and reached for the crutches as she stood on one leg. Within seconds she was racing after Jared, Duke hot on her heels. She was almost at the kitchen door when she looked up and saw Jared watching her approach, his eyes dark and hooded. Yelping, Bella turned and fled back to her room then shoved her arms into her towelling gown, pulling the belt tight around her waist, her cheeks aflame with embarrassment. Her return to the kitchen was much more sedate where she was greeted by a grinning Jared.

'It's nice to know you missed me so much you couldn't waste time to cover up your sexy body.'

Bella was chagrined by Jared's whispered words but at the same time she felt an ache form low in her pelvis. Did Mario hear him? She glared at Jared, unable to think of a suitable retort then moved into the kitchen where she found a chair on the far side of the table as far away from the source of her mortification as she could get.

'Tell me about Izzy. How is she?' Changing the subject was imperative.

'Izzy is fine and very happy. She has married Alvaro Rodriguez, a man who thinks the world of her and they have a beautiful four-month old daughter, Inez. I have a letter for you and I believe there is a photograph in there.' He slid a large envelope across the table but kept his fingers on it as Bella reached to grab it. 'Before you open it I guess I'd better let you know I told her almost everything but without the gory, descriptive details. She insisted.'

After sending him another glare Bella slipped her forefinger in the back of the envelope and slit it open. Ever changing emotions almost overwhelmed her as she scanned the neat handwritten words and stared at the two photographs. She felt such sadness, joy and at the end surprise, accompanied by a heating glow in her cheeks. The last few words brought a rush of intense heat to her face as she glanced up at Jared and seeing him watching her, just as rapidly glanced down again. What did he say to Izzy? She re-read the postscript at the bottom. *I very much like your new man. I hope you are very happy with him.* Taking care to refold the letter she replaced it in the envelope then hid it in the pocket of her dressing gown with her mind spinning in turmoil. When she glanced up again Jared was standing in front of her.

'I like your new cast.' Squatting on his haunches he lifted the edge of Bella's gown to reveal the new plastic cast that had replaced the heavy plaster, stopping when he reached her knee then deliberately brushing his fingers against her skin.

Sucking in her breath, Bella felt a warm coil of heat spring out from her insides and the heaviness in her pelvis deepen. Even though she had never been able to physically consummate her marriage she knew all about the physical hunger of desire and hers was escalating so much, so quickly. How she wished Jared felt the same for her. How she wished she had the gumption to reach out and run her fingers down his face but the very thought of him jerking away from her touch, stopped her.

'Mario had me dress to look like Janet then took me to a private doctor. I was supposed to have had an X-ray a week after the accident but things seemed to always be getting in the way. The break has set well and is healing nicely and this cast is certainly a lot easier. I can get it wet then take it off to dry my leg. Janet has been wonderful in helping me. How long before I can go home?'

'I'll call Mario and tell you both what I've found out, but you are going to have to stay in hiding until we find the rest of this little gang. Your place is not safe and nor is mine.'

'We only have to find one more. We traced the man who tailed you and is owner of ten of the accounts. He's a sitting Member of Parliament.'

'Strewth! I thought I recognised him.'

'We also have James Carthew - Bart's accountant, Bill Hudson who is Bart's brother and business partner and his secretary, Joan Brady. She used her dead mother's name on her account. Then as we had already guessed, Travers and

Walker own ten accounts each. We assume the other one is the fourth person who was at the meeting in Hudson's office because after seeing photographs of all the others I am certain he was none of them.'

'But that doesn't add up to a hundred accounts, what about the others?' Jared dropped the edge of Bella's nightie and rested back on his haunches.

'It actually makes ninety. Tracing business names, we discovered that each person does in fact own ten accounts.'

***

'You have been busy.' Jared spoke over his shoulder as he went in search of Mario, finding him holed up in his office. 'How about a coffee while I show you what I have? I've found out how they did it.'

'You two had enough time alone?'

Nowhere near enough, he thought then added aloud, 'I think Bella would appreciate your company, she's finding being alone with me a little daunting and I'm finding it very difficult keeping my hands off her, so please come and save me?'

Mario laughed aloud as the two men returned to the kitchen, causing Bella to look up with a quizzical look on her face. Jared withdrew the papers he needed from a folder he retrieved from his bag then spread them out on the table in front of Bella. Mario moved behind to peer over her shoulder.

'This page is the Offer and Acceptance form signed by Inez Duarte when she accepted the offer for her home. Have a look at the amount. This other sheet is what Juan Perez stole from Bart Hudson's office. Closely look at the amount. Both have original signatures on them. This is Hudson's signature as the real estate salesman but we can't make out the other scrawl above it, which is the purchaser's name. All I can figure out is the double l in the middle. The home was resold a month later for the original amount. The second purchase is legitimate. Hudson only paid Mrs Duarte the lesser amount and she died a few days later in mysterious circumstances. Juan investigated and must have gone to Hudson's place of work. His death two days later is just as mysterious. I believe this is what Hudson was looking for and thought you, Bella, had in your possession. I have made several copies and sent them to various people on our team and Isabella has a copy locked safely away.'

'Phew, it's so simple it's ridiculous,' murmured Mario. 'Who would check the amounts on the duplicate copy when they sign these things? We need to track down original owners of all the other properties Hudson has had dealings with and see if this was his standard method of dealing. Damn, but I wonder how many deaths occurred if sellers began complaining. Hell, this gets messier and messier. Then we need to see if we have a ninety thousand dollar amount on any of those daily deposits around that time.'

Before Mario finished speaking Bella pushed her chair away and left the room. She came back with a file held under her arm. Flicking through a couple of pages, she quickly found what she was looking for.

'There it is. On the day of Juan's funeral fourteen accounts each received six thousand, four hundred and twenty eight dollars and fifty-seven cents. Two received an extra cent each. I knew I recognised the total. Now we know what we are looking for it should be easier to collate things together. I'll start first thing in the morning. That scrawl – does it look like any of the other nine names or could it be the tenth person?'

Both men peered at the scribbled signature then at the list of names Bella pulled out from the same folder but none of them could match it up to any of the names on the list. Jared declared that his eyes were too weary to be trying to sort anything out and asked Mario if he could drive him to his car. At Mario's agreement Jared packed away the papers then pulled out a small package from his bag. Bella had already crutched her way towards the door when Jared called her to stop. Carrying his bag towards her, he handed her the beautifully wrapped package.

'A gift for you from Colombia. Izzy helped me choose it. Good night. I won't be able to come to see you very often; it's too dangerous. I'll ring. Take care.' Jared headed towards the front door and called Duke to him. 'Duke, come!'

The dog looked from Bella to Jared and then back again, his allegiance seemingly torn. Jared stood at the door stunned at Duke's disobedience then called Duke to him again.

'Come, boy, it's time to go home.' Duke took a few steps and then sat on his haunches staring up at Bella who in turn grinned at Jared.

'I thought you said he was well trained.' She then rubbed Duke behind his ears. 'Go, boy.' The dog obeyed instantly.

'You're both traitors,' Jared mumbled as he stalked away, Duke following and Bella laughing out aloud as she made her way back to her bedroom.

***

Itching to open her gift, Bella perched on the side of her bed, dropped her crutches on the floor then reached over to switch on the bedside light. Her fingers were shaking as she slipped the silver ribbon down to the bottom edge then dropped it on her lap. Deep green embossed paper was wrapped around a small oblong box. Not wanting to damage the paper, she turned the parcel over and lifted the edge of the tape then peeled it away. The second piece of tape received the same treatment then both were tossed into the bin next to the bedside table. Anticipation wracked her as she turned the box over and carefully lifted the lid.

Nestled on white velvet was a pair of square cut emerald earrings set in fine gold filigree. 'Oh, Jared, they are beautiful,' she whispered as tears sprang to her eyes. She fingered the beautiful deep green stones as an unrelenting ache settled in her heart.

Her fingers shook so much they fumbled as she pulled the backs from the diamond studs she usually wore then poked the shafts of her new earrings through the tiny holes in her lobes. After clipping the backs onto the studs she groped around for her crutches then sped to the bathroom, her hand reaching up to flick the switch for the light as she passed through the doorway.

Standing in front of the long mirror, Bella turned her head from side to side, studying her ears. The green and gold earrings were stunning. Returning to her bed, she lifted the receiver from the phone and dialled Jared's mobile number, something she had craved to do for the past week. It only took two rings before she heard the deep tones of his voice.

'Bella, you should be asleep. Are you all right?' She looked down at the receiver, puzzled and then suddenly twigged that her number must have shown up on his phone.

'Thank you so much, Jared. They are quite stunning.'

'You are very welcome. I'm looking forward to seeing you wearing them when next I see you. I'm sure the real thing is far better than my imagination. Go back to bed and sleep well. I'll ring you some time tomorrow.'

'Good night, Jared and thank you again.'

Chapter Twenty Five

It took three days before Jared was forced to make a phone call. 'Mario, can you please take Duke back? His doleful eyes, persistent whining at the side of Bella's vacant bed and refusal to eat enough food to sustain him, are driving me nuts. He's pining for Bella.'

Mario laughed, causing Jared to swear down the phone. 'How about you, Jared, are you eating?'

'Not funny, Mario!' Jared mumbled then added more softly, 'Yeah, this place is like a mausoleum.'

'Okay, same place as before?'

'No, I've spied the same pale blue sedan in too many places to make me feel comfortable. I'm sure I'm being watched.'

'Where then?'

After much discussion they agreed on a time and place, meeting that night at midnight after Jared had taken Duke on a long run in a densely wooded park halfway between the two houses. Duke changed hands with the word *Bella* being all it took for Duke to go willingly with Mario.

'Lucky bugger,' Jared muttered as he handed over his traitorous best friend and watched him depart with a wagging tail. Mario's snorts of laughter didn't help. Jared maintained a slow jog through the thick forest until he reached his car, empty-handed. At the same time he pressed the remote to open the door he heard an echoing noise from behind, back in the dense undergrowth. The sharp snap sounded like a branch being crushed underfoot. Rooted to the spot he attuned his ears, waiting and not daring to turn around. What the hell was he supposed to do?

Deciding to stall for time he eased the door open then rested one foot on the sill. Bending at the waist he made out he was retying the shoelace on his running shoes. He figured that if he was a target for shooting his vital organs were out of the line of fire. As he changed feet another sound, a definite footfall this time, seemed closer. His muscles automatically tensed as he dropped his head so he could look backwards under his stretched out arm.

It took a few seconds of swinging his eyes around before he saw a shadow move from one tree to another. 'Damn,' he whispered under his breath then wondered how long he had been observed. Did they see Duke with him as he entered the forest? Had they followed him, or Mario, if they had been followed at all? But who else would be here in the middle of the night and the stealth of the movements made it obvious whoever was out there didn't want to be seen.

Without standing upright, he eased awkwardly into the seat then slid two fingers into the corners of his mouth and emitted a shrill whistle as though calling for Duke. Terrified he was about to be the recipient of a bullet he dared to turn his head to make out he was searching the area for the dog. The slightest flash of gunshot, untoward movement or sound and he would be prostrate in a split second.

Adrenaline surged when the shadow moved again. It took him a few seconds to realise the person was moving away from him. Reaching over to the passenger seat he scrimmaged under the sweater he'd tossed there for his mobile phone and rang Mario. As he waited for Mario to pick up he whistled again then watched from the corner of his eye, following the stealthy retreat.

'Mario, one of us was followed. I can see one person.' He twisted around for signs of a vehicle in the car park. 'No vehicle visible. You need to be extra vigilant. I've whistled for Duke as though I'm waiting for him so I'll sit here for a while. I'll let you know if anything evolves.'

It was then he heard the rumbling of an engine from the other side of the park. Figuring it to be Mario he waited. There was a pause before a door slammed. He swung his head slightly to the right in the direction of the noise. What sounded like a heavy 4WD revved up and sped off. The thumps and bumps telling him it wasn't traversing a smooth road but more likely a bush track. Gut instinct told him that Mario had probably been spotted with Duke.

***

After a long roundabout journey home with his eyes constantly searching in vain for signs of a tail, Mario had no hope of keeping Duke's presence a secret until morning. The moment Mario drove into his garage, Duke was whining at the door to be released. Mario attempted to climb out of his door first but found four furry paws and a massive weight on his lap the moment Duke heard the click of the lock opening. Duke shoved the door open and was at the front door in an instant, his tail thumping the ground and his head on one side staring at Mario to hurry up. His hand in Duke's collar to hold him back while Mario slipped the key in the lock was a futile exercise. Duke wrenched his collar from Mario's fingers and bounded through the crack in the door, shoving it back on its hinges. Rapid clicking of claws along the polished wood of the passage, a skid on the slippery floor as he rounded the corner into Bella's room at full pelt then an almighty leap and Duke landed fair-square on Bella's prostrate body, waking her instantly. To really make sure his beloved Bella was awake, Duke ran his wet, slobbery rasp of a tongue up the side of her face several times.

'Down, Duke!' Bella yelled in between her squeals and laughter. Finally managing to get the exuberant dog onto the floor she turned towards the open door with a hopeful look on her face, only to find a grinning Mario standing there. Bella couldn't hide the disappointment on her face.

'Sorry, Bella, Jared isn't here. Duke was pining for you so Jared asked if he could come back until after the Court hearing. It was too risky for Jared to come. As it is we are not sure whether we were observed swapping Duke from one to the other, even though we were very careful.'

There was no way he was going to tell Bella about Jared's two phone calls. Someone knew of the dog swap and was probably tracing number plates, if they didn't already know. He was going to have to be extra vigilant although it was only the dog they'd seen and Duke had been with him several times before. He snorted, as if it didn't look suspicious handing the damn dog over in the middle of the damn night in the middle of the damn bush.

'Duke hasn't been eating since he left here. Jared used quite a few colourful words as well as things like, traitor, treachery, turncoat and double-crosser. I think most of them were describing Duke but I couldn't swear to that. Duke probably needs a feed.'

Turning away, Mario headed down to his own bedroom to rejoin his wife while leaving Bella to tend to the dog. He heard the pair of them head for the kitchen and laundry as he curled up against Janet's soft warm body.

*****

Preferring the quietness of his office building to the acute emptiness and utter loneliness of his house, Jared worked late every night while putting the finishing touches to his case for the upcoming Court hearing where Bella's accusations against Bart Hudson were to be heard in front of a judge. It had surprised him that Hudson had opted to not have a trial by jury. The matters pertaining to the fraudulent activities of the accounts Bart had set up were to be heard at a different hearing, but all the evidence was being just as carefully collected and collaborated. While Jared worked in his office, Mario worked at home while keeping an extra vigilant guard over Bella. Simon and Dan did the legwork interviewing the original sellers of six years worth of property and business sales that had gone through Bart Hudson's company. The rapidly building mountain of evidence was overwhelming and shocking. Why all these disgruntled people hadn't reported Hudson beggared belief. Then maybe some of them had for an alarming number of sellers were no longer alive. And maybe the last person they were seeking was someone in authority in the complaints department of the relevant government body. It was worth the time to investigate so Jared jotted down a memo.

With only a week to go before the hearing, Jared needed to spend considerable time with Bella, going through every detail and discussing the likely questions. Once again elaborate plans were made for the two to meet in a secret location. Just in case, he'd taken to wearing the small firearm he took as precaution against wild animals on climbing adventures. It didn't sit well going armed in public, especially when he knew he was such an appalling shot.

***

Feeling weird dressed in Janet's clothes, Bella sat on the edge of the cushioned seat, twitching with apprehension while she waited for Jared to arrive. Two weeks had passed since she had last seen him and even though they had spoken each day on the phone she felt uptight. Such businesslike and impersonal calls had convinced her that Jared didn't feel the same way towards her as she did him. Their conversation was always stilted. Apart from the normal, how are you going, there was never any hint of caring, no words of feelings, not even so much as I miss you.

With the wait seemingly interminable, Bella became overanxious and unable to sit still. She began roaming around the hotel room and reading every sign and information sheet she could find. She opened the bathroom door, switched on the light and peered in to see what the amenities were like. Deciding to make use of the facilities while she waited, she closed the door behind her - anything to break the intense edginess of her nerves. After washing her hands, Bella backed out of the luxurious room then stopped, suddenly feeling as though she wasn't alone. She slowly turned around, fear causing the hairs on the nape of her neck to take on a mind of their own.

Jared stood by the curtained windows watching her. Dressed in tight fitting denim jeans and a casual short-sleeved shirt that highlighted his magnificent physique, Bella was struck dumb by how wonderful he looked. Her blood began thrumming around her body, her knees felt so weak she didn't dare move lest she fell.

On the other side of the room Jared stood still then swung a chair around to face the other one then plonked his long frame into it.

'Come and sit down, Bella. This could take some time and you need to be comfortable. I've ordered refreshments from room service.'

As Bella moved across the room she could feel his eyes never once leaving her face. She felt ridiculous about being so darn nervous. His voice softened as he spoke. 'How have you really been?'

'Bored. I'm heartily sick of this whole thing and am yearning to have some freedom, to find another job and go back to work, go back home, have a coffee in a café, be able to walk around the shops. I want my life back.'

'I'm really sorry it's had to be like this but at least you've been safe with Mario and Janet. Only five more days to the hearing and I'm hoping if everything goes to plan it will all be over. Our only big stumbling block is the tenth person. Nobody has been able to figure out who it is. You have no idea how many government departments have had their personnel records searched but we haven't been able to track any person to Hudson's little empire. Three are in jail for other crimes and the other six are under constant surveillance but any of them could have hired someone to find you. In fact we are certain of that.'

Even though she already knew most of this, Bella couldn't help the hiss as her breath sucked in.

Jared glanced at her then added in a softer tone. 'I thought you knew that Simon and I have both spotted someone watching and following us, hoping we lead them to you.'

'I did but you saying the words just made it sound scarier.'

'Tonight, I'm booked into this hotel with my so called lover.' Jared smiled at the second gasp that whooshed out of Bella's mouth.

'She's an undercover cop and is next door keeping guard over you courtesy of the Commissioner of Police.'

Suddenly Bella realised something that had puzzled her, why she hadn't heard Jared arrive. 'You came through the door over there?' Turning around in her chair she pointed to the connecting door. A loud knock on the main door startled her and sent another frisson of fear skittering across her shoulders.

'It's probably room service. Stay there.' Jared kept the door on the security chain to check who was there before opening the door wide. He took the covered tray, closed the door and carried it to a small table, which he pulled between the two chairs before settling down in his own chair once again.

Without wasting any time Jared began detailing his trial strategy as they ate. Bella was continually amazed at the details of the investigations, strategy and planning undertaken by a larger group of people than she had initially thought. She had been aware of the work done by Simon, Dan, Mario, Jared and she, but she soon discovered all about the high level police involvement as well. The charges Jared had laid on her behalf were quite extensive but were only the beginning of a far more serious set of white-collar crimes involving members of high society and the legal fraternity.

After ploughing their way through a particularly complicated set of papers, Bella sat back in her chair rubbing her aching head with her eyes closed.

'Are you all right?' Jared reached over and touched her arm. 'What's the problem?'

For a moment Bella remained still and silent. She took her time raising her eyes to him. 'It's all beginning to sink in. I now know why my evidence is so crucial, why my being a witness is so important and just why Bart and his cronies were so keen to get rid of me. This is all so unbelievable and all because of one mistaken identity. I feel like I'm in a vacuum or having some bad dream. And it's not going to end at this first hearing is it?'

Sitting back in his chair, Jared clasped his hands together, closed his eyes then inhaled and exhaled three very deep breaths. 'No. This first hearing is going to deal with what Hudson and the two coppers did to you. We hope, with the amount of concrete evidence we have, Hudson will see the sense in pleading guilty to all charges. We pray he will co-operate, but we have taken a lot of care in planning this in the hope of catching others in the group. I'm betting most of them will turn up as audience to find out how much you and we know. Unfortunately for those who do turn up, we have a little surprise for them. If things go as we have planned, you probably won't have to say very much at all. They already have your very extensive and detailed written statements and DNA from the branch and my house positively identifies Bart Hudson.'

'Am I going to be safe in the court room?'

'Absolutely. Apart from the armed undercover guards you will have, all personnel will have to go through quite rigid security checks before being allowed in the building. You and I will be entering through a back room.'

'And later? You said this was only the first hearing.'

'You may be asked to testify about what you have found in the computer files. There could be more Court hearings but with you as a witness. This is the one where you have laid the charges. The other trials are based on what we have discovered. I'm not going to lie to you, Bella, this is not going to be easy.'

'It's going to be a damn sight easier than having to fight for my life all the time.' Using only one crutch as a walking stick, she stood then limped restlessly around the room.

'You're using your leg. You never told me.'

Stopping in the corner, she turned and stared at Jared. 'Probably because you never asked.'

Jared blushed with guilt. 'I'm sorry. It certainly wasn't because I didn't care. When does the cast come off?'

'Hopefully the day after the hearing but we may have to change the appointment if things go on too long. Can we have a break? My brain feels like it is going to explode.'

Jared sat back in his seat then nodded. 'We have these rooms booked for a couple of days. Why don't you lie down to relax for a while or turn on a movie or listen to some music? I can go next door.'

'That's some love-in, a couple of days.' Bella's quiet sarcasm resulted in Jared laughing as he piled up the spread out papers on the table and shoved them in his briefcase. Before leaving the room he moved over to Bella. With great deliberation, he studied her face then reached up and caressed the emeralds in her ears.

'They look better than I imagined. You are quite a stunning woman, Bella Perez.' He dropped his hand and turned away. 'Take as long as you want. I'll leave the connecting door unlocked. I could do with a break myself;

it's been quite an arduous few weeks. I'll order a meal when you're ready.'

He left via the connecting door, leaving it ajar a fraction while Bella stared after his retreating back, wondering why the dramatic change in demeanour from looking and sounding as though she meant something to him, to business-like in a split second.

***

While Jared lay back on the bed chatting to his supposed lover, who was sitting in an armchair with an open novel on her lap, he heard the muffled tones from the radio in Bella's room and then there was silence for quite a while. Feeling an urge to check on her he wandered back into her room, knocking before he entered. Bella lay curled up on one side of the enormous bed, sound asleep. He pulled one side of the cover over her then stood watching, his feelings for her unmasked and wishing he had the nerve to lie down beside her. Instead he re-arranged the chairs in the room, sitting in one and resting his long legs on the other then settled back, enjoying being able to observe the woman he now knew he loved deeply, in her sleep.

When her eyes finally opened Bella didn't move. 'What are you doing?' she asked.

'Watching you sleep while I think.'

'Thinking about what?' Bella pushed the cover aside and sat up, swinging her legs down to the floor.

'You.'

'Care to be more explicit?'

Damn, that was a stupid thing to say. 'No, not yet, I'll order us a meal.' To avoid further questioning, Jared pushed the two chairs apart and made his way over to the desk where he perused the in-house menu. 'What do you fancy?'

After reading out the menu he then went next door to ask Sandy what she would like.

The three ate together before Detective Sergeant Sandy Wilson returned to her room leaving Bella and him to complete their planning for the trial. Mental exhaustion had set in by the time Bella was whisked down the service elevator and out the back entrance to the waiting car with two different plain-clothed officers who were in charge of returning Bella to Mario's home without being observed.

Chapter Twenty Six

Too exhausted to sit chatting with Janet and Mario, Bella retreated to her room where she showered and then read for a while in a desperate bid to ease the turmoil spinning around her head as well as her heart. Duke had been exuberant at her return but now settled down on his cushion by her side. Not long after she switched off her lights she heard Mario and Janet retire to their room and the house settled into the quiet darkness and solitude of a peaceful night.

Only a half-moon shone in the sky. The light filtering into Bella's room created fascinating patterns on the walls and furniture. With the lights out she was able to make out the shapes of night on the outside. Sleep was elusive with vivid memories of the little exchange after she had woken in the hotel room running around her head again and again.

What did Jared mean? Why wouldn't he elaborate? Why had he been sitting there watching her? What had he been thinking? The thought of him watching her caused a variety of emotions to flood though her body. It was so wonderful seeing him again but how she wished things were different.

There was a sudden low growl from Duke. He stood with his hackles up, the soft belly growl unceasing. Leaning up on one elbow Bella reached out with her other hand to curl her fingers through his hair, attempting to calm him but Duke moved towards the window, his growl deepening. Alarm replaced the pleasant thoughts of a moment ago. The moment she went to sit up Duke flicked around and padded towards her. Then he lifted his paws up to her chest, pushing her back down on the bed.

'What on earth is the matter with you?' she asked.

His reply was to shove her in the side of her stomach with his nuzzle. When he continued budging despite her attempts to shove him off, she rolled to the other side of the bed thinking he just wanted to lie next to her, something she knew Jared would have a fit about if he knew. But when Duke followed, belly crawling onto the bed and then kept shoving she couldn't figure out what was wrong with him. She slid onto the floor between the bed and the wall, shivering as bare skin brushed against the cold floor.

'What's wrong with you?'

Duke growled so low and deep the hairs on her arms stood on end and a shimmer of unease settled into her belly. Something was wrong. She made to get up, glancing around at the same time. Fear turned to dread when she noticed a dark shadow pressed up against the window. Too scared to move Bella suppressed the whimper that was trying to force its way out.

'Get Mario,' Bella whispered in Duke's ear.

The dog slid to floor beside Bella then padded on silent paws around the end of the bed before fleeing out the door at the same moment as Bella heard a tinkle of glass cracking and a quiet ping. Thinking a small rock had been tossed against the glass, she dragged her body against the side of the bed and curled up to make herself as small as she could, checking that all her body was below the edge of the mattress. She heard Duke tear down the passage and a door being pushed aside.

***

'What the hell?' Mario mumbled as he woke with a start to feel two rows of teeth wrapped around his wrist. 'What's the matter with you?'

A silent growl and a harsh tug at his wrist had Mario instantly alert that something was very wrong. Duke had never come to him like this before. He grabbed the loaded pistol that was never far from his reach and whispered to Janet to hide in the closet before following the agitated animal out the door. Mario crept duck-like with his knees bent and his eyes searching every nook and cranny while swinging his sighted weapon from side to side until he reached Bella's door. Seeing her bed empty, Mario's adrenaline began pumping but years of practice in the military and as a personal bodyguard had taught him not to panic.

'Bella,' he whispered.

'Over here by the bed. I heard glass breaking and a ping. What's happening?'

'Christ!' Mario cursed then whispered, 'Keep below the mattress as long as you can while you crawl over here, down the passage and into my room. Janet is in the closet.

Join her but let her know you are coming. I'm afraid your whereabouts has been discovered.'

He dived across the room then grunted when the air fled his lungs as he dropped prostrate to the floor, skidding the last metre until he was hidden behind the end of the bed.

He waited until Bella reached him then he peered at the window. 'Now,' he whispered. While Bella moved like a stealthy cat across the floor on all fours and keeping as low as she could, Mario hovered between her and the window while keeping his eyes glued to the glass. The ping could only mean one thing, a shot from a silenced gun. Only waiting until Bella was safe with Janet, Mario then used his mobile to scramble Simon and Dan from their beds.

'Duke, here, boy,' called Mario in a harsh whisper. With the dog by his side he made hesitant rounds inside the house. A low rumbling growl from Duke when they entered the lounge room told Mario that whoever had fired the shot was still lurking around. Decision time. His eyes ran over the curtained windows searching for any sign of a moving shadow or one that shouldn't be there. It was imperative he protect the women; it was his number one priority and he hated being down the other end of the house from them. What to do? 'Come on boys, I need you,' he whispered. Despite his fervent wish, Mario knew it would take a minimum of ten minutes for Dan to arrive even with the low middle of the night traffic that wouldn't hinder his progress. Not knowing all the commands Duke had been taught, Mario vowed to learn them as he grasped a hold of the dog's head and looked into his eyes.

'Duke, you follow that bastard and let me know where he is'

Some word in his command must have registered for Duke immediately padded out of the room, pawed at the closed door of a spare bedroom and then emitted a deep, low rumble. Mario slowly turned the handle then pushed the door open with his hand, keeping his body protected against the passage wall. Duke waited in the doorway with his ears pricked at alert and stared at the window then he shot down the passage to the next room. Praying Duke was tracking the gunman, Mario sped down the passage back to his bedroom, the one taking a lot of Duke's keen interest. Mario crawled along the floor and positioned himself between the bed and the closet, whispering his presence to the two women he figured would be feeling terrified.

Mario dared to dial Dan's number. It would make little difference if he was heard but since Duke had left the room, he doubted their pursuer was outside his window.

Dan had the good sense to know Mario was probably not in the position to talk and so asked questions requiring two taps on the mouthpiece for a yes. From his questions, Mario was able to let Dan know that the gunman was still there - outside, that so far all three were unharmed and Mario was guarding the hidden Bella and Janet.

A low growl from the vicinity of the doorway alerted Mario to the slow moving shadow outside his room. He concentrated on the curtained window, searching for an indication the man knew he was in the room and not daring to breathe although he was certain the man wouldn't be able to see inside. Shooting his gun unnecessarily in a suburban home was not the wisest thing to do and from this distance the glass would probably deflect his shot to some degree.

With his mobile still plastered to the side of his face, Mario didn't respond to any more of Dan's questions in case the sounds were heard outside thus giving his position away. Dan would know why. He hoped.

Being much darker on this side of the house, he found it very difficult to discern much movement in the darkness. He prayed it meant the man had gone and wasn't interested in this particular room. It would be too much to hope he had disappeared altogether.

Then a much darker shape moved closer, almost to the glass and shot across the expanse of the large picture window, pausing in the centre. In the split second, Mario wondered whether or not to take a shot. Too late! The shadow fled. Duke spun on his paws and padded in the same direction.

'E.T.A?' Mario whispered harshly into the phone.

'Two minutes,' Dan yelled back. 'Is he still there?'

'Yes.' Mario slid across the floor to the door, anxious to see where Duke had gone. The dog was standing outside Bella's room with his head peering around the corner. Damn! The window was already cracked, making it too easy for the intruder to enter. Dropping the phone he rolled onto his stomach and using his feet in a commando crawl, skidded across the slippery tiles to join Duke. He stretched out on the floor and flicked his head into the door opening to ascertain what was happening.

His movement must have been noticed for there was a sudden, 'ping, ping.' Small lumps of plaster fell onto his head at the same time as he yanked his head back.

'Shit!' He grabbed hold of the scruff of Duke's neck to keep him back. The tinkling of small slivers of glass followed the sound of another shot.

Duke shook free of Mario's grasp, then launched himself at the window like a torpedo, crashing through the remaining glass with an almighty growl. Crouching down low, Mario followed with his pistol ready to fire. Shards of glass shattered all over the floor and desk, the curtains keeping most of it headed straight down near the wall but it was too dangerous for Mario to walk on with bare feet. He sped out of the room then raced towards the lounge-room, catching his elbow on the doorframe then bouncing off the far wall as he tried to regain his balance. Reaching the glass door he twitched back the edge of a curtain to see the intruder fleeing towards the back fence, a snarling, angry beast rapidly gaining on him.

There was a sudden loud report of a gun being fired as the intruder scrambled up the rear fence, Duke doing his best to fly after him. Mario spotted the shape of a second man rushing towards the fence from the vicinity of the garage. Recognising Dan, Mario unlocked the door and flung it backwards and called out, 'He's only just leapt the fence.'

Dan followed, leapfrogging the fence by using one hand. There was a thud and muttered oath when Dan landed on the other side. Duke moved backwards, paused then launched himself over the fence, barely clearing the height. A slamming of a door, the gunning of an engine, a squealing of tyres and Mario knew the intruder had escaped.

Simon Adler joined him in the back yard a few moments later. 'What happened here, Mario?'

'Intruder fired shots into Bella's room. Dan went after him, so did Duke. We'd better go to find Duke. Jared would never forgive us if anything happened to his dog.'

'I'd forgive you a lot less if anything happened to Bella. Is she safe?' The deep anxious voice came from behind.

'Jared, how did you know?' Mario queried.

'Simon called me. Bella? Please tell me she is unharmed.' Jared was brooking no hesitation, the tone of his voice demanding a positive answer.

'She's safe cowering in my closet with Janet. We'd better go and drag them out, but first we need to check on Duke. He went over the fence in pursuit.'

At a loud ear-piercing whistle from Jared, Simon and Mario flung their hands over their ears. Three loud woofs replied, followed by a cylindrical shape flying over the top of the back fence. Within seconds Duke was sitting obediently at Jared's feet, a supercilious grin on his face.

'Good boy, Duke.' Kneeling in front of his dog, Jared ruffled the fur vigorously around Duke's neck. 'Find, Bella.' Duke was off like a rocket. The three men waited while Dan scrambled back over the fence far less enthusiastically than he had leap-frogged over before, then they followed the dog inside, Dan limping rather badly.

It took plenty of persuasion to coax the two terrified women from the relative safety of the wardrobe. Janet crawled out first, seemingly not caring about standing in front of four men in her cotton nightgown. Relieved, Mario wrapped his arms around her in and held her tight before kissing her then grabbing her robe and holding it open. Adrenaline was still surging but he felt intense relief as she slid her arms into the sleeves. Her hands were shaking as she knotted the belt. Who could blame her?

'Come into the kitchen. I think we could all do with something to drink.' He slung his arm around her shoulder, needing the contact to convince his mind that they were unharmed. Simon and Dan followed them down the passage leaving Jared and Duke to wait for Bella who was crawling out on her knees.

***

Unaware that Jared was watching, Bella shoved the high-spirited Duke out of the way then pulled herself up onto one leg, unable to walk more than a couple of steps without the crutches she had left in her room.

His sharp indrawn breath alerted her to the fact that someone else was there. She lifted her eyes. 'Jared? What are you doing here? How did you know?'

'Mario called Simon. Simon called me. I was in my office working. Are you all right?' He rubbed a hand down his face. 'You don't know how beautiful you look to me right now. I was so scared you had been harmed.'

She looked down at the beautiful bit and then looked abashed. In an automatic defensive action her hands crossed over her body as she dropped her eyes in embarrassment. 'I'm unharmed but petrified. What happened?' Too embarrassed to move she just stood there. 'Could you please get my crutches for me?'

Instead of turning around Jared took two steps towards her then before she could protest, lifted her into his arms and immediately headed down the passage. Switching on the light of her room with his fingers as he walked in the door he grimaced at the shards of fallen glass on the floor. He swung Bella around, taking in every detail of the room. A shudder wracked his body before he gently dropped her feet to the ground.

'Lean against the wall for a moment,' he said then checked she was comfortable and balanced before moving across the room to inspect the damage. He lifted her crutches from the floor and brushed off all the glass. 'Christ'!

"What is it?'

Jared changed direction then leant over. Bella followed his line of sight. Her pillow was shredded. 'What happened?'

Leaning forward, his fingers felt in the hole then closed tight around the hard metal object he found in the depths. All traces of blood left his face.

It must have been his lengthy silence that had unnerved her for the next thing he knew Bella hopped over to Jared's side, coming to a standstill when she saw what his fingers held. Then her eyes moved down to the pillow. She gasped then staggered. A long arm reached out, snaking around her waist, drawing her close to Jared's body.

'That was in my pillow?' she squeaked.

'How did you know to get out of the way?' Jared's voice sounded strangled.

'Duke. But how did he know? He growled then pushed me with his paws. Then he shoved me with his nose over to the other side of the bed. He wouldn't stop until I was on the floor on the other side. I heard a ping and the glass cracking but didn't hear a loud bang.'

'They used a silencer. God, Bella!' His arms enfolded her to his chest, his body shuddering as he held her close.

It wasn't a romantic hold, more one of need and Jared didn't know who had been the more scared, him or her. Unaccustomed moisture sprang to his eyes as Jared rested his chin on her head. So close, so terribly close! When will this horror end? He fought for control over emotions that were seesawing so much, he felt nauseous. When he finally opened his eyes he spied Mario standing in the doorway watching them.

'You need to call John Wright. I found this in Bella's pillow,' Jared said as he held up the bullet with Bella still in his arms. 'We have to get Bella out of here tonight and find somewhere else to hide her. Any ideas?' He eased his hold on Bella then grasped her hand. 'Come on let's get out of this room.' Before leaving, he found Bella's robe and held it up while she slid her arms into the sleeves then he handed her the crutches he'd dropped so she could make her own way to the kitchen.

It was quiet, very quiet, when they reached the large homely kitchen. Janet was busy filling the kettle and setting out the doings for a hot drink, the rattling of the mugs as she set them down the only indication she had little control over shot nerves. Mario drew the Venetian blinds shut, his lips drawn tight in a thin line as though he was angry for allowing an intruder to come so close. Dan and Simon could be heard outside checking the property to ensure there was no one still skulking around. Bella's eyes landed on Jared who was unconsciously rubbing the tips of his fingers through the thick fur on Duke's back. Duke was lapping up every moment of his master's attention, pushing his head into Jared's hand for more every time Jared slowed. Pulling out a chair next to Duke, Bella sat but he noticed her face was stiff and her fingers unsteady. To hide the signs of her nervous tension she clasped her hands together in her lap in an attempt to stop the shaking.

'Are you all right, Bella?' Jared's hand moved from the dog's head, reached over and clasped around Bella's fisted hands. A furry head immediately plonked itself on Bella's thigh, big brown eyes staring up at her.

'I can't get the sight of my pillow out of my brain. If it hadn't been for Duke...' The sentence went unfinished while she stared into space for a moment. She shuddered then turned her attention to her saviour. 'I'm going to buy you the biggest, meatiest bone I can find when this is all over, Duke.'

'Ruined for ever! The mutt is already nuts about you. How am I ever going to win back his affection after that kind of reward?' Jared's gentle teasing broke the intense maudlin atmosphere, bringing a smile to everyone's face.

'He misses you.' Bella couldn't hide the cheeky smile on her face.

'Sure, and just whom does he miss more? How come I had to bring him back here?' Jared lifted his fingers, cupping them around Bella's chin as he turned her face to look at him. He smiled at the guilty blush shooting up her face.

She was saved any further embarrassment by the arrival back inside of Simon and Dan accompanied with John Wright and a small team of five other police officers. All the men disappeared into Bella's room, leaving Janet and Bella sitting in silence together whilst taking small slow sips of hot chocolate.

***

The sky was beginning to lighten and twittering birds had started their morning scrounge for insects and titbits when a parade of cars left Mario's house, Bella hidden in one of them. Seeing the bullets that had been dug out of her room had put the wind up her. She still couldn't believe she had survived yet another attempt on her life. The bullets were safely ensconced in plastic evidence bags. The room had been stripped of all her belongings. Both she and Janet had dressed in identical outfits of long skirts and hooded jackets, each limping with one crutch being used as a walking stick. They moved from car to car hidden by a group of eight men. The idea had been to confuse anyone still stupid enough to be watching from some hidden niche not already searched by the police. It was doubtful anyone was there for the search had been long and thorough but just in case whoever was observing the carefully orchestrated shenanigans, they certainly wouldn't have been able to tell which car Bella ended up in. Even Mario's car was used in the getaway. The only person left in the house was a police officer guarding the broken window.

The six-car motorcade headed along the road to the main intersection where they peeled off in three different directions. As each smaller group arrived at the next intersection they all turned down different roads again, each individual driver heading home or back to base.

Duke had pride of place in the front passenger seat next to Jared, the wind from the open window whistling through his hair, his sensitive nose twitching at all the early morning scents, his tongue lolling out the corner of his mouth. He was one very happy dog on his way home with his master as well as Bella, who was lying across the backseat smiling and feeling content at the thought of spending the next few days back in Jared's house. This time there would be four armed guards keeping watch over her, twenty-four hours of the day. The first shift of men was already there, ordered to check out the property to ensure unwelcome visitors were not lurking around.

Chapter Twenty Seven

utterflies had been flying in a frantic eddy around and around in Bella's stomach since early morning. First, she had been escorted into an unmarked police car before sun-up. That manoeuvre alone had given her the willies. Then the entire drive to the rear of the Courthouse had kept her nerve endings so taut she thought a single sound out of place would have shattered her into a million pieces. Even the presence of three armed men riding with her did nothing to ease her trepidation. Just the sight of the bulky lumps hiding firearms had her clamping her eyes shut.

According to intricate plans, Jared followed a couple of hours later with an armed policewoman at his side dressed to look like Bella. He'd had a police escort, both front and rear.

While waiting, nothing she did eased the tension in her stomach. She'd tried reading, watching TV, pacing, writing, listening to music – none of them worked and she was feeling rather nauseous now that it was almost time to enter the courtroom. It was ridiculous to feel that way since she now had so many armed minders that she was safer now than she had been for the past six weeks. Yet her nerves were more on edge now than ever. She forced her mind to think of what was supposed to be going on outside.

Every single person entering the cordoned off courtroom was being searched both physically and with metal detectors before being allowed entry. Simon and Mario were scanning the people entering, noting where each sat and whether each matched the photos of the nine account holders they already knew about.

A knock at the holding room door had Bella jerk around. Dan stuck his head inside.

'As expected, those not already in jail are present.' He scoffed. 'They're trying so hard to look as though they are merely curious members of the public that their guilt is obvious.' He paused and smiled at Bella but neither his relaxed face nor his news eased her tension one iota.

When the door closed again Bella went over some of the facts Jared had told her. A closed hearing would have been more than acceptable practice but this way all the proverbial eggs would be in the one basket - except for the one, as yet, unidentified man. And it was that factor causing her so much grief. Would she recognise the man if he turned up? Much as she'd tried, she hadn't been able to bring an image of the man to the forefront of her mind, even when a police artist had asked her questions and she'd stared at mug shot after mug shot. She retreated back to the chair she'd been in and out of so many times in the past hour.

***

Jared surveyed the room with a critical eye. He spied Superintendent Jack Watson slip in the door at the last minute to sit at the very back near the door. Probably for an easy escape, Jared thought as he swung his eyes around again. The audience hushed as Bart Hudson and his lawyer entered the room, sat and whispered together. All eyes turned to the door on the other side of the room when it opened. An armed uniformed officer stepped in followed by a very chastened Bella, her jerky movements making it obvious that she was alert for the slightest move of aggression. She kept her eyes downcast all the way across the room then almost fell into the chair Jared pulled out for her. She grabbed the arms, twisted into the seat then grasped her hands together in her lap.

'Relax, Bella,' Jared whispered.

'All right for you to be able to relax,' she hissed back without daring to glance at him.

The Clerk of the Court asked everyone to stand for the Judge. A sense of unease prickled along Jared's nerve ending as he watched the man stride from his own antechamber, stand in front of the packed room and then nod to his audience before sitting confidently in his large winged leather chair. At least someone felt confident today. Jared heard Bella gasp and turned to her. She was glancing at the audience behind them. He followed her line of sight. A large number of people were standing shoulder to shoulder. As they sat her eyes kept scanning the faces, finally resting on one in particular.

A strangled gasp whooshed out of her mouth and the curled fingers of one hand flew to her lips trying to stifle the sound at the very moment the clerk asked everyone to sit. Jared stared at her as he sank down then had to drag the unmoving woman back into her seat.

'Shh, keep quiet,' he whispered through the side of his mouth.

'But …' Bella clamped her mouth shut then reached over in front of him, grabbed his gold pen and open pad then scrawled two words on the bottom margin. *He's here!* Shoving the pad back in front of him, she nudged him in the ribs then pointed to the words.

Who? Jared wrote back.

The fourth man. Now those words did get his attention. He stopped listening to the opening proceedings, turned in his seat to be eye to eye with Bella then mouthed the word – where? Keeping her hand below the edge of the vast wooden bench they were sitting at, Bella pointed in the direction of the man. Jared's eyes popped open really wide when he followed the direction of her pointed finger. He stared at the man dressed in a smart, pressed black suit, pristine white shirt and dark tie.

'Mr Manning?' The question jolted Jared back to the proceedings. Glancing up, he noticed the judge staring at him, his fingers drumming with impatience on the desk.

Jared leapt to his feet. 'Sorry Sir, I need a quick word with my client.'

As he sat down again under a withering stare from the judge, he heard a deliberate loud snicker from the opposing lawyer. Jared understood why – only a lack of preparation would be requiring a lawyer to be consulting with his client in the first minute but he was prepared to withstand the obvious silent tirade to ascertain what Bella was trying to tell him. He leant over to Bella's ear.

'Are you absolutely certain?' For his troubles he received an equally withering stare from his own client. Of course she was certain otherwise Bella wouldn't have said anything.

'This changes things quite dramatically,' Jared whispered back as he searched through his pile of evidence papers, finally finding what he was looking for and after extracting it he placed it face down on the desk in front of him. So much for all the hours of preparation he had put in. How was he supposed to handle this situation? He turned the piece of paper over and stared at it, seeing if the scrawled signature on the bottom could really be that of the man Bella had pointed out. He wrote a few words on a blank piece of paper and handed it to Simon, who was sitting behind them.

'Are we ready yet, Mr Manning?' The question from the judge sounded sarcastic and very audible.

'Yes, Sir, my apologies for the small delay.'

Jared was beginning to feel like a Jack-in-the-box with his having to stand every time he spoke to the judge. He sank down again slowly, his brain frantically trying to think about a different plan of attack. Somewhere in the background of his consciousness he heard the charges being read out and Hudson's lawyer respond for his client that Bart Hudson was pleading not guilty to all charges. It was expected for no sane person would plead guilty to any charge despite the evidence. It was now up to Bella, at Jared's careful questioning, to make the judge believe her. Knowing she was more nervous than he's even seen her, he wasn't looking forward to the next few hours.

'Before we proceed, your Honour.' The interruption was almost shouted out. Jared turned to see Peter Marshall standing at the defence table. A pen was tapping dramatically on the wood, ensuring everyone had his attention. Now what was he up to? It wasn't up to him to start.

'Yes Counsel, you have a problem?' Jared didn't like the sly smile on Marshall's face as the Judge responded.

Peter Marshall turned half way around, sneering at Jared. 'Yes, Sir, I believe we have a conflict of interest here with Counsel for plaintiff. I believe Mr Manning shouldn't be acting on behalf of someone he's having an intimate relationship with.'

The loud gasps from the audience were followed by a deathly silence. Glancing at Bella, Jared noticed her visibly pale then a look of sheer anger spread across her face. Her lips tightened, her brow creased and her eyes screwed up tight. Watching her reaction Jared took his time in standing, pulling on all reserves to dampen down his anger but he was suddenly given a lifeline. He was going to turn this accusation around to his advantage.

'Don't you dare say a word,' he hissed at Bella before straightening. 'Your Honour, I would appreciate it if Mr Marshall explained exactly what he meant.' It took an enormous effort to keep his voice slow and controlled but years of practice came to the fore. He ensured his eyes were icy as he stared back at Peter Marshall.

'Your honour, it is well known that Mrs Perez has lived in Mr Manning's house on more than one lengthy occasion and that they have had secret assignations in a well known hotel and at the home of Mr Mario Basile.' He lifted a pile of papers. 'I have photographs here as evidence so I suggest this hearing be postponed until Mrs Perez can find herself an independent lawyer, one she isn't sleeping with.'

Noticing a movement from the corner of his eye, Jared reached out with one hand, pushing it on Bella's shoulder to keep her from leaping up from her chair. He could feel the white hot anger emanating from every pore of her body. Peter Marshall's words had just given him a great deal of information about how well they'd been watched and why. Shoving his own anger away, he stepped from his seat and moved to the side of the room where he could face the audience, Hudson, Marshall as well as the Judge.

'Your Honour, my learned friend, since such a vicious accusation has been made against both Mrs Perez's and my reputation, I assume the entire court deserves an honest, complete response, giving all the intimate details.'

Bella's eyes flew open, glaring at him at the same time as snickers and gasps came from all directions. It took more than a few seconds for the rumble to cease.

'I first met Mrs Perez almost two months ago when I was working as an officer with Air and Sea Rescue. It was my job to rescue people from difficult situations. With Mrs Perez, I had to abseil down a cliff face. She had fallen from the top onto a small ledge. Mrs Perez was seriously injured and unconscious when I reached her. As a trained paramedic it was my job to feel all her major bones for fractures and tend to her cuts and abrasions. If I didn't do this, I wasn't doing my job. Yes, I physically touched her with my gloved hands, set the compound fracture of her tibia and fibula, stabilised her leg in a brace then cleaned and covered her cuts. Then when her body went into shock I wrapped my limbs around her in an effort to get her warm while I rubbed her uninjured limbs to get her blood circulating. When you are stuck alone on the side of a sheer cliff there are no other means of warming a body which has gone into shock.'

Jared turned to stare at Bart Hudson. 'I wondered how Mrs Perez managed to get herself into such a precarious situation. I asked her. Do you know what she told me?' He spun around and opened his arms in question to all the audience. He knew he was over dramatising but what the heck.

'Her boss, a Mr Bartholomew Hudson,' Jared turned back to the man he was talking about, 'whacked her on the head with a dead branch, twice, then dragged her across the ground, hefted her over the safety fence, ignoring the three strands of barbed wire, dangled her over the edge of the cliff and when she looked him in the eye, he released her hands and shoved her so that she fell.'

'Hearsay!' yelled Marshall.

Turning back to the hushed audience, Jared continued. 'Not hearsay when we have a witness and those are the words the witness used. Unfortunately for Mr Hudson, Mrs Perez landed on a ledge and survived to tell her story. What is also fact is that Mr Hudson left his DNA on the end of the branch he used to whack her with and her DNA was in the traces of blood left on the other end.' Jared paused by pacing a few steps to the right then the left.

'But my touching Mrs Perez didn't end there. I managed to get an abseiling harness on her moments before the ledge collapsed and guess what ladies and gentlemen? I wrapped my arms in a very tight embrace around her body and held her very, very close as we swung wildly around, seventy metres off the ground on the one rope that was holding us up there. Do you really think I was worried about how intimately close to my body Mrs Perez was? Do you honestly think she was thinking we were making love? Believe me, her screams were not of pleasure for she was as frightened as I was and I can assure you, I was terrified. I have never been so scared before in my life. That we managed to abseil down together, on one rope, was due to the will of God and an incredible bravery on the part of Mrs Perez who was not only petrified but also in a great deal of agony.'

He paused for effect while he prowled around for a moment as though he was deep in thought but he wanted to maintain the dramatic. He ceased his pacing then paused again before continuing. In a quick glance towards Bella, he noticed that she appeared to have shrunk with her shoulders hunched over and her face hidden. He had no doubt she was feeling mortified.

'Once at the bottom, I did it again. I held Mrs Perez in my arms.' Sarcasm dripped off every single word he uttered. 'She was in agony, she was upset so I held her to comfort her and it got even more intimate when I held her under the shoulders as she followed a desperate call of nature. Without the use of one leg, she wasn't able to hide behind the nearest tree, or to squat down – what would you have done in the same circumstances?' He spun around with his arms open wide, begging the entire audience to respond to his question. He was met with astonished looks but not a sound came back in response.

'Mrs Perez was taken to hospital where her leg was set under anaesthetic and I dared to sit by her bedside until she came round. A man tried to kill her, had been witnessed by her in the act. Did I think he was going to leave it at that? Would you if you knew you could be recognised? He came back and tried again - this time by injecting a poison into the bag containing her fluids and antibiotics. Unfortunately for Mr Hudson, she was awake at the time and watched him through half closed eyes and through her resourcefulness, she survived a second attempt on her life. When I reached the hospital after receiving her distress call – guess what I did? I actually held her in my arms again until the terror, shaking and fear left her body. Shame on me!

'But it didn't end there. I had to continue with my intimate assaults on Mrs Perez. Mr Hudson stole a key to her home so she wasn't going to be safe living by herself and, unable to walk she was in no fit state to be able to escape if he broke into her house. Having no other relatives or family with whom she could stay, I took her to my home to care for and protect her. The only people who knew where she was were the police department; our wonderful, caring, community protectors who take an oath to uphold the law.'

Jared shook his head as though in disbelief while wandering around the room. He stopped, looked up then mock whispered in a loud voice. 'Two of those police officers informed Mr Hudson where Mrs Perez was. Waiting until I was at work, Hudson drove up to my house then stalked Mrs Perez with a garrotte stuffed down his shirt.'

'A garrotte?' was squeaked from the direction of where Bella sat. No one had told her what they'd found. He hadn't been game to.

'That garrotte is listed as evidence. Now why would he have one of those if it were a purely innocent visit as he claims it to be? Can you imagine what was going through Mrs Perez' mind as she sought a hiding place in my home, unable to run because of her leg? She locked herself in the only room with an inside lock – my toilet. But Mr Hudson didn't have evil intent, oh, no. That was why he found a metal bar and bashed a hole in the toilet door - just to talk to her.' To give his story dramatic effect, he snorted in derision.

'I have to give it to Mrs Perez - she is one very resourceful lady. Not only did she have the presence of mind to ring my mobile number when she first noticed Mr Hudson wandering around my property, but she raided my kitchen for two very sharp knives and took my police trained dog into the room with her. Nice and cosy, very intimate while they sat there in silence listening as Mr Hudson searched my house, pulling out drawers, throwing my belongings onto the floor, smashing things but all the while he was giving me time to reach the house. Big mistake on your part, Mr Hudson.'

Jared stood right in front of Bart Hudson, relishing in the fact that the man wasn't able to look Jared in the face. His fidgeting body language gave away a great deal.

'An even bigger mistake was underestimating Mrs Perez. When he slipped his hand in the hole he had made to unlock the door, Mrs Perez attacked with the knives. Yes, she admits she stabbed repeatedly at his hand and in the process Mr Hudson's index finger was sliced severely, but she denies she cut it off entirely. My police trained Alsatian admits to taking the finger in his mouth and yanking it off. Duke has great taste - he spat it out. Yet Mr Hudson still denies he was there. He left the first two joints of his finger behind, flesh and skin hanging from the remains of my door and a bucket load of blood spattered all through my house. DNA has proved it is all his and yet he pleads not guilty. Amazing.'

Jared moved towards the judge. 'Here's another of my admissions, your Honour. When I, and two of my fellow workers found Mrs Perez sitting on the toilet seat she was in a catatonic state, rocking backwards and forwards, her arms wrapped around her body, covered in Hudson's blood and unable to speak. I stepped over the bounds of propriety and lifted her from the seat, carried her outside and sat with her nestled in my arms for almost an hour while I was whispering in her ear and rocking her like a baby until she came around. I can even get the police to attest to my actions. They were there watching me. So yes, I'm guilty of holding Mrs Perez in my arms.

'Your Honour I could go on and detail every other time I've had to touch Mrs Perez but I think every person present in this room has got the picture. On each of these occasions I was not acting as Mrs Perez's lawyer. I wasn't even practising law at the time and Mrs Perez had no idea I was a lawyer. I didn't reveal my legal status until the same two corrupt police officers illegally took Mrs Perez into custody, drove her to an abandoned house in a remote location and tried to force truth serum into her. Those two police officers are now in custody and I am not at liberty to discuss the matter any further due to legal restraints. Suffice to say, I have never been intimate in any way with Mrs Perez. We have never slept together, touched each other sexually or even kissed.' A wash of guilt rose for he had kissed her on her head. 'Your Honour, I am certain you have read Mrs Perez's medical report and I'm sure you are well aware of the last finding on it?' Jared turned to stare at the judge, awaiting a response.

'Yes, and I didn't believe it. Mrs Perez was a married woman and you expect us to believe she is still a virgin?'

Jared heard the loud indrawn breath coming from Bella behind him. He hadn't told her about her medical report and she was going to hate him that her intimate secrets had just been made very public.

Jared's voice softened. 'Your Honour, if you ordered an independent medical examination today, the result would be exactly the same. Her husband was already terminally ill with a very aggressive spinal cancer when she married him. He was paralysed from the waist down after the cancer had destroyed his lower spinal cord and he was unable to be intimate with the wife he loved so much. I imagine it distressed him to the nth degree, so yes, I expect you to believe the medical report is accurate.'

A loud gasp of denial from Bart Hudson had Jared swinging around to face him. 'Ah, Mr Hudson, you appear surprised by the revelations. You had us stumped for quite some time as to why you were so hell-bent on pursuing Mrs Perez. Allow me to introduce you to Annabella Perez, wife of Raoul who died from cancer six months after they were married. You should have done your homework a little better because Isabella was the wife of Juan Perez, the man whose life was deliberately cut short after he discovered what you were up to. I have tracked Isabella down and she has handed over the papers you have been so assiduous in searching for in Annabella's belongings. You attempted to murder the wrong Bella.'

Jared turned to face the Judge. 'Sir, I'm wondering if Counsel for the Defence is still concerned about my ethics or if he is going to withdraw his unfounded accusations?'

The Judge asked Peter Marshall who had no choice but to withdraw his objection. Jared was delighted because now he could play his trump card. He returned to his desk, stood behind his chair, withdrew a small pile of papers from the top of his larger pile then attacked.

'I'm pleased, your Honour because I would now like to ask you to consider that Mr Marshall has a conflict of interest and shouldn't be representing Mr Hudson.'

The cries of shock were not so quiet this time. Jared looked around with intense eyes, noting the stillness of a few people and the nervous fidgeting of a couple of others.

'And your evidence, Mr Manning?' asked the Judge.

'Your Honour, in our very extensive investigation into why Mr Hudson was so intent on murdering Mrs Perez, we discovered that Mr Hudson and Mr Marshall are partners in a corrupt business. Mr Marshall has been accepting rather large amounts from the proceeds of crime. Unfortunately, because the details are a matter undergoing legal investigation by the authorities, I am prevented from publicly giving any details. I do have here, a copy of ten accounts for which Mr

Marshall is the signatory, and which are in the form of Trust accounts in the name of deceased persons. The maiden name of his wife is the password for each account. Over the past six years, over two million dollars has been laundered into these accounts and been withdrawn by Mr Marshall. The other signatory on transaction papers referring to those accounts is Mr Bart Hudson and it is through Mr Hudson's companies this money is being laundered. So I believe Mr Marshall could not possibly be an unbiased legal representative for Mr Hudson. Oh, and since Mr Marshall is about to be arrested for illegal activities, I don't believe that legally, he can represent anyone.'

Jared stopped, nodded his head and a plain clothes detective read Peter Marshall his rights, handcuffed him, then led him outside. There was a flurry of activity amongst the audience. Jared noticed anxious looks between other members of the corrupt little gang and Superintendent Jack Watson attempted to leave. The doors had been locked, preventing anyone from exiting the room. The man had no choice but to resume his seat.

Jared raised his voice to be heard above the hubbub. 'Your Honour, our discoveries didn't stop with these two men. Thanks to Mrs Perez's excellent accounting skills and sharp intelligence we were able to find one hundred such Trust accounts and were able to trace nine of the owners of those accounts, each person being signatory for ten accounts each. And isn't it a coincidence all nine of those people were curious enough to discover what we had found. They came along to listen in on today's hearing, well except for the two police officers already in custody. Bart Hudson is the owner of ten of those accounts as is Mr James Carthew, his chief accountant, Joan Brady, his secretary and Bill Hudson, brother of Bart and a partner in his firm.'

As Jared read out the list of names each person was approached by a police officer and arrested. He waited while each person was removed from the room before continuing. This was going far better than he'd ever anticipated.

'Now let me see,' He rifled through his pile of papers and picked up a pile pinned together with a large paper clip. He waved them around in the air. 'These ten accounts here belong to James Smith, a Member of Parliament and the man who has been tailing me on and off for the past few weeks.'

Jared paused, waited for the arrest then flicked another pile of papers in the air for effect and to regain everyone else's attention, although the Courtroom was being emptied at a rapid rate. 'These ten, talk about casting aspersions on me. Who would believe such a high ranking police officer would stoop so low. I'm sorry Superintendent Jack Watson but your signature matches the withdrawals on these accounts here.'

Jared waved the pages in front of Watson's nose as he was arrested. Loud cries of shock drowned out any more talk so Jared ceased speaking until the court was calm.

'Your Honour, request to approach the bench?'

He waited until the permission was given. He walked forwards, coming to a standstill in front of the high desk. A hushed silence filled the room. He leant over the front of the bench and whispered so no one else could hear his words.

'Your Honour, because of your position I'm going to spare you the embarrassment of being arrested in public. We weren't able to name you as the tenth account owner until today when Bella recognised you as the fourth person at the meeting in Hudson's office. If you'd had the good sense to excuse yourself from this case, as you were legally required to do, you might have gotten away with your complicity. As it is, I believe it is your signature on this Offer and Acceptance form, which I was able to obtain from Isabella Perez. You people pursued and attempted to murder the wrong Bella Perez and I hold you as much responsible for what Annabella has been through as Hudson. I now understand why Hudson elected to have only a trial by judge. You were going to find him not guilty despite the overpowering evidence. Now, I suggest you find Mr Hudson guilty on all counts and discharge this court. Then I suggest you make a hasty retreat to your little room back there and allow the two police officers waiting there, to arrest you. Could I also suggest you call off all your little minions from any further attempts on Bella's life? None of you will gain anything by her untimely death. In fact, so many people know about this now, I suggest her death will only make your guilt even more obvious. Your phone calls will be traced and we will arrest every single person you have been in contact with. Good day.'

Jared returned to his seat, asked Bella to stand while Judge Collins handed down his judgement then watched as the man walked proudly, head held high, through his personal side door. Pandemonium broke out amongst the remaining people in the room. Bart Hudson was re-arrested on a different set of charges and taken away before the Court usher tried to empty the room of the few remaining people. Jared sat in his chair, refusing to speak to the stunned woman beside him until they were left alone.

When silence reigned in the room, Jared turned to Bella. 'It's all over, Bella, and you didn't have to say a word.'

'I'm stunned and speechless!'

'Well, that has to be a first. You are usually ready to argue every point.' Jared grinned at her.

'Yes, well there are one or two points I was going to bring up.' He watched, amused, as Bella began to fire up. Her face changed from amazed to defiant in an instant. His adorable Bella was back.

'Save it for later. We need to get out of here. I'm looking forward to your arguments when we get back to my office. How are you feeling?'

'Very relieved but is it really all over?'

'I believe so, yes. You may still have to testify as a witness to different sets of charges but Hudson has been found guilty of all the charges of attempted murder against you. The Super and the Judge will be placed in protective custody. In a normal jail they will last a matter of weeks, if that long, before the inmates attack them because of their positions in the legal hierarchy. You are free to pursue a normal life.'

As they departed, Jared's hand hovered then settled into the small of Bella's back. The moment he got her back to his office he intended to kiss her senseless and begin the process of wooing her. It was such an old-fashioned word but boy, so appropriate and he was going to enjoy every minute of his pursuit.

His hand jerked back in shock when she said, 'I think I'll go to live with my parents in England.' She shot off like a rock from a catapult and headed down the corridor.

'Huh?' He was stunned. Then when the meaning finally registered he raced after her. 'Now just wait a minute!'

Chapter Twenty Eight

All of a sudden, Jared was very afraid. This was the last thing he had expected and where did she think she was going? Her clothes were still at his place, she had no car and couldn't drive in any case. What was going on here? Why this sudden desire to escape?

'England? You can't!' Shock caused Jared to stand in his tracks, unable to get out any more words. Where on earth did this England nonsense come from? Bella had said nothing about it before. Yes, her parents lived there but she'd refused to tell them of her trauma during her weekly phone chats. They didn't even know she'd fractured her leg. Thoughts of her leg reminded him that she had a medical appointment to have the cast removed, so where did this London trip come from?

Hope surged as Bella stopped, turned and faced him. 'Can't? Last time I looked, I was a twenty-seven year old widow who has no ties here, no family, no job and no one who cares a damn about me. I don't need anyone's permission. At least in England I have my parents who love me. They don't physically jerk away from me every single time I touch them.' He spied tears welling in her eyes.

'Do you know how much that tiny action hurts?' was squeaked out before she spun around on her one leg and almost ran down the passage, her crutches working at a furious pace and with her using her almost healed leg in an ungainly hop and waddle. Somehow, he knew the tears she so stoically kept at bay even under the strongest of duress of the past several weeks were now falling. But what really gave him hope were her words. He felt sure she hadn't realised how much she'd given away. For his actions to hurt her then she must care a lot more then she'd let on. It could only mean she had strong feelings for him.

'Bella!' he called after her then began chasing, not stopping when she turned left then shoved a door open. The heavy wooden door slammed in his face but he thrust his shoulder against it and shoved it open. Not caring where he was, he entered the room as Bella locked the door to her cubicle in the ladies' room. 'Bella, can we talk? Please?'

'Go away!' She tried to yell but a sob made it sound more like she was choking.

'I'm not going anywhere until we discuss all the nonsense you just spouted.' He leant up against the end wall nearest where Bella was, one foot casually crossed over the other, his arms folded and with a wry smile on his face about exactly where they were.

'I need to pee. Go away and give me some privacy.'

'My presence hasn't stopped you from peeing before

and you have far more privacy now than a couple of other times I can recall. I'm staying, so pee away and while you're doing it would you mind telling me what all that nonsense was about me not liking you touching me?'

'I already told you.' Then she sniffed and snorted.

'I don't recall ever telling you anything of the kind.'

'You didn't have to tell me in words. Your body language says it. Every time I touch you, you wince and pull away. I'm truly sorry you find my touch so distasteful, you don't know how sorry but I think it would be better if we say goodbye now.'

After all his years in law, Jared knew how to read unsaid innuendos. He was delighted. 'Bella, you were my client. It isn't ethical for me to have even an inkling of a relationship with my client. You saw the way Hudson's lawyer tried to have me thrown off the case because of a perceived relationship with you.'

'Your over-inflated sense of what is right and wrong sucks, now go away.'

He was doing no such thing but her words brought a smile to his face. In fact he felt as though he was grinning like some idiot. If he was reading things correctly then she did want more from him. The very thought warmed his heart. 'I take it by your words that you would have liked me to be less ethical. That gives me hope, Sweetheart and just so we set the record straight, I love it when you touch me. I love it so much that all I want to do is wrap my arms around you and kiss you senseless. Those winces, as you call them, are my body reacting to you. Every time you touch me it's like being hit with a bolt of electricity. My hormones pound through me. My wanting you but not being able to have you because you were my client and in my care, caused me an enormous amount of heartache but I wouldn't have been able to represent you if I had given in to my very deep desires.'

'Oh, so sweet.'

Startled, Jared glanced up towards the next cubicle. He hadn't even thought that someone else was in the room. He heard Bella gasp and figured she had been just as surprised – and probably feeling mortified that their conversation was being overheard. Tough and she had no way of escaping so he intended ploughing on.

'Bella, the bit about no one here wanting you or caring about you is so wrong. Duke will go berserk if I don't take you home and more important, I want you. I want you to stay in my home, in my life, in my bed. I want you as my wife. I love you, Bella. I think I fell in love with you when I first saw you up on the ledge.'

Jared stopped when he heard the lock of Bella's cubicle turn. The door opened a fraction. He moved away from the wall and stood eyeing the door.

'Would you mind repeating that bit?' Bella's voice had softened.

Jared couldn't see her but knew she was standing just behind the partially opened door. Her toes were peeking from underneath. He straightened his body, a smile tugging at the corners of his mouth. 'Which bit? That I want you to marry me?'

'No, the other bit.'

'That I want you? Come out here and I'll show you exactly how much I want you.'

'No you fool, the bit with the four letter word starting with the letter L. Men can be so obtuse at times, thinking the woman wants all the bells and whistles when all they need is to be told they are loved.' These words came from the third cubicle down.

Jared couldn't help but laugh as he gently pushed the door open and watched his beautiful, adorable Bella standing there on one leg, her face streaked with drying tears. 'I love you, Bella. I'm hopelessly in love with you so please marry me and spend the rest of our lives together so I can go on showing you how much you mean to me?'

Bella stared up at him. He could see the love in her eyes, but he could also see her firing up.

'You're proposing to me in the toilet?' she squeaked. 'And you've never even kissed me, ever! You even told that to the whole world in the courtroom. How can I marry a man who has never even kissed me?'

Jared reached out to take a firm hold of Bella's hands, his eyes softening as did his voice. 'Well, I had planned on somewhere a little more romantic but you took me by surprise before I could ask you to join me at the nice romantic dinner I had planned. I had also planned on rectifying the lack of kisses as soon as we had made it to my office but once again you put a stumbling block in the way. Besides I have kissed you twice before.'

'Oh, for heavens sake, just kiss her. Then she can't argue any more and we can get out of here!' Cubicle two sounded as frustrated as Jared felt.

'What an excellent idea, thank you, ladies.'

One sudden movement and Bella was drawn into his arms, her startled open mouth covered, smothering any further protests or arguments. He made sure the kiss was very long and very passionate but it left him feeling as though he were on fire and with no doubt about her feelings by the way she kissed him back. They were still embraced when he heard the two other ladies emerge and wash their hands. He lifted his head, giving both women a wink and a smile.

'Oh, my! You are so good looking, if she won't have you, I will.' Cubicle three looked overawed as she spoke.

Jared burst out with a loud shout of laughter as the young woman walked out. 'Not a chance, my heart belongs to Bella.'

Smiling at the gooey look on Bella's face, he bent down to lift her up into his arms, crutches and all, then carried her outside, settling her onto her feet in the middle of the corridor. Not caring where they were, he cocooned her face with his hands then kissed her once again and then stood with her held against his chest, lapping up the feel of her soft curves against the hardness of his own torso.

'Now, my beautiful love, can we start over again? Will you please come out to dinner with me tonight? Before you answer that, let me make it official - you are no longer my client.' He waited for the muffled yes he heard against his chest. 'Are you really planning on going to England?' This time he was very relieved to hear the quiet no. 'Just as well, because I would have followed then pestered you until you agreed to come back, but maybe we could make it a honeymoon destination so I can meet your parents.'

For his comment, he felt a soft punch to his ribs. Bella lifted her head. 'I haven't agreed to marry you yet.'

'But you haven't said no, which gives me hope.' Her sweet mouth was too irresistible. He swooped down. This time he was far gentler; his tongue tasting its way along both lips, then he nibbled, first the top and then the bottom followed by an exploration, tasting, seeking, giving, accepting. He felt as though he was drowning in pleasure and Bella wasn't hesitant in giving back exactly the same.

When he finally lifted his head, Jared murmured, 'What if we find somewhere more appropriate for me to ask you again?'

Bella thought for a moment then smiled a slow, cheeky grin. 'I might need a few more kisses to help me make up my mind.'

He lowered his head until he was only millimetres from Bella's mouth. 'It will be my very great pleasure.'